CAJUN JUSTICE

CAJUN JUSTICE

LEE R. HADLEY

Based upon a concept by Michael Cagle

BookWise
publishing

BookWise Publishing
Riverton, Utah

www.bookwisepublishing.com

Story Concept: Michael Cagle
Viper Photo used by permission of Daniel Rosenberg to create the cover illustration
Cover Illustrator and artist of viper: Brian C. Hailes, HailesArt.com, bchailes@gmail.com
Cover and Interior Designer for print: Francine Platt, Eden Graphics, Inc.,
www.edengraphics.net
Interior Designer for E-pub: Dayna Linton, Day Agency, Dayna@dayagency.com
Editors: Stephanie Clarke of Precision Editing, Lehi, Utah
and Karen K Christoffersen of BookWise Publishing

Library of Congress: 2016956264

978-1-60645-160-1: Paperback
978-1-60645-161-8: e-Pub
978-1-60645-164-9: Jacketed-Hard Cover

First Edition: 2016

10 9 8 7 6 5 4 3 2 1

Printed in the United States of America

DEDICATION

LET ME TELL YOU about Michael Cagle. He is a 4th Degree Black Belt, a good neighbor, friend, and the person you want to have with you in a dark alley, and *especially snake-infested swamps.*

Cajun Justice is based on one of Michael's ideas. One day we were visiting on his driveway when I took note of his tee shirt. With a shiver running up my spine, I exclaimed, "How can you wear that shirt?"

His shirt bore the image of a very large rattlesnake. In the past, we had talked about my books, *The Towers Series,* and after hearing the shock in my voice, he said he had a great idea for a book. In a few moments he gave me the premise for what became *Cajun Justice.* So, thank you, Michael for the idea that ignited the creativity of my intellect into a mind-shocking, shiver-shooting story spawned by dishonesty, *rattlesnakes,* and the application of justice. Michael, this book is dedicated to you.

ADDITIONAL NOVELS FROM LEE R. HADLEY

Origins available now

Morning of Despair 2016

Providence 2017

CAJUN JUSTICE

PROLOGUE

MY FRIENDS CALL ME Jensen, at least my close friends do. I live in San Francisco. Dr. Michael Benson, a leading theoretical physicist, had contacted me about a very strange experience I had in New Orleans nearly a year ago. The secrets of the event were kept from the press and the public, but Dr. Benson had learned of them and wanted to know more about what really took place.

I had traveled to New Orleans, and out of curiosity, took a detour to the swamps of Louisiana where I learned that the bayous could be both fascinating and terrifying. At the end of the road, in the heart of Cajun country and the heat of the swamp, I met an "o-wom'n"—Mothe' Moses—a clear-minded woman of the swamp who introduced me to her "li'l babies," and my life changed forever. I left the swamp with a load that is far heavier than I ever thought I could carry. The load was accompanied with a hiss and rattle that pierced my nerves and rattled my soul.

Back in New Orleans, and without realizing it, I dragged my best friend, Bob, and his wife, Anne, into a terrifying balancing act; in this case, it was the balance of the scales of justice. After a week in the city, they saw first-hand that the application of Cajun justice is far different than the justice meted out by the United States judicial system. We all learned we are a composite of our experiences and choices, and that justice might be applied in ways and means that are completely undreamt of, and certainly unexpected.

I will never forget the sights and sounds of the living bayou, including its slithering creatures, the musky scent of foggy, black swamp water, and the questionably joyous revelers on Bourbon Street. Had you been there, it would have grayed your hair and left you in a cold sweat. I had explored a world of previously unknown punishment and encountered the concept of mercy in a way that was unexpected, terrifying, but, in the end, justifying.

The information that Dr. Benson gained from our interview became powerful evidence to the premise of his theory and research because I told him the entire story.

The Heart of the Swamp

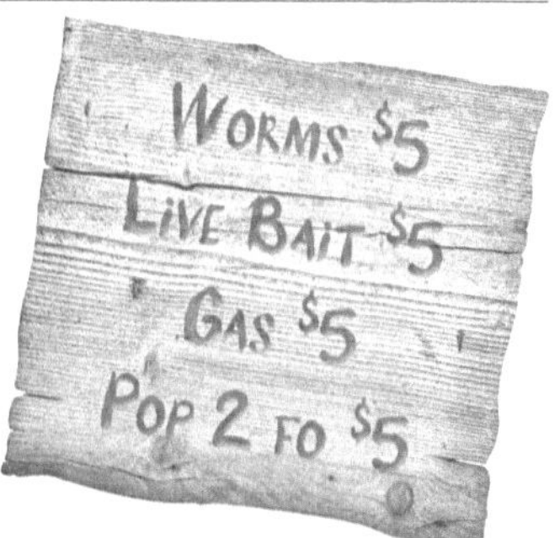

THE WORDS ON THE old sign were written by hand, but they still caught my attention; that and the need to relieve myself slowed me to a crawl. The weathered sign was hanging askew near an old gas station, similar to run-down stations depicted in old movies: outdated, dilapidated, and without any hint of prosperity. The prices for their apparent bestsellers had been scrawled in now dingy gray paint. It might have been black in an earlier year, but time had silently slipped past, and the paint had lost its fresh appeal. Long ago, the words had been hand-brushed onto whitewashed plywood that had been nailed to an ancient power line pole. As with the line of letters and words, little attention had been paid to presentation. It was crooked, washed out, and gray, similar to the other-worldly land around it, which lay twisted and curled amid swamps, bayous, trees, and brush—un-designed, un-managed, and un-kept. Everything was helter-skelter without any seeming order. Even the power poles leaned in haphazard stances, the lines dipping dangerously close to human reach.

I'm Jensen, and I crept over the edge of the broken road and onto the gravel of the rundown gas station. My SUV still had half a tank of gas, but my side trip had already taken longer than I'd planned. I thought it best to fill up while I could. The $5 per gallon gas price was steep but seemed a bargain when compared to being stranded in this strangely uncivilized land.

I'd been pampered by the cool, air-conditioned dryness inside my Durango. Although the last few miles had been rough and winding, the ride had been comfortable and the environment accommodating. My extracurricular drive resembled nothing of my metropolitan home in San Francisco, but it was fascinating and intriguing—until I opened my door. I was not prepared for the suffocating affront of humidity and the aromatic pungencies of life, both thriving and rotting. For a short time, I'd lived in Phoenix where locals dismissed the high temperatures with the statement, "But it's a dry heat." I was now in the midst of a wet heat, the kind that breeds bugs and rots everything. My palms were instantly moist, my slacks quickly stuck to my thighs, and beads of sweat began to trickle down my spine.

Full-service gas stations are a relic in my cosmopolitan world. Over the last few years, I'd seen every large city in America. I was an independent businessman, and I thought I had seen it all. This day would prove me wrong. *Very wrong.*

Motion caught my eye as a man's head popped up from the rusty carcass of a pickup truck, apparently in the process of repair. I wasn't sure what to look at first, the old clunker that should have been traded for cash or the gray-haired, gray-eyed, dark-skinned, and excessively-whiskered face that was peering at me from under a dingy baseball cap.

I stopped dead in my tracks. Had I more presence of mind, I might have laughed, but the entire scene left me stunned and unresponsive. The man, older than he looked, or younger than his age—I cannot say which—started moving toward me while wiping his discolored hands with a greasy rag. There seemed little purpose to his slow, ambling pace. He wore no smile, nor did a greeting escape his lips.

As he passed from the shade of the single bay garage and into the sun, I remembered why I had stopped and realized I was standing in the burning sun, the source of our mutual outdoor sauna. My pores were fully open, releasing a cooling sweat.

I stayed in my place as the man's feet crunched across the gravel, his more than 300-pound bulk pressing rock into rock. I remembered the muted sound of my tires rolling over the same rock. Really, it was a bit of a surprise. So much of the land was dirt and sand rather than rock. My eyes flicked around the premises, and my suspicions were confirmed; a layer of gravel had been spread around the gas pump and in front of the single overhead door of the small service station.

New Orleans is a city to which I had often traveled. As I made my reservations over the phone, I was continually reminded that the language of this bayou state was foreign to me. A mix of Creole, old Indian dialects, French, slave slang, and southern white English, I had struggled through many calls attempting to understand the person on the other end of the line.

In an even *more* incomprehensible version of the jargon to which I had become accustomed, the man asked, "Wha dya nee, man?"

I couldn't help but notice the immense muscle mass of the man, who must have just offered to sell me gas. Despite the humid air around me, my mouth had become dry, and I could only croak, "Fill it up." I don't know why I felt intimidated, but I was. I was out of my element and uneasy because of it.

In an unveiled attempt to avoid excessive effort, the giant man pulled opened the gas tank cover of my car, removed the cap, and turned back to the pump. There was only one class of gas so there was no point in discussing octane requirements. An old lever was lifted, releasing the gas pump nozzle from the pump housing. In a minute or so, gas was flowing into the tank of my Durango.

"Do you have a restroom?" I humbly croaked.

The answer was a slight nod toward the building.

The rock crunched under my feet as I walked away from the solitary gas pump and toward the shade of the old station. I was surprised to see a screen door as the only barrier to the small office area. It squeaked on its hinges as a slight breeze disturbed its rest. I walked past the squeaking door to the corner of the building and turned left where a second blighted sign read: "Toilet." A smile crossed my face, and I lost track of the crackling of my feet across the graveled surface.

Rounding the corner, the path took me under a covered breezeway. The gravel path changed to dirt that looked like it had been soaked in oil. Within a few steps, I was at the door of the restroom and found it to be just as my mind had conjured. The graying paint, which might have once been white, was peeling from the surface of the ill-fitting door. A pull on the loose handle announced my entry with a screech, and the scene I suspected would be uncovered, was now fully realized.

Years of grease served as the coating on the concrete floor. Nearly as many years of grease stained the cracked, porcelain sink with its single cold-water spigot. Dead flies lay on every horizontal surface and an old strip of flypaper hung from the ceiling, covered in dead flies. The toilet seat had undoubtedly been used by the 300-pound hulk still pumping gas into my rental. It was cracked and discolored. Then I learned that the door didn't close and latch properly.

A roll of toilet paper sat on the floor. I wondered what manner of insect might have crawled over, or worse, into the humid and swollen roll. *Which is worse,* I asked myself, *covering the seat with tainted TP or sitting on the bare seat?* Desperation drove me to make a decision. I began my balancing act on the unsteady seat behind an unlockable door as a host of flies buzzed about my head. Had my business not been urgent, it would have been left undone. It might have been a better idea to locate a secretive thicket of brush behind which to relieve myself, but then I tried to remember what poison ivy looks like and realized I wasn't sure. Being in direct contact with a poisonous plant would have been a serious mistake. *I'm better off on this seat,* I decided.

There was no soap and no paper towels. I wondered about the bacteria count on the single faucet handle. After flushing and rinsing, I left the restroom. I considered rubbing my hands in the dirt; it was surely cleaner than the grotesque spigot. I resisted the impulse and wiped my wet hands on my expensive designer slacks instead.

Moving from greasy dirt, to rock, and around the corner, I looked back to the gas pump. The large man was still standing there, pumping gas. I wanted to apply a name to him. His old worn bib overalls partially covered a soiled, but once white, tee shirt. There was no nicely embroidered name on his clothing that I could see. I thought of several service station character names from old television shows, dismissed them all, and decided upon Mr. Hulk, although I didn't dare call him that to his face.

Then I remembered my third need, a cold soft drink. I peered through the dust-filmed windows into the office and saw a chest pop dispenser. As I expected, the screen door screeched when I pulled it open. Once inside, my mind conjured up old brands of soda pop, like Nesbitt's and Grape Nehi. I even added Orange Crush to the list. It wasn't hard to imagine those products as I looked at the ancient dispenser. I'd heard my father talk about such vending machines.

My hope for a cold drink was dashed when I could not hear the hum of the compressor. I touched it and wasn't surprised to find it was warm. As I opened the lid, a foul musky odor wafted up from the empty cooler. Void of soda pop, the old metal rails where bottles once hung were still in place. If there had been a quarter in my pocket, and if there had been soda in the ancient cooler, and if it had worked, I would have moved my selection along the track to the point where it could have been lifted up and out of the cooler. That is, if I had actually deposited the quarter, which would have unlocked the mechanism, releasing the soda. I closed the lid.

Still thirsty, I turned and opened the screen door, walking back out into the hot Cajun sun. The door escaped my grasp, swinging closed with another screech and a bang. The banging of the door made me jump, but Mr. Hulk never looked up. His non-reaction and slow-motion methods reminded me of a tree sloth. I smiled a little at the thought. Mr. Hulk finally pulled the gas nozzle from my car, replaced the cap, and closed the lid; then he replaced the nozzle in the pump housing. I was back at the Durango before he had finished.

He looked up at me and quietly said, "Fifydala."

I reached for my wallet, anticipating Mr. Hulk's response as I pulled out my plastic banker.

"Cashony."

He nodded toward a faded handwritten sign that read, "Cash Only."

He wasn't rude, but I was becoming irritated. His short quips and uncaring demeanor were a little annoying. I opened the cash compartment of my wallet and hoped I had exactly fifty dollars. I couldn't imagine getting him to make change. I'm sure he wasn't dumb; he just spoke a dialect foreign to my cultured ears. But getting change would mean I'd have to stay longer than I wanted. I found two twenties and a ten, which I handed over to Mr. Hulk, while I silently offered a word of thanks that I had correct change, sending it out into the world of Karma, not being a believer in God.

I resisted making a symbolic gesture of raising a bottle to my lips to indicate that I wanted a pop and merely asked, "Where's your pop?"

His gray eyes registered the question, and he turned to his left, nodding toward a building with a long wooden porch, "See da o-wom'n." The building was joined to the station on the other side of a questionably safe breezeway.

I couldn't see an old woman, but I guessed that was what he meant. I looked at Mr. Hulk, his long gray, wiry hair pushing out from under his old baseball cap. The cap was missing a logo of some sort; the shadow of which had been mostly lost to sweat and grease. I thanked him with a nod, which he returned.

I decided it wouldn't be right to leave my vehicle in front of his single pump, plus I wasn't all that comfortable in his presence, so I started the Durango and drove it the twenty feet to the front of what appeared to be some kind of general store. I should have driven down the length of the old store, but I didn't. I opened the door and left my automotive sanctuary once more.

The structure was about fifty feet long. It was an archaic, wooden, once whitewashed building with a long raised and covered wooden boardwalk along the front. The boardwalk, which served as a porch, stood about a foot and a half above the ground. The windows of the building were coated in dust and checkered with a number of old, torn, disintegrating fliers, illegible newspaper ads, and outdated handwritten signs. I wondered about the state of the store. *Was it open or closed?*

At the far end I could see what looked like an alcove built into the structure. Protruding slightly from the alcove was an old woman sitting in an ancient, squeaking rocking chair. She was whittling a piece of wood. *She must be the o-wom'n,* I thought to myself.

My eyes shifted back to the gas station, to Mr. Hulk, and once again to the unrepaired building with the long boardwalk. I had two choices. I could step up and onto the porch, with its loose, warped, bare, and treacherous-looking boards, or I could walk down the partially graveled, earthen frontage to the point where the old woman was rocking and whittling. After surveying the scene, I almost gave into the idea that I should have driven to the other end of the structure.

I admit that my imagination was taking over. I noted the blackened space under the porch and wondered what manner of creature might be lurking there. Having seen more than one Hollywood representation of such places, my mind conjured up the horrid buzz of monstrous, malicious rattlesnakes, each waiting for me to pass; each waiting to strike with its venomous fangs. I moved to the end of the porch where two wooden but open steps covered the blackness. I skipped the two steps and hopped directly onto the porch.

I was startled by the groan of the wood, as though it had been tortured by my landing. The first step was no different. A lover of all kinds of movies, I pictured the danger of walking over a thousand-foot ravine on a rope bridge, stepping on wooden slats that were old, decayed, and undependable. In my real world of crossing the wooden porch, but certainly not in rational thought, I considered the possibility of falling through the boards into the blackness below to be bitten by hundreds of conjured rattlers. The fear of snakes slithering below me began to overshadow my vision of the deep ravine. I forced myself to focus on crossing the weathered boards of the boardwalk.

I knew from experience that the porch would be strongest near its supports at the end of each plank. I had two choices, and it seemed a no-brainer. I could walk on the front edge or up close to the building fascia. I pushed up close to the facade of the building. The old wood on the face of the building was twisted and warped. There were gaps between and behind the boards. I eyed the gaping cracks with mistrust. Begrudgingly, hugging the face of the building, I began a high-alert journey toward the old woman.

The sound I emitted was not so much a scream as it was a loud and peril-ridden grunt, but it was accompanied by a quick jump to the outer edge of the boardwalk. A large tarantula had popped out of the open knothole. It was fully six inches wide, or so the limbic part of my brain cried out; in reality, it was a mere four inches from leg tip to hairy leg tip; recognizing that didn't make me feel better.

Chills ran down my spine, and the hair on my arms stood on end. I was in full fight or flight mode. There was no way I was going to fight that evil arachnid, so my instinct for flight had taken me to the edge of the porch where I was precariously balanced. At that moment, the possibility of a rattlesnake was secondary to the reality of a spider as big as my hand.

After some deep breathing and an attempt to calm my mind, which continued to play nasty tricks on me, I thought of the snakes again.

I had never seen a rattlesnake in the wild; but both tarantulas and rattlesnakes are part of the southwestern desert outside of Phoenix, where I lived for two years. But I was a city guy and seldom ventured into the wild. My infrequent desert ventures had been made in a cool and comfortable SUV. I once asked an experienced desert dweller if I would recognize the warning buzz of a rattler's tail. "Yeah, you'll recognize it. It'll stop you in your tracks, and you'll know what it is without a moment's thought," he'd told me.

I thought of his words and hoped they were true. As I stepped lightly and carefully down the outside edge of the boardwalk, I surveyed the surrounding area. Across the road, I spotted what was little more than a turnout. In that turnout were the remains of an old, barely standing building, the rusting nails and rotted wood hanging together more by tradition than strength. Down an overgrown dirt trail, I could see an aging mobile home. It had seen better days, but an open window and slightly shifting curtains made it look like someone actually lived there. I wondered if it belonged to Mr. Hulk.

At the thought of Mr. Hulk, I looked again toward his domain. I noticed a propane tank on the other side of his dilapidated business, beyond that was a shack. It was raised up from the ground on stilt-like supports. I wasn't sure if I liked that idea. I mused that it must be better to have a home built on a slab of cement that secured the underside of the house. But then again, the close proximity to ground level, where snakes and spiders freely roamed, simply felt wrong. I remembered seeing a TV image of an earthen-floored home in Africa. Some kind of poisonous snake was stalking rats, slithering around sleeping children. I shuddered. Maybe a house on stilts is better. At least it was up and away from the lurking, crawling, and slithering things of the Earth.

The wayside was small. The swamp and the trees seemed to have marched up to the very edges, hedging it in. It was a solitary place. Its only paved access was the broken asphalt road that had brought me to what I now considered to be the edge of civilization. Beyond, the wayside the road turned into a rough-looking dirt road. The trees were typical of the swamps I'd seen in documentaries and horror movies, depending on the selected cable channel. Scanning the area, I identified the famous Cypress trees of the swamplands. They were tall, dominating, and like most trees there, draped in Spanish moss. I shuddered once more at an image of the trees and mist on a moonless night, a swamp creature lumbering after me. I quickly shook off that idea and paid attention to the more solid land that was covered in a variety of shrubs and trees.

The setting was like nothing I had ever seen before, which was precisely the reason I had left the Interstate. I wanted to get a look at the famed bayou. It was even stranger than I had expected. I knew there would be trees and lots of undergrowth, but I was surprised at the heavy, oppressive atmosphere of the swamp.

I remembered the swamp came up close to the back of the dilapidated gas station; I had seen it from the restroom. Although I couldn't, at the moment, see the swamp behind the store, its presence was unmistakable. The sounds, the scent, and the humidity all seemed to emanate from the dark, and mysterious waters of the bayou. To me, the water felt like the driving force in the aura of my surroundings. I came to feel that everything drew its life force from the swamp.

O-wom'n

IN MY SURVEY OF the wayside, I had stopped moving toward the old woman. I began, once more, to sidle over to her. As I got closer, I thought the squeaking boards of my slow advance would certainly announce my presence, but she had not looked up. She continued her steady rocking over the squeaking and croaking porch. I began to wonder if she might be deaf, although she apparently could see well enough to whittle on the nondescript piece of wood she held in her old and weathered hands. I continued, step by step, each one squeezing out a new groan from the loose boards, until I was but three feet away.

I stopped and simply stood there. I had forgotten about my thirst. I was captivated by the shriveled old woman, who for all intents and purposes was ignoring me, or unaware of my presence. I believed the first thought and doubted the second. I continued to watch her. Her hands were bony but appeared to be strong as she manipulated the knife and wood. She was a trifle of a thing, just the opposite of Mr. Hulk. With her head turned down toward her whittling project, an unruly cascade of scraggly gray hair was her most dominant feature. That hair sported veins of black that streaked from under her wide-brimmed hat, which was pulled tightly down upon her head. I took another step toward her, and another board shrieked under my weight.

"Ehhh—whad yuh wan', sonny?"

"I, ah, I was told you had some cold drinks here?"

Her hand shot up and back, pointing to the rear of an alcove.

"Back 'ere—in da coola. Hep yuhsef."

I wasn't exactly sure what she said but the gesture made it clear. I thought about my phone calls to those New Orleans businesses and realized their speech, though sometimes difficult, was easier to understand than Mr. Hulk and this old woman.

I took a tentative step toward the cooler. The flash of foreboding started at the base of my spine and shot up my backbone. I couldn't see the danger. I felt it, though, and hunkered down, suppressing a heavy grunt, not knowing what to expect next. Then I realized the source of my terror. It was the buzz. My friend in Arizona said I would recognize it, and I did. Rattlesnakes! The recognition had come, but much later than the first sense of danger. Fight or flight had once again been invoked, but I didn't know where to flee, and I certainly wasn't going to fight! I was slightly crouched, my heart racing, and my muscles tense, waiting for directions from a wildly terrified mind.

Within a second of my grunt of terror, the old woman picked up a cane that had been propped up against her chair. She raised it high and smashed it down upon the hollow sounding boards. She hit the boards once, then twice, and then a third time. She uttered a phrase that I cannot repeat or claim to understand. Seemingly, with her intervention, the buzzing stopped. She inclined her face toward me for the first time.

"Dey gets a li'l p'otective at times. Ah remind 'em 'oos boss."

She must have seen the terror showing on my face, but she didn't speak of it. In an effort to better explain the circumstances, she added detail, "Dey rattlahs—dey get p'otective an' Ah remind 'em 'oos boss."

Still slightly crouching, I felt my knees about to buckle, and I looked for a place to sit. The only spot I could see was the old stained cooler that supposedly held the drinks. I half stumbled, half fell onto the cooler. The moment I sat, a new chorus of buzzing erupted, and the old woman pounded the boardwalk once more. The buzzing stopped.

"Don' worry, sonny, dey won' bite. Dey knows de boss."

I struggled to make sense of what had happened. This tiny, gray-haired, sun and weather-etched woman, with too few teeth, and seemingly too much hair, was telling me that the rattlesnakes knew her and obeyed her. It made no sense. I sat there for what seemed an eternity of terror-driven gasps and a racing heart. I sat there long enough for the sweat to begin to dry and for my heart rate to subside. I began, at length, to feel almost normal and merely cautious, not terrified. She apparently understood my discomfort and was content to let me rest and regain my wits.

I noticed that she looked up at me several times as though examining me, profiling me, or simply gauging my nerves, while never saying a word. However, at last she said, "Hep yuhsef to anoda' pop. Dey two fo five, like de sign say."

I'd forgotten about my thirst, but her reminder confirmed its existence. I rose slowly, turned and opened the lid of the cooler. There was one choice, a mainstream cola product that I was happy to have. I opened the can and quickly downed a great portion of it before coming up for breath.

Without even looking up she said, "Yuh migh'y thirs'y."

For the first time I opened my mouth to actually speak to the old woman. "Yes, yes, I guess I was."

She continued whittling, the motion of her knife never changing, "Yuh goin' fishin'?"

Shaking my head, I answered, "Ah, no—no, I'm not going fishing."

Focusing on her work, she asked, "Wha' yuh doin' here?"

"I'm, a—on my way to New Orleans. I'm going to a convention there. I sell shirts."

Seeming more interested, she spoke up, "Yuh sell shirs', eh? Wha' kine shirs'?"

At last I could speak about something from my world. "Oh, nearly any kind of shirt—from tee shirts, to expensive dress shirts, and anything in between. I sell it all."

Watching her whittling more than me, she said, "No' much call fa fancy shirts in de bayou."

Looking around the wayside, I quickly agreed with her. "Yes, yes I can understand that. I just wanted to see the bayou so I pulled off the Interstate, followed my GPS and, well, here I am."

"Yuh falla yuh GPS?"

Looking back to her turned down face, I responded, "Yes ma'am."

"Pretty neat ting, GPS. Goo' fa swamps."

As she responded, I laughed inside. Here I am, Mr. Big City Guy with the expensive car, a worldwide traveler, a regular 5-star hotel occupant, and yet I'm deferring to this little old woman like she was my mother. Now, laughing out loud, I thought it would make a great story to tell my friends.

"Sumpin' funny, sonny boy?"

Hoping not to offend her, I quickly replied, "Oh no, not funny, I—I'm just amazed at my good fortune to stumble upon this place. It's not on the maps."

"Na, we no' ona map."

"Does this place have a name?"

Without missing a knife-stroke, she answered, "Na, no name. We jus' sell gas, po'pane, 'n some bait; mos'ly to loc'ls."

With a smile on my face, which she could not see, I added, "You live in an—interesting place."

She didn't seem affected by my statement; she just kept on whittling. I was beginning to feel more comfortable. The sugar and caffeine in the soda had replaced some of the energy lost in my bout with terror.

After a moment of silence, I asked, "Do you live here?"

"Yuh, live hea' ma whole life."

"How do you live? I mean, how do your support yourself?"

She looked up from her whittling, which hadn't stopped since she had pounded on the boardwalk with her cane. Her eyes settled into mine. Suddenly I felt naked.

"Ah use' ta sell wittlin'. Now, ah sell a li'l gata' meat 'n gata' pa'ts. Ah sell rattlah meat, some live uns, too. Preacha man, he come. Buy live rattlahs. Ah hea' some man got bit' 'n die. Dey no p'otec'ted so good."

I looked around for a real place to sit down and spotted a chair close by. "Mind if I sit?"

Still working on the wooden shape, she said, "Na, Ah don' min'. If yuh got a fiva, dey's anoda pop fa yuh."

A bit worried about change again, I decided I would have one for the road. "Thank you, I—I think I will have another."

I watched her whittle for a few more minutes. Nothing was spoken. At last I broke the silence, "What are you making?"

"Ah'm makin' nuttin'. Jus' passin' time. Ah wait for nex' cus'ama. Wittlin' keeps ma fingas stong. Ah tink Ah ca'ved ever' creacha on Ea'th. Ah used to sell 'em, but Ah ca've too many. No' wo'th it. Fingas strong, bu' no' like dey used ta be. Now, ah jus wittl'."

The more she talked, the more interested I became, and I began to pick up on her swamp dialect.

"So you've carved a lot of creatures in your life?"

"Ya, lots."

"I'm sorry; I should have introduced myself. My name's Jensen."

"Hmmm—Jensen . . . yuh fus' o' las' name?"

"Well, it's actually neither. It's just a name I got tagged with in college. It stuck and, well, that's just what my friends call me."

This time she looked up at me. "Yuh ga' frens?"

I struggled to understand what she was saying but decided she was asking about friends.

"Yes, I do. Well, I think they're my friends. They say they are."

Her eyes, which had shifted back to her whittling, lifted up to mine.

"Ard t' know 'bout frens; sometimes frens, 'n sometimes no frens. My frens no' like ma li'l babies."

She nodded toward the boards, and I realized she was talking about the snakes, referring to them as her little babies. I admit it kind of freaked me out.

"Ah cun coun' on my li'l babies unda po'ch. Na' so lucky w' 'uman frens."

I thought about what she had said, thinking it odd that she depended more on her rattlesnake friends than human friends. Surely, over the apparently long span of her life, she had developed good friends. I let that thought fade away and asked another question. "So, are you alone here?"

"Naw, yuh met ma son, Henry. He sells gas 'n po'pane, ' n fixes o'd tucks, bo't engine, any'ting."

I considered the size of the woman and then turned toward the garage. I couldn't see the man I had dubbed Mr. Hulk, but I wondered how a woman so small could give birth to a man so large. It was unthinkable.

Turning back to the old woman, not daring to use the name I'd given her son, I asked, "Does Henry get your (and I slipped into her vernacular, even began thinking of her now as the o-wom'n) "gata meat for yuh?"

"Na, ee too big ta get'n da wadda w' gatas, bu' once 'er on land, taint no gata' 'ee cahn't tame. Naw, Ah got anoda fo' dat. 'E fetches gata meat t'me. I keep em on ice 'n dat otha cooler or' der. Ah don' advertise gata, jus' fo people oo' knows to come 'n get it."

After her last statement, the old woman stopped her whittling and looked at me once more. It was unnerving. Her eyes were a pale green, and they pierced mine in a discomforting way. After a long look, she seemed to have come to some kind of conclusion.

Shirs'

"Yuh sell shirs'?"

"Yeah, that's my game."

"Ah go' some shirs'."

I turned my focus to the o-wom'n in earnest. "You have shirts? You have shirts here . . . to sell?"

Appearing unimpressed with my enthusiasm, she said simply, "We try t'sell some, bu' mos' did'n like 'em. Dey fears 'em."

The intensity of my focus increased. "Afraid? They were afraid of a shirt?" I scoffed at the idea.

"Das what Ah sayed. A'feared."

My interest was more than piqued. I couldn't imagine what kind of shirt an old woman in a swamp would sell. Add the concept of fear to the mix, and I had to see these shirts.

"Can I see one?"

"Yuh shua 'bout dat, sonny?"

"Yes, of course."

"Sh'oot, dey scares yuh, too."

Strengthening my voice, sitting up more straightly, and almost laughing at the challenge, I said, "Try me."

She pointed back over her shoulder to a door that opened into the dilapidated building.

"Der a stack a boxes insi' dat door; bring one out 'n see fa yuhsef."

My interest waned a little as I considered walking across the wooden floor. I wondered if my steps would raise another chorus of buzzing rattlesnake tails. I swallowed my pride, toughened my senses, roused my courage, stood up, and walked tentatively to the door. There was no buzz this time. I was relieved.

The door was just like every other object I had seen at this unreal roadside stop. It was old and its paint had flaked and fallen away. It hung slightly askew and didn't close properly. I wondered how it could possibly keep out the creatures of the night, which surely must look for warmth and food in the dark of the evening hours. Pushing that thought aside, I pulled the screen door open. It whined and creaked like a banshee wounded in a mortal fight. My hairs stood on end and goose bumps welled up again.

The interior was gray, like the paint on the door. I could find no light switch and very little light trailed through the dirty, paper-covered windows. Hidden in the partial light, and true to the old woman's word, there were boxes stacked just inside the door. The top box was dusty. I tentatively brushed it off and carefully picked it up. It was heavy, like a box of shirts might be. I carried it outside and set it on top of the cooler, near the old woman, who was still whittling.

"Op'n it, sonny."

The top flaps had been folded over. I grabbed two of them and pulled up. All at once, the terror I had known just twenty minutes before took my legs out from under me and I dropped to the floor. A new chorus of buzzing filled the air. The old woman slammed her cane against the porch planks once more. The chorus stopped, but my heart rate had doubled, and new sweat broke out on my forehead.

I sat, paralyzed, on the wooden planks of the porch. I knew there were rattlesnakes beneath me, but what had I just seen in the box?

"Go on, t'won' bite yuh."

Her demeanor was matter-of-fact. There was no caution in her voice or equivocation in her tone, but she did have a slight smile on her face, as if to say, "I told you so."

I looked at the box. What I had seen, and how I felt didn't mesh with her cavalier attitude.

"Ah say t'won' bite yuh."

I nodded my head in the affirmative, while silently disagreeing with her assessment.

"C'mon, big city man. Look a' de shirs'."

Her persistence spurred me to one knee. I warily turned my attention to the box. It was full and something bizarre was at the top of the pile. I rose to both knees, cautiously peering into the darkened container, questioning the shadowed contents. I lifted myself up, getting both feet under me. I was in an awkward stance, but I was upright. I braced myself for what I was about to do.

I squeamishly gripped both flaps. It must have been my imagination because no cane came down to silence any rattlesnake buzzing. Slowly, and very carefully, I pulled aside the flaps, and looked into the shadows. I resisted the screams of terror that erupted from my wary mind.

The scene was senseless. My eyes and limbic system couldn't correlate the contents. My limbic system was convincing my right-brained imagination to run away. It was trying to tell me that the box held a lurking danger that would quickly strike and kill me. But, the left-brain, the logical side of thinking, suggested there was no danger. The carton was indeed filled with shirts. The color of the cloth was a familiar and neutral cotton color, but on the front of the shirt was the most realistic snake head I had ever seen. It looked more than alive. The ancient man in me kept demanding that I run away, but the modern, enlightened man understood that it was just an image—even if it was a realistic, terror-filled image that made me cower.

It was the eyes that fixed my attention. They reeked of a nasty, evil streak of pure hatred. They didn't blink or quail. They pierced my mind and held me like a charmed bird. The eyes said, without bluff and bluster, that I was a dead man. The open mouth with flashing fangs bore witness to the truth of that statement. At least, that's how my inner, ancient psyche saw it. My contemporary side looked upon the massive head, open jaws, and bristling fangs with awe, but my primeval parts swore that the forked tongue flicked, ever so slightly. I had never seen a more expertly painted image of a Southeastern Diamondback Rattlesnake. The venomous eyes demanded me to yield or be taken. The large thick body snaked down and across the front of the shirt, the rattles standing upright with a sense of hysteric buzzing. I felt the presence—the malevolent presence—of a creature that wanted nothing more than to sink its two-inch fangs into my muscle, pumping me full of venom that would surely kill me within minutes.

I turned and looked at the o-wom'n, "You're right, that thing scares the hell out of me."

"Told yuh t'wud," a teasing smile spreading across her face.

She kept looking at me, once more holding me in her gaze. After some uncomfortable minutes, she spoke, "Can yuh sell 'em?"

I was stunned at the quality of the shirts in the box, the excellent graphics and printing, and the incredulity of the idea. I'd only ever seen the small Western Diamondbacks in Arizona, and they were behind glass. Most of the western rattlers are only an inch thick and little more than two feet long. They are far smaller and less intimidating than the menacing image in front of me. The semblance of the snake revealed a massive body that appeared to be four inches in diameter. Its head was a big as my fist. Its pale orange eyes, with black slits in the center, bore through me just like the o-wom'n's eyes had done. I looked again at her. She was concentrating on her whittling. I looked down at the wooden porch and understood even more intensely the terror that lurked beneath those boards. I sent out a Karma-laden prayer of thanks that I hadn't walked along the front of the dark, open boardwalk.

I still hadn't reached down to pick up the shirt, but my mind was cataloging its details. It wasn't a cheap tourist tee shirt. It was a high quality polo. The shirt that I had pulled out was a 2XL. It was an excellent canvas for the life-like image.

Even though I had seen very few rattlesnakes in my life, one might surmise that each one had terrified me, and this image was giving me the creeps. With my skin crawling and my spine tingling, I continued to gaze on the top shirt. The detail was astounding; the aura of the shirt was intimidating, the realism inescapable. As evidence to those statements, I couldn't force myself to reach down to pick up the shirt on the top of the stack.

"Yuh gonna pick it up?"

That question was still unanswered. The ancient Mr. Limbic screamed not to touch it. Mr. Right-Brained Imagination screamed a thousand types of tortured conclusions about the boxed apparition. Mr. Left-Brained Logic stood his ground, suggesting there was no danger. As long moments passed, the left side of my brain was slowly taking control.

I had to force my hands to move down, but even as I reached toward the amazing shirt, Mr. Limbic continued to scream, "Stop, stop!" I admit my muscles were tense, and I was holding my breath. Then a new fear took me; I began to wonder what was under the top shirt. Maybe there were snakes hidden below. Mr. Limbic and Mr. Imagination were working overtime.

Using all the bravery I could muster, I reached deeper into the box. My fingers had barely touched the shirt, but my mind began cringing back and away from it. I forced my body ahead. Cautiously, I pinched the collar between the thumb and fingers of both hands. Applying courage that came from some unknown source, I lifted it carefully, which allowed the cloth to partially unfold. While fearfully watching the eyes and fangs, the body was fully revealed with the unfolding of the shirt. It took all the fortitude I possessed, but as the shirt unfolded, I draped it over my left arm.

I had done this a thousand times before, but none of those experiences compared with this harrowing adventure. I had to fight the imagination of feeling the scales scrape across my forearm. I had to fight the sound of the buzzing rattler tails in my ears. I fought hard to push down the fear of being bitten and refrained from tossing the shirt into the wind and running back to the safety of my air-conditioned and fully gassed SUV. I was reminded that, in moments, I could leave this green, creature-infested hell and be safely on the Interstate. The frantic call of full flight filled every muscle in my body. Still, I held my ground.

With an impressive effort I stifled the sense of flight and forced the fight senses to take on the duty of investigation. Ignoring the image as best I could, I looked at the stitching. It was amazing. It obviously came from the sewing machine of a highly skilled craftsman. The material had been perfectly cut, and the seams were exact. In every way, the shirt looked to have been created by an artisan of the highest skill. It was a masterpiece.

The business side of me went to work. *How much can I sell these shirts for? How many are there? What will she charge me? Is there a profit to be made?* As an independent distributor, I dealt with these questions on a daily basis. I had a solid estimate of an appropriate sales price, but I didn't know how many shirts the old woman had, and I didn't know how much she would charge. I also questioned whether this would be a one-time deal, or if there were more shirts to be purchased. In the end, the most nagging question became, *where did she get these shirts?*

Before I could begin to make a deal with her, I did a quick analysis of the o-wom'n. I reminded myself that her nearly unintelligible dialect didn't mean she was stupid. In fact, I determined that she just might be a very smart woman. I finally responded, "Yes, I can sell them."

Mothe' Moses

BEFORE ASKING ANY QUESTION of the o-wom'n, I had actually played a number of scenarios around in my mind. In the end, I simply wanted to buy them. I wanted to pay her, take the horrid, nasty, but beautiful shirts, and leave. I wanted to sell them at the convention in New Orleans. It seemed to be a very profitable venture.

"How much do you want for them?"

As soon as the words had escaped my lips, the breeze stilled. I became aware that no birds were singing, no alligators bellowed, even the insects had stopped buzzing. The bayou had become deathly quiet. It was as though the entire world was holding its breath for this one moment. All time seemed to stop, waiting for the answer that would seal or break the deal.

Keeping her eyes on the still carving knife blade, she said, "Ah wan' fif'een dolla' p' shir'."

Inside I choked, wanting a better deal, but kept calm. "That's a lot," I said, but it wasn't, and I knew it.

"Fif'een, take er leave."

Excitement grew in my guts. "How many shirts are there?"

Without emotion, she said, "Five box a twen'y-fou'."

"Do you take credit cards? I'd like to get my Sky Miles."

Clearly in control of the moment, and still looking down, she responded, "No cads. Fif'een dolla' e'ch."

Liking the deal but feigning amazement, I blurted out, "That's $1,800.00. I don't have that much cash."

Her solution was simple. "Go ta yuh bank an' come back. Dey still b'ere."

My mind raced as I thought about the convention where I would use them to my advantage. I nearly blurted out the words, *"I have to be at the Convention Center tomorrow; I could never make it in time."*

Speaking as though the sale meant nothing to her, and caring little for my predicament, she said, "Come back anoda day."

My mind raced. Somehow, I had to make the deal, and I had to make the deal today, not some other day. "Will you take a check?"

She lifted her face once more, peering deeply into my eyes. She held her gaze for the longest moment. I felt it impossible to remove myself from her stare. For just an instant, I thought I heard a light buzz from below the planks. I began to wonder which was the most skilled charmer, the image of the snake or the old woman? In the end, I decided it was the "o-wom'n."

"Pu'snal o' bidness check?"

"Business."

"Then you make da check fo two tousand."

I pretended to gasp at the price. I feigned disappointment and distress, but at last I agreed.

"Okay, $2,000.00."

I hesitated before asking my next question. It was odd that I stopped to think about grammar, but I was in her world not mine so I simply asked, "Who do I make the check out to?"

"Mothe' Moses," she said without a flinch.

Now, I was the one looking deeply into her eyes, and something changed in my mind. I gave up any possibility of cultured English. Not only had she become the o-wom'n, she was now Mothe' Moses. *What a strange woman.*

Thinking of her now in her own dialect, I said, "I'll be right back. I have to get my checkbook from the car."

"Dat a nice ca."

I nodded in agreement and hurried down the boardwalk, forgetting about the loose, creaking, and weakened boards that covered the heads and fangs of massive, cranky rattlesnakes. It was only thirty feet, but I felt out of breath as I quickly pressed the key fob, which unlocked the doors. The engine started, the transmission slipped into gear, and within seconds I had backed up to the boardwalk.

"Are the other boxes in that same room?"

"Dey be all dere."

I scribbled out the check without a moment's regret. I tore it from the register and shoved it toward Mothe' Moses. She grasped the check in her left hand, but with her right, she grasped my wrist with a strength that was unsettling. Once again, her pale green eyes bore into mine. It was disquieting.

This time she looked up at me as she spoke. "Ah hope you a on'es' man."

"Oh, I assure you the check is good."

"'Tis goo' now, bu' tamora?"

I looked back with my best, honest-looking, non-bluffing poker face. "Yes, it will be good tomorrow, too."

She subtly tapped her foot on the planks. A chorus of buzzing arose, "M' li'l' babies ah very p'otective. You be shua da check be goo tamora, too."

Calculating possible profits, I asked, "Can I buy more of these shirts?"

"Not shua, mayba no."

In my mind I cursed. For this to be a really good deal, I needed a larger supply.

"I will come back to see you. We will talk about more shirts."

"We see."

I heard her words, but I'd learned a thing or two about reading people in my time. She was holding back. What is her hesitance? I wondered. Maybe she can't come up with more of them. Heck, maybe she stole them. Maybe the gata killer guy got them for her. Maybe some traveling salesman is rotting in the swamp while I haul his stolen shirts away.

And then I stopped short, realizing that I had used the word "gata" in my mind.

She has taken over my mind; I've begun to talk like her.

A hundred thoughts raced through my head as I loaded the five cartons into the Durango. It was already quite full with other merchandise and brochures, but I made quick work of re-organizing the contents and stacking the five cartons safely inside.

Mothe' Moses had not changed her demeanor or activity. Although the check had been quickly tucked into her dress, she had resumed rockin' and wittlin'.

I closed the door, shaking my head and wondering why I was thinking in her dialect. I looked toward her, "Thank you, Mothe' Moses."

She didn't look up but said in a muted voice, "Ah 'ope yuh still tankfu' 'n a few daze."

I stood quietly for a moment, looking at the amazing o-wom'n. *Who is she, really? Where did she come from?*

It's like she was an alien who had settled into the backwater world of dark mysteries. As I quietly watched her, she simply kept wittlin'. It was clear that she had no more to say. I broke the silence of the moment, said goodbye again, and climbed into the SUV.

— CHAPTER TWO —
TUESDAY: JENSEN'S RETURN TO NEW ORLEANS

Back to the City

I WAS TEMPTED TO stomp the accelerator to the floor, purposely peeling out through the gravel and onto the road. The rattlesnakes were my impetus, but consideration for the o-wom'n gave me second thoughts. She wouldn't appreciate the gesture, though it wouldn't have been directed at her personally, but I didn't want to get on her bad side. Mr. Logic became the master, and I pulled slowly onto the road.

As I passed the gas station, Mr. Hulk was standing by the pump, wiping his hands with what must have been the same greasy rag he'd held earlier. His eyes locked onto me as I passed, but his face wore no expression, his head on a pivot, watching as I drove past him and out of his life. I wondered once more where he might live. Was it in that rickety old shanty next to his weathered station, or did he live in the station? My bet? He lived in the station.

I was anxious to get back to New Orleans. There was much to do and the convention was just a few days away. I'd flown into the Louis Armstrong New Orleans International Airport from San Francisco, just the day before my bayou adventure. Early this morning, I had driven to Baton Rouge where a shipment of goods awaited me. The cheaper freight costs to Baton Rouge more than paid for a rental vehicle and a drive from New Orleans. I had spent a considerable sum ordering a luxury vehicle with second and third row seating capacity that would fold down, providing the space to carry my international cargo. It was this extra capacity that made it possible to load the five boxes of shirts that I purchased from Mothe' Moses.

When I left Baton Rouge on I-10, I headed southwest with no specific destination in mind. I just wanted to visit a bayou. As I had told Mothe' Moses, I had a GPS in the Durango to keep me from getting lost. I had heard about the swamps near Houma in the Atchafalaya Basin and thought that might be good area to see some swampland. Going well out of my way, I drove west to Lafayette, then southeast on Highway 90. I left I-90 and ended up on the road that took me to Mothe' Moses's wayside. Now I needed to find my way back to 90, which would take me through the outlands of Louisiana and back to New Orleans. Thank goodness for my GPS.

The drive out of the bayou was similar to the entry, except that I felt pressed for time, and that caused me to hurry. The broken road would have been harsh in a lesser vehicle, but the Durango easily smoothed out the bumps. The highway skirted great Cypress trees in between open waterways and around murky swamps. In my hurry, I found myself negotiating the curves a little faster than I should have. My loading had been somewhat slipshod and the freight shifted. As one of the boxes tumbled, Mr. Limbic took over, allowing the breakout of great Eastern Diamondback rattlesnakes into the cargo area. I felt exposed. There was no barrier between the cargo area, Mr. Limbic's conjured snakes, and me. I decided to slow down, but not for the reason you might suppose. It was certainly not due to the limbic-spawned snakes, but rather because I didn't want the cargo damaged. Slowing down actually calmed my nerves, and I began to enjoy the drive.

Snakes aside, but still in my mind, the swamp was actually quite beautiful. My automotive environment was controlled, and I enjoyed cool, dry air and a satellite radio. Ensconced in the familiarity of the vehicle, I settled back to enjoy the sometimes-close brush with trees and water.

My mind shifted to artists' renditions of dark and foggy nights in the swamp, where humid air hung like a stifling blanket. I envisioned old stilted shacks with angled chimneys and wispy smoke cycling up into the darkness. I had heard stories of gata bellows and imagined them echoing across the blackened night with the occasional flapping of owl wings and the scream of some unlucky rodent, speared by sharp talons, driven by muscular legs and feet. With a start, I snapped back to reality as I saw the body of a very long, thick snake, stretching almost entirely across the road.

There was no time to stop, and I don't know if I could have willed myself to stop, so I punched the accelerator and hurried over the nondescript reptile. There was no feeling of sorrow for killing the serpent, but rather a shiver up my back as I thought of the monster being caught up in my tires and finding its way into the car. Mr. Limbic was working way overtime, and I quickly tried to dismiss him, but in a last ditch effort to scare the crap out of me, I heard what sounded like a very distant rattlah buzz coming from behind me. I thought once more of Mothe' Moses and mused that she'd had an unnerving way of sticking with me.

As I traveled along the road, I saw lots of trucks parked along the narrow shoulders. Most were scratched, dirty, and mud-caked, looking as if they had spent countless hours in off-road romps through the mud and brush. I wondered how many snakes those knobby tires had run over, and I actually pondered whether or not a snake fang could puncture a tire. *Nah— that's stupid.*

I finally found my way back to Highway 90, a divided highway with long straightaways and gentle curves. The road split agricultural land, where narrow ribbons of farms dotted both sides of the highway, but did not run deeply into the swampland. I began to understand that this culture had a healthy respect for the swamp and the creatures that surrounded them. Their civilized corridors were narrow and surrounded by a world that was more hostile than friendly.

Highway 90 had long lengths of frontage road on each side, and in some areas, I could see a railroad track. I wondered why railroad tracks would have been built through the swampland. Then I saw what looked like sugarcane plants. I hadn't known that Louisiana has a flourishing sugar cane industry, but suspected the purpose for the trains was to service the sugar cane farms.

I noticed a road named Black Bayou Drive. It was a reminder that, though woven with beauty, the land had a dark side as noted by that particular name. My adventure had been exciting, but I would be glad to get back to civilized metropolis of New Orleans.

As I pressed east toward the city, my mind finally separated from the bayou. I began thinking of the week ahead; I needed to have a good week. The economy was tough, and I was desperate for a good sales week to make a balloon payment on some shirts I had fronted for a customer and to defray the costs of my personal brand of shirts. Everything was costly: the travel, the extra-large Convention Center space, and the large, expensive display where I would be laying out my samples. As for the samples, I simply could not take the chance they might not arrive on time. Missing samples had been a deal-breaker early in my career, and I had sworn to prevent that at all costs. Of course that meant pre-convention shipments and freight storage expenses. In New Orleans, the freight had to be transported both into storage and out of storage by union workers. In addition, it was policy that large displays, like mine, had to be set up by union members. I was perfectly capable of putting the display together, but strictly prohibited from doing it. All in all, it was going to be an expensive convention, and I needed to secure some big orders, or I would be facing a financial setback.

My mind flipped back to the rattlah shirs', and once more I fell into her vernacular. The rattlesnake shirts simply became the shirs'.

It crossed my mind that there could also be black shirts depicting Cottonmouth pit vipers with their white mouths wide open, displaying their bristling fangs. Gata shirs' might also be a big hit. I pondered the idea of adding them to my start-up shirt brand. Surely I could contract out the sewing to cheap labor in Asia. However, the higher quality of American seamstresses might trigger more sales. And I had to use highly skilled artisans to either silk screen or embroider the incredibly realistic snake creatures onto the material. *What would the startup costs be?*

With a twinge of remorse, I thought it was too bad I'd just spent $2,000 on these shirs'. Unless I got some big orders, my bank account would be terribly thin at the end of the convention. The cost of the hospitality suite was another consideration. The two grand paid to Mothe' Moses could have been used to pay for all the free food and booze I would soon be serving to clients and prospects.

Highway 90 took me all the way to New Orleans, where it became the West Bank Expressway, which circled to the south of New Orleans, then to the north, and, ironically, west again over the mighty Mississippi. The Mississippi River snaked around New Orleans and under the Crescent City Connection Bridge (CCCB), a two-span bridge system with one span for each direction of traffic. I found it difficult to keep my eyes off the river traffic and on the cars around me.

On the north side of the river, I took a right-hand, downhill exit, which curved to the left and under the raised freeway. Making a complete U-turn, the off-ramp ended at Convention Center Boulevard. After turning left onto Convention Center Boulevard, I found myself in the shadow of the towering overhead Interstate structure. Moving forward, I sensed the electronic buzz of overhead power lines, now in a chorus with the imagined buzzing of my cargo. The concrete roadway was divided by a lush green median, which gratefully offset the stark face of the Ernest N. Morial Convention Center, now lined with mostly gray and dull silver cars and trucks. After an interminable drive past the bland frontage of the Convention Center, the scene changed to a pleasant ocean mural on the walls of the Audubon Aquarium of the Americas. The humpback whales beckoned me to turquoise waters and azure skies. Enthralled with their implied cavorting, I temporarily forgot about the backseat buzzing that wouldn't leave me alone. I made my way to Canal Street and finally turned onto Bourbon Street.

Bourbon Street

DAYTIME BOURBON STREET barely resembles its nighttime reputation. Like me, there were supply trucks making their way to, and double-parking in front of, the many stores and restaurants on the bawdy street. I had reservations at the Royal Soncsta Hotel, an elegant four-star hotel on Bourbon Street. I believed it was the perfect location for our hospitality suite, since the convention would coincide with the French Quarter Festival.

I stopped on the street filled with daytime delivery trucks rather than revelers. Horns blared as I double-parked, exited the SUV, and darted around the front to the concierge on my right. I made arrangements for valet parking as chorus of horns and curses continued from behind my Durango. Oddly enough, all that noise was accompanied by a feeling of the buzzing of rattlah tails.

I quickly shrugged off the thoughts of buzzing and walked under the balcony-covered facade and across the red tile of the entryway where a friendly man opened the door and introduced me to the gorgeous lobby of the hotel.

The first thing I saw was an architectural feature simulating a medium-sized fountain. The raised fountain was encircled by what looked like exquisitely polished Italian marble laid out in triangular shapes of tan and dark browns and arranged to form a radiating star. The fountain was non-functioning, but filled with greenery typical of New Orleans. The center of the fountain erupted, not with water, but with an incredibly extravagant blooming floral arrangement. Hanging from the low ceiling above the floral fountain was an elegant crystal chandelier. The ceiling of wood, laid in large dark squares with light-colored centers, was reminiscent of New Orleans architecture from the early 1900s.

Stepping into the lobby was a contrast in worlds. The air was dry and cool. On my right was a restaurant, making preparations for the evening. On my left was a beautiful arched hallway, lined with columns, all finished in rich yellows and light tans highlighted by warm incandescent lighting. The ambiance exuded a rich and warm invitation to enter, relax, and enjoy the charm and hospitality of a home away from home.

I was impressed. It was even better than I expected. I had reserved a large hospitality suite on the second floor with an expansive balcony overlooking Bourbon Street. I wanted to instill a party atmosphere into the hearts and minds of those who came to my suite, which would be stocked with free food and booze. The second floor was close to the action and excitement of Bourbon Street, yet up and away from it at the same time. The tone of the four-star hotel was unabashed opulence and a stark contrast to the Bourbon Street frontage with its exploitive debasement of life and morals. The storefronts of Bourbon Street were more utilitarian in nature, designed to be alluring to festival attendees with copious amounts of food, booze, and sex.

A Decision

I'D BEEN TO THE French Quarter many times. It is a contrast of openness and closure. During daytime hours, heavy wooden doors in greens and blues lock the inner world away from peering eyes. Daytime doors were more for suppliers than party-goers. The metamorphic transition to nighttime hours is something to behold, and I imagined the change that would soon occur. As the nighttime doors opened, the humid air would fill with world-famous New Orleans jazz and other lesser-known musical forms. Cajun cooking would scent the air, and, with the coming weekend, the excitement of a carnival would begin to invade the streets.

The convention planners had picked this week for a reason, and I thought they were very smart about it. It was the week of The French Quarter Festival, which would reach full stride on Friday night. It is said that the festival sports two hundred hours of free music of many styles on seventeen stages. There would be food, dancing, and laughter, setting the perfect moods for convention travelers. I was pleased to have landed the hospitality suite overlooking the party atmosphere of French Quarter Street Fest, as they call it.

So many thoughts and ideas filled my mind. Interspersed with the excitement around me, I kept thinking about those amazing shirs' and their stunning artwork. I wondered again and again, *where she had obtained them.* I mused the question a hundred times in my mind. *Could they be duplicated?* The artwork was magnificent, and I knew it would take a master artist to recreate the image. Printing it on the shirt would prove just as difficult, but I knew I could find a way. After all, the o-wom'n, Mothe' Moses, had done it, or so she said. Throughout the drive to New Orleans, I had been considering a variety of plans to have the shirs' recreated, and as I walked the final steps to the check-in desk, I decided I didn't need the o-wom'n. I could recreate the shirs' without her.

As I handed my credit card to the hotel clerk, I cringed at the thought of the $650 per night room cost; and that was just for the room. It didn't include the food and drink, which would be, not inexpensively, catered by the hotel. As I rode the elevator up one floor to my room, I recalculated the cost of the convention and the French Quarter Fest. I was sure that the week would cost me more than $10,000. *I need orders* was my overriding thought. As I unlocked the door to my room, I considered the possibility that the shirs' might be the perfect attraction to introduce retailers to my new clothing line and personal brand. I entered my room and stopped short.

The room was incredible! It was decorated with a mix of French Quarter nostalgia and modern luxury. I'd been told that the Bourbon Street Balcony Entertainment Suites were the most coveted and favored hospitality suites in the French Quarter, and now I understood why. I walked across the parlor to the French doors that led to a spacious balcony. Opening the door seemed to suck in the sights, sounds, and smells of a street just beginning to awaken from its sleepy day and stretching into the morning of its long nighttime work cycle. The view of the street was not quite what it would be in a few hours, but my imagination filled the void. I could hear the music, smell the crawfish étouffée, shrimp Creole, and the gata meat. I wondered if any of the o-wom'n's gata meat ever made it to a place like this. *Probably not,* I mused.

I turned back to the room. The wet bar was in its place as promised and looked to be the perfection of hospitality for thirsty visitors. I envisioned the hundred people that would visit my hospitality suite during the evening hours of the convention. I had no way of knowing how many people would actually show up, and I wondered if my costs would indeed exceed my ten grand budget. The expense of the $2,000 to the o-wom'n troubled me once more, but I reminded myself that I had to spend money to make money. It was an old, but too true axiom. There was a lot riding on the success of the week. Would the shirs' help me, or would the cost hurt me? *How can I make the most of it?*

I walked to the bedroom area. It was one of two, also elegant and well appointed. "This place is perfect," I said out loud. Just then, there was a knock at the door. It would be the bellman with my luggage. But there was far more than just luggage. The boxes of goods would nearly fill my second bedroom. The bellman wheeled in his cart and began to unload my special Baton Rouge shipment, which had been flown from Xiamen, China, and the five boxes of shirs'. As he unloaded the goods from one cart and then from a second cart, I thought about the future and hoped it would bring the rewards I had been planning and working toward.

Xiamen, China isn't noted as a big manufacturing center like Shanghai, but I had stumbled across a small factory that made custom-embroidered, collared, pullover shirts, and more. It had an odd name, which had attracted me. *Tu Fiu Trading Company of Showmen, China.* It was an obvious attempt to stand out from the large numbers of manufacturing enterprises. I figured out that Tu Fiu was the English/Chinese phonetic rendition of "Too Few." It was clever and the antithesis of the reality of too many companies to choose from. The last part was just as clever. *Showmen, China* was a play on Xiamen, China. Since the Xiamen factories were away from the hustle, bustle, and limelight of Shanghai, they needed a way to stand out as a higher quality, fair-priced provider of clothing. I had spent a considerable sum on the design and manufacturing of my new clothing line, complete with my own brand and logo. I thought, once again, that the Bayou shirs' might be the perfect marketing tool to launch my own brand.

I handed the bellman a fifty-dollar bill for a tip. The two carts had been full and heavy. I felt he had earned it. I thought once more about the two grand. And then it hit me. *Why pay her at all? I don't need her. I'm sure I can recreate the shirs'.*

Then I remembered the words of Mothe' Moses. It was like I was living it all over again.

"Ah ope yuh a on'es man."

"Oh, I assure you the check is good."

"'Tis goo' now, bu' tamora?"

"Yes, it will be good tomorrow, too."

I remembered her foot tapping and heard a new chorus of buzzing rattlah tails.

"M' li'l babies ah vey p'otective. You be shua, check be goo tamora, too."

"Can I buy more of these shirts?"

"No' shua, mayba no."

"I will come back to see you. We will talk about more shirts."

"We see."

I don't know why Mr. Limbic chose to be so literally coincidental, but I could swear that I had again heard the buzz of rattlah tails. This time, they seemed to be coming from the bedroom where the bellman had left the boxes of shirs'.

I shuddered and decided I needed a drink. The wet bar had already been stocked and since I was paying for it, why not? After long days of travel and stress, the booze and the luxurious bed took over. Within minutes, sleep overtook me, and I was unaware of the rousing nighttime world outside my suite.

— CHAPTER THREE —
TUESDAY EVENING: OLD FRIENDS

Jensen's College Buddy Arrives

I WAS WAKING FROM a deep slumber. I dreamt a dream of party animals whose noise gradually rose to a level I could no longer ignore, but the final lurch into wakefulness occurred when the phone rang.

"Hey Jensen, how yuh doin'?"

It took a moment of cobweb wiping, but I finally figured it was my old friend, Bob.

"Hi Bob, are you in town yet?"

"Just checked in and walked into this incredible hospitality suite! You were right on! This is great!"

A little more wakeful, I mustered up some words, "Yeah, it's pretty nice isn't it? Hey, come on over, our suites are adjoining, and so are our balconies, just like I promised."

"Great, I'll open my side."

JENSEN'S BIRTH NAME WAS Alex McIntyre. He was born near and grew up in Quincy, Massachusetts. A wealthy family tree made it possible for Alex to pick from the better educational institutions without regard for the cost of tuition. His undergrad work was at Boston College. His MBA came from Duke University where brand and retail studies were his focus. Jensen earned a second Master's degree in International Marketing at Erivan K. Haub School of Business with a secondary emphasis on business ethics. It was at the Haub School of Business that he met Robert Preston, originally from Tucson, Arizona.

Robert earned his MBA at Arizona State then, like Jensen, sought an International Marketing degree at the Haub School of Business. They became life-long friends on an international study tour. Of course, they were still comparatively young and looked to have some fun along the way.

Jensen developed an interest in the Jensen Interceptor, an English-built sports car, in particular, a convertible 1974 Mark III Jensen Interceptor. He had one imported from Britain to the United States. It was powered by the Chrysler 7.2 liter/440 cubic-inch engine. It should have been a fast car, but the engine was radically detuned to reduce emissions and insurance rates, so its performance was limited. Not being happy with the performance and having money to spend, he decided to retrofit the '74 model with the three, two-barrel carburetor setup from the '71 Dodge engine, also known as the 440 Six Pack. Still suffering from emission controls, it was faster but not quite a hot rod.

Alex took the Jensen Interceptor to Philadelphia when he attended Haub. The two friends had great times in the Jensen. One of their favorite activities was for Alex to slouch down on the right-hand driver-side of the car, barely able to see over the dashboard. When traffic patterns were just right, Robert would stand up in the convertible on what, in America, is the driver's side of the car. He'd raise his hands high in the air, like he was on a roller-coaster, while Jensen drove the car from the right seat. After a few minutes they would both be laughing hysterically at the responses from oncoming traffic, so much so that they'd pull off the street to regain their composure. One day a traffic cop spotted the prank, pulled them over, and issued a hefty fine to Robert. That was the end of their roller coaster rides but spawned a new name for Alex. From that day forward, he became known as Jensen, in honor of his 1974 Jensen Interceptor with 1971 power and its legends of a headless driver. Similar to the *Legend of the Sleepy Hollow* and the headless horseman in Tarrytown, New York, the Jensen had developed its own driverless folklore.

They remained close friends. For nearly a year, Bob and Jensen shared an apartment in Phoenix, while lining up post-graduate jobs.

I walked to and opened the pair of large French doors that effectually converted one hospitality room into two. The combination of rooms made it possible to entertain at least two hundred people. Our goal was to attract convention retailers to our free food and booze parties in the evenings after the convention hall closed. From the expansive balconies, our guests could stand in the pleasant air and look out onto Bourbon Street. When the need arose, they had easy access to more of whatever Bourbon Street had to offer. Of course, before they left, the plan was to have obtained an address where we could send samples of our clothing line, or possibly write up an order.

"Come on in, Bob! Mi casa, su casa! Let's keep the French doors open the entire week."

Bob responded, "Well, maybe not for the entire week. My wife will be here later and, well, you know, we'd like a little privacy."

"No problem, no problem," I retorted with a knowing and slightly jealous smile.

Bob asked, "So how was your drive to Baton Rouge?"

"It was a nice drive and my custom shirs' were waiting for me. Gratefully, everything is here and ready for the convention."

Bob had been involved with his own preparations and quickly added, "I checked my merchandise, too. Everything is there, including the display. Of course, mine isn't as elaborate as yours."

I nodded my head mechanically but had something else on my mind.

"Bob, I've got something incredible to show you. It's in my second bedroom. Believe me, it will blow your mind."

He appeared interested, "Okay, let's see."

I walked to the bedroom and opened the door. A number of boxes were set around the room. Most were obviously Chinese boxes, made in their own cheap style. But another set was very different.

Waving toward the west, I explained, "I made a trip into the bayou after leaving Baton Rouge. I met an o-wom'n in the swamp . . ."

I stopped cold, realizing that with every passing minute I seemed to be drawn back to the language of Mothe' Moses and her son. I decided in that moment to completely give in to their influence.

Picking up my train of thought, I added, "She's a crazy old girl. Her son called her the o-wom'n, but she calls herself Mothe' Moses. She sold me something I think you'll love. Go ahead and open the top box and have a look for yourself."

Bob's mistrust in me had developed from too many practical jokes. He raised his hands and asked, "Is something going to jump out at me?"

I laughed and said, "Nah, but I'll wait over here. I don't want to get between you and the surprise."

Bob gave me a look that said he didn't believe or trust me, hesitated for a moment, then started toward the box while seeking an explanation, "You said you got it from the bayou?"

In a half grin, I said, "Yes."

Almost hesitantly, he asked, "Is it clothing?"

"Yes," I said, still smiling.

His look implied an "*I don't believe it*" attitude.

I have to admit I stepped back another foot. I would've stepped back even further but didn't want to be too obvious. Bob's suspicion was evident. He gingerly pulled open the last two flaps.

"Holy crap!" he grunted, letting go and jumping back.

A smile erupted from my face. He was almost as surprised as me, but he hadn't had the experience with the rattlahs under the boardwalk to add to his surprise.

He stood for some time, looking back and forth between the box and me. I nodded toward the box, coaxing him to go back to it. Finally, he stepped back to the box and asked, "What the hell is that?"

Taking a step forward, I gestured and said, "That's part of my new line of specialty clothing."

He stood and looked in the box from what he felt was a safe distance. At length, he reached into the opened box and pulled out a shirt.

"You said you got this from an old woman in the swamp?"

"Uh huh, like I said she was a little crazy. She talks to the rattlahs that live under her porch and calls them her li'l babies."

Holding the shirt at arm's length, he asked, "What did you pay for them?"

"Too much."

He looked me square in the eyes. "Spill it."

"Twenty bucks apiece."

He dropped the shirt back onto the box and agreed, "You're right, too much!"

"I felt that same way at first, but look at them. The quality is top tier. The material is a high quality cotton weave, the hems and seams are perfect, and the artwork is like nothing I've ever seen."

I watched as Bob took another look at the shirs'. I was sure the shock of the high price had been a good excuse to drop the life-like snake shirt, now hanging partially in and out of the box. And, like me, he showed reluctance to pick it up again, but he couldn't take his eyes off the shirt. *Good, he's intrigued,* I thought. *The realism has not been lost on him. If he's impressed, then that seals my evaluation.*

At last I said, "These are great shirs'." I couldn't help but use the o-wom'n's slang.

I noticed that Bob seemed to stiffen up a bit as his hands moved back toward the shirs'.

"I don't know if I can actually pick it back up. It gives me the creeps."

I laughed and said, "Go ahead, t'won' bite."

He looked at me oddly and said, "T'won'?"

I left out the laughter that had been building in me, "I guess I've picked up some of the slang of Mothe' Moses, the o-wom'n of the swamp."

He looked at me even more dubiously. "What have you done? These shirts are beyond description. They won't bite! Hell, it looks like they could if they wanted to."

"I told you they'd knock your socks off."

Regaining his courage, Bob held the shirt up again and spread it out over his forearm. "I've never seen anything like them. They really do scare me."

I admitted my own fear. "I haven't mustered the courage to put one on yet."

Still uncomfortable with the shir' on his arm, Bob added, "I can see and feel why you haven't put one on. They are more than mere artwork, almost as though there is some kind of malicious life in them and, I swear, despite the high quality of the cotton, I'm getting a scratchy feeling of scales on my arm."

"That's what makes them so cool!" I exclaimed. "They won't be a mainstream shirt, but there is a segment of the population who will love them and will spend $50.00 or more to have one."

I was pleased when Bob agreed. "You're probably right," he said.

Bob put the shirt back in the box and closed the four flaps, careful not to put his hands in contact with the fangs, bristling from the open-mouthed rattlah.

"Coward," I said.

Without even batting an eye, Bob replied, "You got that right."

Just as he said the words, I sensed, more than heard, that back-tingling buzz once more.

"Did you hear that?" I asked.

"Hear what?"

That answered my question. Mr. Limbic was at it again.

I didn't want to tell him about my—what? Hallucinations? "Oh nothing, I'm just trying to spook yuh'."

"I'm spooked enough," he admitted.

"Bob, I'm thinking of adding other images to these sinister bayou shirts. I'm thinking of a Cottonmouth snake on them, its white mouth wide open with bristling fangs. Alligators and black panthers might also be a big hit."

"That sounds creepy," he said, and shuddered.

With visions of dollar signs in my head, I replied, "Yeah, but I bet they sell well."

Shaking his head, he agreed, "They might at that."

"You should buy some," I suggested.

"Buy some? I should buy some—from the o-wom'n? What did you call her, Mothe' Moses?

From that moment on, Bob fell into the alluring vernacular of the o-wom'n, Mothe' Moses.

He continued. "I can't even hang onto the one you just showed me, and you think I should buy some?"

Bob was clearly dragging his heels, so I simply said, "Yes."

Bob became quiet, and I could see the wheels in his head start to turn. "How? Where?"

"I'll give you the GPS coordinates. You could go there tomorrow before the convention starts."

Still not completely sold, he said, "I'll think about it while we're at dinner. I've got to decide if I can actually pick them up and carry them around."

I responded, with a belly laugh, "Got that right! No picky, no selly."

"Smart—"

Before Bob could finish the pronouncement of my derrière, a loud knock sounded on the door. I walked to the door and opened it.

"Good evening, Mr. Foster. I'm Pierre Ambroise, the hotel manager. I just wanted to stop by to see if everything was as you requested and in proper order."

"Everything's great," I said. "This is my friend, Robert Preston. He's in the suite next door."

"Good evening, Mr. Preston. Is everything to your liking?"

Bob give Pierre a big smile and said, "Yes, it's great! You have a wonderful hotel here. It's French Quarter-ish on the outside but elegant on the inside. It suits me fine."

The hotel manager couldn't have been more pleased. "I'm glad you both like the suites. Be sure to call me directly should anything be amiss. Here is my card. If I'm not on the property, the assistant manager will gladly take care of you. I'll leave you to your work. Have a good day and remember to call me if you need anything."

With that pronouncement, Mr. Ambroise turned and left, closing the door behind him.

Bob looked amazed, "Wow, does he ever look French."

I shrugged, "Yes, but with no French accent."

Bob replied, "He's probably a Harvard graduate."

"Probably," I agreed.

Bob responded with, "Let's go eat. I'm starved."

Quickly agreeing, I asked, "Do you have anything in mind?"

Bob scratched at his five o'clock shadow. "I'd like to hit Jackson Square. There's a small restaurant on the corner with great peel-and-eat shrimp; then, let's have a beignet. They're made fresh at the Square and after that, some French pastries."

I'd already heard the stories but had to ask, "Been here before have you?"

Already headed toward the door, he said with his back to me, "Yeah, and I've loved it every time."

A Walk Down Bourbon Street

LEAVING THE PEACE OF the doorway of the Royal Sonesta and stepping onto Bourbon Street was a jolting transition. The change from refined elegance to garish vulgarity was nearly overpowering, and the real party hadn't even begun. It was beginning to turn dusk. It was only Tuesday, and the French Quarter Fest wouldn't officially begin until Thursday. Most of the conventioneers hadn't arrived and the weekend crowds were notably absent. Even at that, walking Bourbon Street was not going to be a Sunday stroll.

Since I'd arrived first, I wanted to refresh the layout of the French Quarter in Bob's mind. We turned to our right and began to stroll along the red brick sidewalk. Gone were the double-parked delivery trucks and vans. At night, vehicular traffic is prohibited, making the street a nice, wide walkway often filled with street performers. I couldn't keep myself from looking back to the hotel, amazed by the contrast, which had to be experienced to understand. The street surface was cracked and broken, the curbside cement in varied stages of disrepair. Building fronts were generally coarse-looking, like rough construction instead of finely finished cabinets. The Royal Sonesta appeared as a different world. I could still feel the beauty of the décor and the quiet magnificence of the interior of the hotel. But it went beyond what I felt. There was also the way it looked. The paint on the Royal was fresh and carefully applied, not so with the buildings across the street, where garish paint was chipped and peeling.

As I looked across, the chipped and peeling facade of the building was forced from my mind by cabaret music. We began walking down the sidewalk, and I took note of the small diameter metal poles that supported the balconies. I eyed them with suspicion, wondering how they supported the immense weight of the guests who nightly stood over the street. I thought of our own balcony and the numbers of people that I hoped would stress the slender steel poles. How much weight would they support?

We walked away from the city center toward Jackson Square. After we crossed Conti Street, I looked back to the block taken up by the Royal and patted myself on the back once more for securing the reservations. After crossing Conti, Bourbon Street seemed to transform from a mildly bawdy fascination to a full array of New Orleans party life. Building after building boasted a variety of food, drink, jazz, and adult entertainment. We leisurely covered the three blocks to St. Peter Street trying to take in the details without being overwhelmed by the weight of the whole. As I rounded a corner, my eye caught the Bistro across the street, and I remembered their Cajun popcorn shrimp, a fiery dish of battered and deep-fried shrimp that I had shared with a special woman on a far-previous visit.

We had given up the red brick of Bourbon Street to the cement sidewalk of St. Peter Street. Its sedate atmosphere was tuned more to shopping than debauchery. I continued to examine the building facades and wondered if the rundown and chipped paint scheme wasn't a purposeful presentation as it had a charm that I was beginning to appreciate.

We were two blocks from Jackson Square, the part of the French Quarter that I enjoy the most. Like Bob, I had my favorite eateries, but the similarity in our lists was surprising. At the corner of St. Peter Street and Chartres Street, we arrived a touristy version of Cajun and Creole cuisine, a great restaurant that catered more to dining than partying.

After being seated, Bob ordered and received a plate of crawfish étouffée. I opted for shrimp and was served a large platter of cooked Cajun-spiced shrimp with heads, legs, and tails still attached. My mind went to back to an overnight voyage from Hong Kong to Xiamen where Chinese diners, in the common dining hall of an old ocean liner, cleaned their shrimp of heads, legs, and tails with their teeth. On that voyage I was the non-conforming American, and I had awkwardly used my fingers to clean and peel my shrimp, as I did again during this meal.

The smells and sounds were delightful. Jazz played in the distance, and people were cheerful. I saw steaming bowls of Jambalaya and heaping plates of red beans and rice served with a variety of seafood. Given all this fun, there is still one New Orleans tradition that I have never enjoyed. I watched as diners bit the heads off and sucked the juice out of boiled crawdads. It reinforced my position: I don't like the idea. I was satisfied with my spicy shrimp, although I reminded myself that the bodies still contained the dark digestive tract, which I tried to ignore.

After our tasty meal, we walked toward the mighty Mississippi. The broad walkway was lined on one side with restaurants and stores and nearly blocked with Tarot card readers and street performers. Rounding the corner and turning left, we passed the carriages with their accompanying smell of horse dung and sweat. At the café we ordered our beignets. A beignet is a square of yeast dough, deep-fried, served hot, and heaped with powdered sugar. Banishing the idea of calories, we added cups of hot chocolate to our order.

"Bob, there may be other places to buy beignets, but these are the best I've ever eaten." We were in a gastronomical paradise.

After the beignets, I was satisfied, but Bob had one more stop on his list.

"It's this way," he said.

Bob strode away from the café, leading me across Decatur Street and along a line of shops on the east side of Jackson Square.

"They serve the best pastry in the world down here," he said with his back toward me.

I followed as quickly as my already over-burdened belly would allow. Bob was on a mission, and I had to work to keep up. Suddenly he stopped short.

"What? It's gone!" he exclaimed.

The poor man was almost apoplectic. He stood statue-like in bewilderment and obvious disappointment. I began to wonder if he was going to cry.

"There, there now, Bob. It's okay," I said, mocking his devastation.

Barely standing upright, he squeezed out the words, "I was looking forward to this more than you can possibly know."

"A pastry shop? You're torn up this much over the loss of a pastry shop?" I didn't understand the problem.

"This was no ordinary French pastry shop. It was the best. And—it's where I met Anne so many years ago."

I realized that he had indelibly connected the pastry shop to his not-so-recent bride, and I reminded myself that Bob was a romantic, despite his business acumen.

"You met your wife here?"

Still staring at the place where the old pastry shop had been, he responded. "Yes, and I wanted to bring her back here for a—well, to relive a moment in time. A special memory."

I decided that I didn't know Bob as well as I thought I did. I was amazed at his sense of loss. I knew he was happily married, but I had never identified the depths of his commitment to love and romance. No wonder he wants the adjoining door closed.

The walk back toward the Royal Sonesta was a little subdued. I tried to cheer Bob, but he wasn't budging from his self-administered gloom.

"Come on, Bob, you've still got your gorgeous wife. She's not going to leave you just because your pastry shop closed."

His "I know," was more of a grunt than real words.

"What do you say, Bob? Let's go get a drink."

"Sorry, Jensen, I don't feel like one."

"Well, how about some jazz?"

"Nah. Not tonight."

Jonah

WE WALKED SLOWLY AROUND the Square and back to St. Peter Street where we took a right. I was steering us toward a shop I had noticed with a sign that said, "Voodoo Shop." My mind shifted from Bob to the o-wom'n. She hadn't looked like the Caribbean visage of a voodoo witch, but I began to wonder. Those shirs' are perfect and at the same time haunting. Mr. Left-Side Logic began a debate with Mr. Right-Side, the creative freethinker, and Mr. Limbic, the ancient flight or fight proponent, who continually joined the conversation. It was a very confusing, mental tug-of-war, and none of the sides wanted to give in.

There was no doubt that the shirs' carried some kind of aura. *How? Why? What could it be?* I was not a believer in voodoo, but as I walked under the sign, I had a desire to enter the store. I stopped and stood in the entryway. It felt creepy inside. The small store was mostly dark, barely lit with candles and what looked like old oil lamps.

"Hey Bob, I want to look around this store."

"I don't."

"Come on, buddy, help me out a bit. Pull yourself together."

He stopped walking and partly turned toward the entrance.

"What is this place?" he asked.

He hadn't noticed the voodoo sign.

"You know those shirs' I showed you?"

"Yes?"

Waving at the shop, I said, "Well, this place makes me think of them and the o-wom'n who sold them to me."

"Why?"

"Well—you know those shirs' are kinda' freaky."

Still refusing to open up, all I got from Bob was, "Yes, they are."

"Well, I've been wondering *why* they're so freaky. I'd like to recreate them and sell them, but I'm beginning to wonder if that's possible. They may have some mystique that I might not be able to recreate."

Bob had finally noticed the voodoo sign. "Are you saying they're cast with voodoo spells?"

I looked up at the sign at the same time. "I'm not saying anything. I'm just wondering."

With a scowl Bob spat out, "I hate that crap!"

"What crap?"

"Voodoo crap!" he snapped. "I think it's all crap," waving his hands and arms as if to include the whole shop. Bob's mood hadn't changed, but at least he was emerging from his morass.

Pushing him a little more I said, "Come on. Humor me, let's go in."

Bob crossed his arms. "You go in. I'll wait for you."

"Ah, come on."

"Nope!" He remained as still as stone.

"Look, Bob, come in with me, and I'll buy tomorrow's meal and the drinks. Deal?"

He turned his head to me and stared, "You're going to buy?"

"Yeah!"

A wan smile appeared, "I know of an awful pricey steakhouse."

"Sky's the limit, Bob. Come on, let's go in."

Now, I'll admit that I didn't want to buy Bob an expensive steak, but I did want his input on the shirs' so I figured it was worth the money. He made a grudging movement toward the door, and I knew I had him. He couldn't resist one more fit of rebellion, "This is stupid, you know?"

"I'm sure you're right, Bob, but let's just check the place out."

The transition to the Voodoo Shop was just as stark as the transition from the Royal Sonesta to Bourbon Street. The store was actually a great study in marketing. Passing through the door was a step into insanity. I immediately felt flooring that reminded me of a dirt surface in a Caribbean hut. I could tell the floor wasn't dirt; it looked and felt firm and, well, cleanable, but somehow, it reminded me of dirt. There was some kind of herbal odor that filled the shop. It wasn't incense, it wasn't strong or pungent; it was inviting, and complimented by burning candles. My senses began to enliven, but the analytical retail side of me kept track of the detail. I noticed that the oil lamps were actually electric. In the dim, barely illuminating light, there was an assortment of dolls, skulls, skeletons, and braided materials made into a variety of soft structures. There were some wooden cabinets near the walls, not finished cabinetry, but made from branches, limbs, sticks, and woven vines. The cabinets had some kind of indirect lighting that projected hanging shapes around them: more skulls, skeletons, and dolls.

Scattered among the voodoo bric-a-brac were old rum bottles. There were also shapes that looked like animals. I wasn't certain if they were real animals that were stuffed or stuffed synthetic animals that looked real. I finally considered that each animal had experienced life. A variety of beaded necklaces made from what appeared to be glass and plastic, but also from shapes of wood, each gnarled and misshapen, were displayed. I could find nothing that I could label as beautiful. It all looked twisted, misshapen, tortured, worn, weathered, or rotted. It was as creepy as the snake head shirs'.

I turned to look at Bob. He was still standing in the doorway with a look of disgust.

"Come on, Bob. The stuff's not gonna bite yuh."

"Yeah, that's what you said about the snake shirts, but they sure look like they could, and this stuff looks like it could . . . well—I just don't like it."

"A deal's a deal and remember I'm buying."

He cautiously took another step into the shop. I noticed him suspiciously eye the door jamb and the floor beyond. I suspected he was hoping to qualify for the steak without getting close to anything in the store.

I heard a whisper of a noise from the back of the shop. A woman emerged from a darkened corner. She was not what I expected. My traditional image of a voodoo woman from the Caribbean would have been heavy, buxom, and with a broken accent. This woman was none of those things, but she was a little scary.

She was tall, at least 5'10". She was gaunt. Her skin was ebony. Her hair was jet black but with white, not gray, strands of hair running through it. It was long, flowing down over both shoulders to the middle of her back. Her skin was smooth and beautiful. Her features were delicate, but her eyes were large and open, as if in a startled state, like she'd just seen an evil spirit. She wore a robe-like garment with little bits of this and that hanging from it. I couldn't tell at first, what the things were, but as she moved closer, I was surprised to see that they were tiny skulls. Mr. Limbic was screaming to get us the hell out of there.

She really didn't walk toward us; it was more like she *whooshed* toward us. Her flowing robe seemed to sing a song of the summer breeze, and her bare feet barely touched the earthen-looking floor. But of all these things, what surprised me most was the beautifully French-accented, but perfectly executed English that welcomed us.

"Welcome to Voodoo. That is the name of my shop, and I am here to serve you."

I was frozen in place, almost in a trance. I struggled to makes sense and began to wonder if I had been taken by some kind of enchantment. It was Bob who spoke first.

"Jensen wants to buy a voodoo doll."

She looked at me with eyes that were as big and as deep as the black pools of the bayou. "Is that so, Mr. Jensen?"

"Ah, no, not really, I—just wanted to have a look around."

And then I wondered, *how does she know my name?* I forgot that Bob had used it, and it made me feel all the more unsettled.

She followed with, "You may look all you please. You may touch and you may hold." But then with the barest smile she added, "But please don't drop. It would make them unhappy."

That statement sent the same kind of chills I experienced every time I thought of the rattlahs under Mothe' Moses' porch.

Again, it was Bob who spoke up. He seemed to be unaffected by the strange ambiance of the store. "Don't worry; I'll keep an eye on him."

Bowing her head slightly, she said, "My name is Jonah. If I can help you, please ask."

I nodded my head and, for the first time since entering the store, I mumbled, "Thank you."

She courteously nodded back at me and stayed in her place. The shop was silent.

I finally summoned the courage to take some uncomfortable steps. There was actually nothing in the store that interested me, but I had become very interested in Jonah. I walked from this skull to that cat's claw, to a gata jaw with gray-white but seemingly gleaming teeth. I accidentally brushed past a doll that rattled to the floor. You could hear the gasp that came from Bob and my overworked lungs. In a whoosh, Jonah scooped up the doll. She gave me a look like, "Didn't you hear what I said?" But she said nothing, simply putting on a very polite smile.

I decided that Jonah wasn't scary, but she *was* unnerving. She reminded me again of the o-wom'n. There were similarities in their—aura. I smiled back and croaked out an, "I'm sorry." Once more, she nodded her head and held me with her simple smile and jet-black eyes.

With great effort, I broke away from her hold and took a few more steps around a rustic, wooden display case. My bones jumped, even if my skin didn't move. All I saw at first was the wide-open, long-fanged, white mouth. It was a stuffed and mounted cottonmouth, a water moccasin, or was it alive? I couldn't tell for sure, but I remembered that cottonmouths hiss. Since I heard no hiss, I felt some relief that the snake lacked life. Nonetheless, I became attracted to its perfectly white mouth. It was almost brilliantly white. My initial grunt was still echoing through the store, and both Bob and Jonah knew something had scared me.

"Oh," she said, "you've just met Blackie!" she said softly, as if Blackie were her household pet.

Blackie, I thought, what is the deal with these people? One calls rattlahs her babies and another names her stuffed cottonmouth, Blackie. What a strange world.

With the subject of snakes visually before me, Bob spoke once more, "Jensen wants to ask you about some shirts he bought."

While her deep black eyes focused upon me, she opened her mouth and queried, "What kind of shirts? I do carry a few shirts."

Finally, there was some common ground, I hadn't thought of her as being a shirt retailer.

"I bought some shirs' from an o-wom'n out near Houma, in the swamps. They're spectacular shirts."

The woman was good, but not good enough to hide her realization that I'd met Mothe' Moses. Her face showed recognition and then curiosity.

"Oh, you met Mothe' Moses."

"Yes, I met her," a smile growing on my face.

"And you bought some shirts from her?"

At first her statement sounded like an indictment, her look seemed stern, but then she smiled. It was a cautious smile, a knowing smile, and I wondered what she knew.

I felt like I was under a blisteringly hot interrogation but managed to say, "Yes, and they are amazing shirs'."

As if her analytic mind had worked through a future scenario, the smile began to leave her face. It was replaced by a more serious look. "Are you sure you understand what those shirts are?"

I didn't know how to respond.

She saw my quandary and asked, "When did you buy them?"

"Today. Just today," I said.

Her eyes began flicking back and forth from me to Bob, and she asked, "Have you worn one yet?"

"No, I'm afraid to put one on."

Her black eyes stopped on mine and locked into my being. She seemed to be searching my soul. At last she asked, "What are you going to do with them?"

"I'm actually in the wholesale shirt business. I'm going to sell them."

One eyebrow dropped, while the other lifted, "Sell them?"

"Yes."

"In stores? Like mine?"

I was feeling deeply scrutinized. "Well, yes, possibly, and other stores, too. Mostly specialty stores, I guess. I haven't decided for sure."

She turned softly, moving away, still floating more than walking. At a nearby rustic rack, Jonah picked up a dark green tee shirt. As she walked back toward me, Mr. Limbic sounded the alarm, reminding me of my shirs' with the hidden sound of buzzing. As she approached, I wanted to step back, but I determined that I had to hold my ground, a task that became incredibly difficult as she held the shirt out to me.

"Do the shirts look like this?"

The face of an immense Eastern Diamondback Rattlesnake, one with which I was now well familiar, filled my vision and rattled my nerves. In stoic bravery, I reached out, and I took the shirt. In a simple habitual move made thousands of times before, I shook the shirt, and it unfolded before my eyes and the eyes of Mr. Limbic. The was no hiding my guttural gasp as the wide-open, fanged mouth of a great Eastern Diamondback Rattlesnake snapped into full focus. Mr. Limbic screamed, but Mr. Logic kept the sound to a grunt. Then the shirt dropped to the floor.

"That's twice," said Bob.

My hands were shaking, and I felt paralyzed. There was no way I could reach down to pick it up, but I didn't need to. Jonah quickly had it in hand and barely a second later, it was folded over her arm, the snake head hidden.

She looked at me even more deeply, "Why did you buy those shirts?"

"I was amazed by their craftsmanship." I took a gut pill and reached toward the shirt, "Here, let me show you."

Jonah handed me the shirt and with all the composure I could muster, I laid it across my arm. I started into my spiel, just like I was pitching a customer.

I decided to drop the Mothe' Moses dialect. "First of all, the shirts I bought were collared, not tee shirts like this; but notice that this is extraordinary cotton weave. The thread count is high, and the fabric is soft, and it is absorbent. This is, in short, extremely high quality cotton, similar to an Egyptian cotton. Secondly, the stitching is among the finest I've ever seen. The seams are perfect; there are no crooked stitches, no exposed or frayed edges, and no loose thread ends. The artwork is incredibly life-like. A pure artisan with exquisite craftsmanship created this image. Lastly, but certainly not least, the application of the art to the material is superior to anything I have ever seen. The colors are vivid in their hue and tone, in part because of the quality of the cotton and secondly because of the quality of the inks used in the process. This is a magnificent shirt."

There, I'd said it all. In one moment I had summed up all the qualities of the shirt, but somehow the description was lacking. Jonah had been studying me while I lauded the virtues of the shirt. She continued to watch me after I had finished. The silence seemed to last for hours, but was over in seconds.

"You've said much about this shirt; now tell me, what do you want to know?" she commanded.

I was nearly stammering as the question exploded from my mind. "Where did they come from? (And I slipped back into the swamp-talk.) That o-wom'n didn't make this shirt. Where did she buy it, or have it made? I want more of them."

With furrowed brows she asked, "You want more of a shirt that terrifies you?"

Caught between horror and exhilaration, I nearly shouted, "Yes, there is a market segment that will buy these shirts, just for the sheer terror they cause."

She turned and seemingly floated away again, like a dark elf, which had little need for walking. She moved around a display area, stopped, and then turned to face me. Very calmly she said, "I cannot tell you."

Her voice was matter of fact, not a voice of apology for not knowing, but a voice almost unable to speak a truth, or a fact. In my depths I felt the difference, she was constrained by something from answering my question, which meant that she knew the answer.

I decided to challenge her. "You mean you will not tell me because you choose not to, or do you mean there is something that keeps you from telling me?

Her face suggested that she realized I understood more than she wanted to let on.

"I would not tell you if I could, and I cannot tell you, because I am unable to speak the words."

I heard Bob snort behind me, "Come on, Jensen, this is crazy. I've got some things I need to do."

Jonah's eyes were locked onto mine once more, neither blinking nor giving ground. It was miserably uncomfortable, but I weathered the long moment of her dark piercing eyes. At last, they softened.

"Sir, you have stumbled onto something that will become an education for you. I can tell you nothing more than that, except I hope you gain an education that is good for you. Now, is there anything else I can help you with?"

Bob spoke impatiently, still behind me, "Come on, Jensen, she's inviting us to drop it and leave. Take a hint and let's go."

I didn't want to leave. The whole thing was getting under my skin, and there were now two women, one old and one young, each so intriguing as to nearly drown out all else. Well, all else but the shirs'. Despite the desire to stay, I turned and walked out the door with Bob, who was already on the sidewalk, walking toward the hotel. I quickly caught up. At first, we walked in silence. I think we both wanted to talk about the shirs', but we simply didn't know what to say. Eventually, small talk developed, and we began reminiscing about the old days and the great fun we'd had as students as well as the year we'd spent in Phoenix. It became evident that Bob wanted to go back to the hotel, but I wanted a drink. I prevailed, and we stopped at a place famous for its bourbon and jazz. We continued to avoid the subject of the shirs', but in the end, and after the dulling effects of the liquor and the rhythmic jazz, it was Bob who brought them up.

"I'd like to see one of those shirs' again, when we get back to the hotel."

Nearly choking on my drink, "So now your interest is piqued?"

"Yeah, you could say that. I watched an amazing performance back there, you and the—I don't know what to call her. I'm not sure she was human. Nothing about her made sense. Even her name is wrong."

In the wickedest smile I could conjure, I jabbed at him. "So, you've looked over my shirs' and now you want them for yourself . . ...."

Bob laughed, "Well, I admit there could be a big market for them."

We talked too far into the night about the shirs', our futures, directions to the swamp, and GPS coordinates so Bob could go meet the o-wom'n.

When I finally climbed into bed, exhausted by the events of the day, my last thoughts, just before I slumbered off, were about money and the huge gamble I was taking on this convention. *If things don't work out well, I could be in real financial trouble.* The thought of spending the $2,000 suddenly filled me with an anxiety that kept me awake too many hours into the night. What if I stopped payment on the check? As the thought crossed my mind, I thought once more that I heard the buzz of those crazy rattlah tails. With a shiver, I fitfully dreamed through a restless night's sleep. Sounds of the swamp fought for my attention and a vision of a malicious leering viper kept rearing its nasty head, hissing and spiting, causing me to cower in my sleep.

— CHAPTER FOUR —
WEDNESDAY: BOB VISITS THE SWAMP

Breakfast for Bob

I AWOKE EARLY. The one-hour time zone change from New York to New Orleans had given me a slight advantage over jet lag. I felt a little sorry for Jensen. It was two hours earlier than his San Francisco time zone. I thought about calling him but decided not to. I ordered room service instead, which was on time and cooked to perfection. I enjoyed both the flawless Eggs Benedict and the fresh-squeezed orange juice while sitting in the rays of a warming sun on my balcony over an uncharacteristically quiet Bourbon Street. I wasn't aware that Jensen was already awake, nor that he was hatching a plan.

Jensen's Plan

I'LL CALL THE BANK and put a stop payment on the check. She has no phone, no car, and no means of catching up with me.

The convention had indeed been an expensive one to attend. I'd been required to pay most of the costs before the convention even started. Regular business costs continued to soar, and buyers continued to want better and better deals. The profit margin was already slim and getting slimmer. I quickly went through the calculations in my mind. *I can sell half of the shirts for $65 each as specialty shirts. That will more* *than cover my extra shipping costs. I'll take the other sixty shirts and use them as samples for buyers. They are unusual shirts; there is nothing like them in the world; there is no competition; and I won't have to cut the prices. With those sixty shirts, I'll bet I can get fifteen buyers to write checks for orders. This convention may be profitable after all.*

I have to admit that I wasn't the most honest guy in the world. I had cheated a little here and a little there, but the thought of stopping the check on the o-wom'n made me feel a bit odd. A slight chill ran down my spine. Then I heard something. I stopped and listened intently. It almost sounded like buzzing, and it seemed to be coming from the second bedroom where I had stored the shirs'. I shook off the thought and went back to my work. I had much to do.

Bob and the O-wom'n

BOURBON STREET SEEMED LAZY with only a few delivery trucks and vans parked at the curbs, and even they seemed subdued. The street had been relatively quiet last night, which I knew would change as the week progressed. I had enjoyed the quiet and almost dreaded the river of party animals that would soon be present.

Jensen had given me directions and a GPS location of the o-wom'n, as he'd been calling her. The whole story was almost unbelievable—the o-wom'n, the rattlahs, and the voodoo woman, Jonah. It made a more than surreal trilogy. Given the circumstances, it was a trio I had to experience for myself.

The drive wasn't bad; in fact, it was pleasant, especially for a Manhattan-ite. It was nice to get out from towering and sometimes cold, over-shadowing skyscrapers to experience the verdant green of the swamplands. The divided highway was an easy drive. Jensen's Durango had a satellite radio that I tuned to an easy listening channel. If there was no bayou prize at the end of my day, the relief of a low stress, scenic drive was worth the time.

Frankly, I was surprised that the broken road leading to the o-wom'n was in the GPS database, but true to Jensen's word, I was led to the wayside where the o-wom'n lived. I hoped she was there. Jensen had warned me about the price of gas, so I made sure I had plenty in the tank before I turned off Highway 90. I hadn't kept track of the miles from 90 to the little wayside area, but they seemed unending, mostly because the road was twisting and filled with potholes.

It was just as Jensen described. The little wayside was an odd bit of ground surrounded on all sides by the swamp. I was in the middle of countless cypress trees, thick undergrowth, and miles of dark green and brown water. I wondered what I would find if I kept driving beyond the little wayside. I loved knowing what was around the next bend. If time hadn't been a factor, I might have driven on down the road to see where it might lead me and what I might see.

I stopped at the edge of the wayside to take in the entire scene. On the left was the old shack on stilts. Next to the shack were the gray gas station and the infamous sign, at least in my mind, with prices for worms, gas, and pop. I wondered how they dealt with inflation since the sign appeared to be unchanged, other than to be weather-bleached. The old store was on the left, just as Jensen had described it. Across the road and on my right, was the lane with the rusting trailer house.

I drove slowly past the gas station and down the length of the old store. Yes, there was the alcove, and there was the rocker, but there was no o-wom'n. I pulled the Durango up to the front of the building. The gravel crunched under my tires just as Jensen said it would. It was almost like reliving his experience, except that I would not have to come up with cash for Mr. Hulk, nor walk the length of the snake-in-fested boardwalk. The thought of walking the length of the old store porch brought me to a new realization, since she wasn't in her chair, I might have to walk to her door and knock, which I was loath to do.

There was no one in sight. Other than the rustling of leaves from a slight breeze and the unsettling sounds of the swamp, the wayside was quiet. The silence was, however, overshadowed by a profusion of green and heavy humidity. An odd thought came to me. If it was human-made, it was rundown; if it was nature-made, it was verdant green, and all of it was wrapped in a coating of moisture or dust. I would later learn that there were also countless legions of biting bugs.

I sat in the Durango for five minutes and then ten. I really didn't want get out and walk across that porch. I didn't even want to get close to the front of the porch. I thought, just once, of reaching out and throwing a few pebbles across the porch to see what might happen. If the rattlers didn't buzz, would I be safe? I also thought about tossing small pebbles at the front door. Maybe the o-wom'n would hear the noise and come to the door. Or, I could simply honk the horn, but the mood felt too reverent to be interrupted by such an extreme audible fusillade. A little unnerved by the non-Manhattan quiet, I wondered why she hadn't heard the SUV drive up. Even more troubling, the infamous cooler wasn't in its place. She must be gone. I looked back toward the garage half expecting to see Mr. Hulk leaning up against the gas pump, watching me. It appeared vacant, too.

I sat in the Durango for nearly thirty minutes, wondering if I should stay or go. I reclined my seat and opted to wait a bit longer, after all what was waiting a few minutes compared to the long drive I had just made? I left the engine running and thought how absurd that would be in New York with the enormous pressure on drivers to cut down on vehicle idling time. I looked at the surrounding forest and convinced myself that it would recycle the carbon emissions.

I had almost dozed off when I heard the rattling. My jump from near slumber conjured rattlesnakes, but I realized that what I had heard was a vehicle. I looked around toward the barely muffled sound and saw a beaten-up, rust-infected, mud-caked, dirty-windowed four-wheel drive Willis Jeep. A massive man sat in the driver's seat and a willow-wisp of a woman sat on the passenger's side. They, of course, took immediate notice of the Durango. In fact, I'm sure the o-wom'n recognized it. Then the air was filled with a chorus of rattler buzzing, and I thanked God that I had not walked up to the front door.

The Jeep pulled into a space by the gas pumps. Mr. Hulk lumbered out of the Jeep, but the o-wom'n smartly sprang out and onto the ground. She walked quickly toward me and across the gravel with its noisy crunching. She had a not-so-kind look on her face. The closer she got, the angrier she looked, and I considered leaving; but, because I couldn't imagine why she would be angry, I elected to stay.

It didn't take long for the o-wom'n to cross the sixty feet between the Jeep and Jensen's rented Durango. Since she was clearly headed directly toward me, I opened the door when she was still fifteen feet away. She was moving so fast I was afraid I might hit her if I waited to open the door.

As soon as my door was fully open, she stopped. It was a dead stop, and her facial expression changed. I could see that a question had filled her mind. She stood more erectly and exclaimed, "Same ca, diffren' man!"

I realized that she expected to see Jensen in the Durango. I immediately wondered why she was so angry with him.

"Are you Mothe' Moses?" I asked, immediately wishing I had pronounced her name with more respect.

"I be hea. Wha' you wan?"

Her eyes looked fierce. I decided to slip into her vernacular. "You sold some shirs' to my friend yesterday. Do you remember that?"

Without a change in her demeanor she said, "Yuh, I r'memba."

"I wanted to know if you have any more shirts to sell."

And odd smile crossed her face. "Yuh wan buy shirs'?"

"Yes, do you have more?"

The odd smile became almost a smirk. "Yuh wan rattlah shirs'?"

"Yes, if you have them, or even something else."

Her face became serious. "Wha yuh do wit'um?"

"I'll sell them."

With a look of knowing she said, "So, yuh sel shirs', too?"

"Yes, I do."

I saw her eyes move from mine to the running Durango and back to the rear of the car. I pressed the button that turned it off. She looked back to me. The loss of cold refrigerated air immediately opened the pores on my hands and arms. In seconds, beads of sweat trickled down my back. I became uncomfortable with the heat, the humidity, and my own sweat, but most of all, the o-wom'n's piercing eyes. I felt guilty, like a child being grilled by an overbearing father, while in a state of innocence. She didn't speak, and I didn't know what to do. I began to envision a herd, if that's what you call them, of snakes slithering out from under the porch, attacking me at her command. As the silence grew, I felt more and more uneasy. Thoughts of leaving flashed through my mind. At last I gained a morsel of courage and asked, "Have I done something wrong?"

"I d'no.' Ave yuh?"

"I don't think so. If I have done something wrong, I'm unaware of it, and I'm sorry."

She seemed to take an even closer look at me, examining my very soul. I was about to close the door when she said, "Com ta'k." She motioned to the porch.

I more guessed at than understood her slang, but decided she wanted me to go to the porch with her. I didn't want to. It wasn't clear that she had given up her anger, and I had a vibrant memory of Jensen's story about the snakes under the porch, plus there was their welcoming chorus.

I stepped out of the car and onto the crunchy gravel. I eased myself around the door and pushed it shut, making sure the key fob was in my pocket. She started toward the porch, and I slowly followed. I wanted her to take the first step. It wasn't that I thought such a move would have protected me, but I at least felt better about it. Despite her leadership, I found myself frozen at the edge of the steps that led up to the porch as she plopped into her rocking chair.

"C'mon, sonny. Wha' yuh wait'n' fur?"

I honestly didn't know, except that I was more terrified than I had ever been in the back alleys of Manhattan or even the deserts of Arizona.

I cautiously stepped up onto the porch. There was no buzzing. There was a chair near her, and I walked toward it. The boards creaked and groaned, but there was no buzzing reprise. As I sat, the chair groaned but, other than that, silence reined.

"Dat man a good man?" she asked pointing to the Durango.

I assumed she meant Jensen.

"Yes, he's a good man."

"He be yuh fren'?"

"Yes, we're good friends."

"He eva steal fr'm yuh?"

"No, why?"

"He eva steal fr'm othas?"

"Not that I know of."

"Been in jail?"

"No. Never." I thought back to the near miss of being jailed over the car escapades and began wondering about this inquisition. *Oh no, he didn't*, I thought. "Are you angry at Jensen?"

"No an'ry! Mad!"

"Mad. What did he do?"

"He steal fr'm me and ma li'l babies." With that statement she thumped the floor with her cane and the requisite chorus quickly began and just as quickly faded away.

I knew what she meant by her babies.

I quietly asked, "He stole from you?"

"Yuh, he steal fr'm me."

Still surprised, I asked, "Are you talking about the shirs'?"

"Yuh, his check no good. He steal."

I have to admit I was surprised. Jensen usually managed his finances very well. What could have happened? I knew the convention had set him back a ton of money, but I couldn't imagine him letting his bank account get so low as to bounce a check.

I spoke up once more. "Did you go to your bank?"

"Yuh, we wen. Check no good."

I truly felt bad—bad for her and bad for Jensen. "I'm sorry to hear that. I'm sure he'll make it good."

"No' so shua. Banka' say stop pay on it."

"A stop payment?" I was shocked. That didn't sound like Jensen.

"Why yuh come? I gah no mo' snake shirs'."

"Any others?"

This time there was no quick response. Several moments passed, and her anger seemed to wane. Once more, I felt like I was caught as a subject in a character study.

"Yuh on'es'?"

What does she mean? Am I hot? I answered, "Yes."

"He say dat, too. He no' on'es."

I believed she was speaking of Jensen.

"Well, I am and I brought cash."

"Cash?"

"Yes, cash."

"I take yuh to som' weah special. Yuh cum wi' Mothe' Moses."

Having commanded, she jumped to her feet and was on her way. Before she had taken more than three steps I forcefully called to her, "Mothe' Moses!"

She stopped and turned, "Ya, sonny."

Why are you called "Mothe' Moses?"

She eyed me for a moment. It was disconcerting, and I wished I hadn't asked. *Is she questioning my honesty again?*

Her mouth opened but, at first, she did not speak. At last she raised her right hand and pointed back to the old rundown garage. "Se da' man?"

I turned, "Yes."

"He be ma son."

I said nothing; I was shocked.

"Hi name be Moses. I be Mothe' Moses."

It was all so simple, except to wonder how such a tiny woman could give birth to such a massive man.

Into the Swamp

SHE TURNED AND WAS once more on her way. I rose and followed her to the distant end of the old closed-down store. She rounded the corner and scuttled over a trail that took her back and behind the building. I noticed a short dock where a ten-foot boat with a small outboard motor was tied up. She was obviously walking toward it.

"We go fo bot ri'e," she said with her back to me.

I froze in my tracks. I am not a waterman. In fact, I hate water. If the water is over my shoulders, or I can't see the bottom, I am terrified by it. Add the experience of the last two days, and it felt like sheer suicide to get into the boat with the o-wom'n. I just couldn't do it.

Mothe' Moses picked up the rope securing the small boat and turned toward me. She saw my obvious hesitation, looked long and hard at me and finally said, "Yuh 'fraid wa'er?"

I shook my head, *yes*.

"Yuh 'fraid snakes?

Yes, I nodded again.

"Don' ned be 'fraid. No hurt w'me hea."

I shook my head again. This time it meant a tentative *maybe*.

The following events were more surreal than real, I must admit. It's almost like I was watching the scene from behind a silk curtain. As she walked toward me, she opened an old bag she had been carrying. She pulled out a smaller bag and removed something that looked green. She held out her hand and showed it to me. It might have been some kind of green moss. She said not a word, just held out her hand. I didn't react. She turned, walked back to the water's edge and rinsed the green stuff in the water. She began rubbing it in her hands, like soap, occasionally reaching down, taking up water and dripping it onto the stuff. When she came back, she had green goo in the palm of her hand. Without a word, she began wiping it onto my forehead. It felt cool, but nothing more. Then she took my hands, placed the green mush in them.

"Now, yuh rub hans t'geder."

I did as I was told and after a few seconds of rubbing, she spoke out again.

"Now, yuh rub on fo'ead."

It was hard to deny her, and I didn't try, I simply rubbed the green goo all over my forehead.

After a moment, she stopped me, and just looked at me. I silently and motionlessly waited. After a few more moments, I felt the panic abate.

"How you feel?"

"I feel better."

"Good, I rubbed you with very special herbs that are helping you fight the fear, the bugs and the snakes."

I looked at her, smiled and asked, "How does that work? Do you realize what that would be worth to drug companies?"

"Yes, I know. Won't work for them."

Arching my brows, I said, "It won't work for them, why not?"

"One day, maybe one day, you understand."

Suddenly, I realized that her speech had become intelligible.

"Now you get in the boat. We go for ride."

It was true. The fear was gone. I had been afraid, but I now felt no fear, even though the boat rocked badly when I clumsily scrambled aboard.

"You don't know boats, do you?"

"No, I don't."

"You learn."

From that moment on, the o-wom'n became more than an old woman. She deserved a more respectful title and, to me, it would be Mothe' Moses.

Mothe' Moses was at the helm, if that's how you describe it. She was certainly in control. She deftly maneuvered the small boat in and around a confusing mass of trees and waterways. Sometimes the channel was broad and open, and sometimes things were very close and personal. We often ducked under branches and limbs. After about forty minutes of boating, she powered the boat onto a muddy slick.

"This where gators go in 'n out."

Oddly enough, I wasn't frightened by the thoughts of sharing the boat landing with a twelve-foot gator. We got out of the boat, and she started off through the varied terrain. It continually changed from wet, to dry, to mud, from open grassland to heavily forested areas, and from solid earth to swampy marshes. One thing that seemed not to change was that the entire land was littered with bogs, which we walked around. We crawled over and under a variety of bushes, logs, and brush, more than I could ever imagine. I had noticed the swarms of bugs that circled around us kept their distance. Strangely, none of them tried to land, and I suffered not a single bug bite, although a buzzing gray cloud seemed always to be present. I asked Mothe' Moses about them.

"They no like your blood after the herbal rub. It too bitter."

I marveled at the miracle herb. I wondered what it was called and was about to ask, but just then she stopped. Ahead was a very thick copse of brush with a large area of soggy, swampy water surrounding it.

Using a directional nod with her head she said, "We have to get over there."

"Where?" I asked.

She pointed to a stand of bushes. "To the brush."

"Okay." I was already far into the excursion, why hesitate now? Besides, I felt no fear.

"You take off shoes and socks here or you lose them."

I obediently took off my shoes. Hers stayed on, but they were hiking shoes with heavy laces that would hold them onto her feet. My first few steps told the story. The mud was from six inches to two feet deep. It was a difficult slog. I was soon sweating more water than my body could afford, I was covered from head to toe in mud and becoming exhausted. As I stumbled, lurched, and fell into the mud, quickly losing my strength, I was surprised to see her move at will, across the muddy stretch between the brush and us. Mothe' Moses was so light that she seldom sank into the mud. It also looked like her boots were bigger than normal. I hadn't noticed this before. I wondered if they acted like snowshoes.

After an exhausting effort, I made it out of the mud to the stand of brush. I flopped onto the ground to rest.

"You not in good shape, sonny."

I rolled over onto my side to face her, "Not as good as you."

"You have soft life."

I agreed with her but didn't speak the words.

For the first time, it appeared that she looked at me with some level of kindness, not a brusque business demeanor. "We rest for a minute, then I show you treasure."

I silently agreed, closed my eyes and tried to ignore the buzzing insects that never landed to suck my apparently bitter blood. I was glad for that small blessing, even though I hated the constant buzzing.

"Your home in the desert?"

My eyes opened and shifted to hers. It was the first time I felt comfortable looking into her eyes. "I grew up in Tucson, Arizona. How did you know?"

"You look and feel like you comes from the desert."

Arching my shoulders, I said, "I didn't know desert dwellers have a look and feel."

She said offhandedly, "Most people not notice."

Questions filled my mind. "Mothe' Moses, have you ever been out of the swamp?"

"No."

She said nothing more, so I asked, "How do you know the look and feel of a desert dweller?"

"I watch, I listen, I understand. Most people tell more by not talking than when they talk. I keep track and remember for my whole life. I met many people in the swamp and remember most of them. They all tell a story, and I remember stories. I've seen your story before. You from the desert, you hate snakes, water, and gooey earth. There's more that you tell, but that's enough for me to repeat."

I had been nursing an unspoken question from the beginning. I knew it was rude to ask but felt compelled to know.

"How old are you?"

"Now you insult me."

Nervously shifting, I was at once embarrassed. "I'm sorry, but you don't strike me as the kind of woman who would care about her age."

"You right, I no care, especially 'cause I'm older than you think. You guess?"

"Sixty-five?"

"No, much older."

My mind filled with wonder. He skin was wrinkled and a dark tan from too much sun, but she had a physical vitality, clear eyes and an incredibly sharp mind. I no longer wanted to guess, but I did. "Seventy-five?"

"Still older."

Not wanting to insult her any more than I already had, I simply stopped the game. "I give up, you tell me."

"I am older than the broadest Cypress and younger than the smallest sapling. I have no age; I just Mothe' Moses. I have no birthday, and I remember no parents. I just am. I remember no day that say how old I am. I just am. That's all I know. So I can be as old as I want, or as young as I want. It never matters. I just am. I just be Mothe' Moses. Kinda' like God, no beginnin' and no end."

Inside, I smiled, but kept it from my face. I was developing a deep affection for the woman I now called Mothe' Moses. I already had a deep respect for her, but she was filling a soft and treasured spot in my heart; one I knew would not likely be cast out.

She must have sensed my thoughts. She looked at me with eyes that were now very tender and said kindly, "You a good boy. It good we came here today. You help yourself, and you help your friend, and you help many others. Good we came. And now we go just a little farther."

She quickly rose and, tired as I was, I followed. We hadn't gone fifty feet when she stopped and squatted. I stood behind her. She appeared to be looking for something. She rolled forward onto her knees and started crawling, first to the left and then to the right. I watched and waited. She hadn't told me to do anything yet. It took perhaps ten minutes, and then she stopped. She began to finger something in the thick mat of undercover. I moved closer to look at whatever it was that had caught her interest.

Treasure

MOTHE' MOSES WAS PARTING the grasses around a small clump of very unusual vegetation. She patted down the grass in a circle. As she did so, a tiny spindle of a plant became apparent. The plant had one tiny bloom on the tip of its main stem. It was a fragile-looking plant, and the bloom was very small. Mothe' Moses took out a bottle from her pocket. She scooped a bit of mud up and placed it in the bottle. Then she very gently picked the entire plant, roots and all, out of the ground and put it into the bottle. She also sloshed a tiny bit of water into the same bottle. The lid had tiny holes in it. She looked at me kindly and said, "This be for you."

I felt like a child receiving a gift without any comprehension of its nature. "What is it?"

"I have no shirts for you, but this be better. Better for you and better for everyone." She allowed me to look at the tiny white bloom for a few moments. Then she reached out, took it from me, and put it in her bag. "We go now."

With that she turned and headed back across the bog. I tried to follow closely but simply could not keep up. After much toil I caught her on the other side of the bog. She gave me no time to rest but started out immediately. She had become very quiet. I made a few attempts to talk to her but it became apparent that she wanted quiet. It was as though she was in the midst of a great internal debate. At last we reached the boat. She promptly pushed it back into the water and stepped inside. She motioned for me to get in, and I did so as quickly as I could. She pushed the boat farther away from the alligator slick with her oar. We began to float freely in the waterway. She sat down and retrieved what looked like a burlap bag. She reached in and pulled out a plastic bottle filled with water.

"You ne'ly de-hy-drated. You take a drink."

I knew she was right, so I took a drink from a bottle whose cleanliness I doubted. The water was stale, but satisfying. I took another drink and handed the bottle back to her. She quickly took a chug from the bottle and slipped it back in the bag. Very adeptly, she grabbed the rope, gave it a swift pull, and started the engine. We were apparently on our way back to her place.

We traveled in silence, while questions mounted in my mind. For those few moments back at the bog, I had felt close to her, now she was miles away in a world I was not privileged to enter. After forty wordless minutes we arrived back at the store. She tied the boat to the old dock and stepped out.

"Come on, sonny, we get you cleaned up."

I was a mess. Most of the mud had dried, but it was caked on everything.

"Here's a hose, wash yourself off, go around back. Take off your clothes and put on this robe. We'll hang up your clothes to dry. They be dry in an hour or so. While they dry, we have coffee."

I felt a little like an eight-year-old boy at home with my mother. I simply did as I was told without questioning her reason.

Mothe' Moses was sitting in her rocker when I came around from the back of the store in the old frayed robe. She got up, took my wet clothes and hung them on a nearby clothesline. She motioned me toward the chair that stood next to her rocker, and she sat back down.

"The coffee be ready in a few minutes, but we must talk."

I expected her to start in, but she just sat there looking at me. She wasn't even rocking, just sitting, and there was no wittlin' in her hands. My view of this Mothe' Moses raced through a hundred variations, from respect, to love, to mistrust, to disbelief. Who was she, and what was this all about?

"Can I trust you, sonny? Are you a good man?"

"I thought you already said I was a good man."

"Yes, I said that. But do you think it, too?"

The guilt of a thousand mistakes flashed across my mind, but in the time she gave me to think about it, I remembered that I had tried to be, by and large, a good man. It could be that my very worst act was standing in the Jensen, scaring people to death in the suburbs of Philadelphia. Not that the act was so bad, but the results could have been terrible. For some reason, I went through a quiet introspection as Mothe' Moses watched me.

The one area where I had concern was in my marriage. I had always loved my wife and had always been faithful, but, for some reason, the relationship was growing out of sync. I couldn't point to a definable reason, it just seemed like life had begun taking each of us down different paths. If there was a weakness in my life, it was my regard for my wife. I thought, once more, about the pastry shop and realized that the extreme morass of its absence was founded in the dimming of our marital relationship. I had secretly hoped that a return visit to New Orleans might rekindle the candles of love.

I lifted my head, being unaware that it had drooped and looked at Mothe' Moses. "Yes, Mother Moses, I think I am a good man, not a perfect man, but a good man."

Waiting for her reply, I laughed inside. I had called her Mother Moses when speaking her name out loud.

She replied softly, almost lovingly, "It take a good man to say that."

Without another word, Mothe' Moses got up and went through the door. After she left, my mind went back to Jensen's experience with the rattlers. I hadn't heard a peep out of them. A few moments passed, and she returned with a bent and tarnished coffee pot and two dingy, formerly white, glass mugs. She poured the two cups and handed me one.

"You take it black. Sugar will react with the herb and make you sick."

"Black's fine," I said.

I was in a very strange and bizarre world and felt it foolish to quibble over black, creamed, or sugared coffee. I'd rather have had cream, but like I'd told her, black was fine.

"You be walking back to a hornet's nest. You don't know, yet, but Jensen's set bad things in motion. His dishonesty do it. He may be friend to you, but not always good friend to all people. It be your job to control the events that are coming; that's why I take you to swamp."

"I don't understand."

"No, and you won't until more days pass. Then you understand."

"What do I do and when?"

Mothe' Moses took the small bottle out of the bag she had been carrying. She held it up toward the sun and appeared to look through it toward the sun. "This be life," she said. "It be life to maybe a hundred 'n twenty people."

My mind latched onto the number, and I said out loud, "One hundred twenty people? That's the same as the number of shirts that Jensen bought."

"Yes, you good man, and a smart man."

I looked at her and smiled. "Then why do I feel so dumb?"

I hung on my personal self-derisive viewpoint and ignored her "good" and "smart" labels.

She smiled back. "Because you be humble."

The statement caught me off guard. Incredulously, I looked at her more closely while raising my shoulders and hands, "What?"

"Yes, I say humble. You willing to go with me, take herb, and settle down in a rickety boat. You willing to walk through sucking mud and lay in grass while we talk. You not high and mighty, you the right man, you set things right."

I was bewildered. "You keep talking like I understand, and I have no idea what you are talking about."

She had a way of looking into my soul, and she looked once more. "I make it simple. When people start to die, you take this plant to Voodoo Shop in French Quarter and ask for Jonah, but not before people die. You tell her it from me. She know me, and she understand. You do as she say. She save you and save other people. She may save Jensen. We see."

The name, Jonah, caught me by surprise. We had already met Jonah! I knew where the Voodoo Shop was, but the rest made no sense. I decided to say nothing about our visit with Jonah, but as I contemplated that idea, my view of the world was beginning to change. I felt like I was rolling through a veil of fog. Mothe' Moses kept talking, but after some minutes her words became harder to understand. The transition was slow, but I felt it, nonetheless. At length, she stopped talking, and I remained quiet. I couldn't fathom the meaning of it all. It appeared that all I could do was walk unknowingly through future events, watching and waiting for a sign that told me to do what she told me to do.

Mothe' Moses broke the silence, "Yuh bes' get yuh clothes. Dey dry now."

I walked once more behind the store, pulled my still dirty clothing from the line and put it on. It was still damp, but I didn't care. The experience of the day was clear in my mind, but I had undoubtedly been under the influence of something I didn't understand. As I walked back to the front of the store, and perhaps with the miracle of the herb wearing off, my more frightful side listened for the rattlers. Once more, I hesitated to step up and onto the porch.

"Ya, ma li'l babies sti' be hea. B'don' be fraid. Dey no hur' yuh. I in cha'ge 'n dey no' it."

I shook my head as if to clear it. Mothe' Moses's dialect had reverted. It was no longer easy to understand her. I thought about the herb and the clarity it brought and wished the effects were still in force. The little bottle was sitting on the small table, along with the coffee mugs. I knew that I must retrieve it, but I once more felt unnerved.

"Come, ge' it, sonny. Ma li'l babies respec' yuh."

I stepped up and onto the porch. The wood creaked, and my senses expected a chorus from her babies, but none came. I shivered, reached out for the bottle, but she raised her hand to stop me.

"Now, yuh pay, sonny."

Now it was me who looked into her eyes, "Pay? How much and for what?

"Yuh pay fa bot'l n blos'm. Yuh pay fo seven utter people and ma-be yuh fren."

"How much?"

"How much yuh bring?"

"Two thousand dollars."

"Dat be nuf."

Hesitation stalled my actions. I was to pay her two grand for a flower with a bloom in a bottle that will surely shrivel and die before I get to the hotel. I don't know how much time I used to think over my next step. During those moments, it dawned on me that I was paying for Jensen's sins. My mind struggled for the correct path in a world of insecurity. *Why should I pay a lot of money for a plant when I came to buy shirs'?*

Breaking the silence, Mothe' Moses motioned to the bottle and nodded her head as if to say, "Pay me 'n take it."

Like an obedient child, I pulled out my wallet, counted out the two grand, and handed it over to her. I reached for the bottle and picked it up, just as she had commanded.

My eyes had been on the bottle, but I shifted them to look into hers. After a fraction of a heartbeat, I turned to leave the porch. Once more there was buzzing in my mind, but as soon as I stepped onto the ground, it stopped. I pulled the door of the Durango open and looked back. She was sitting in her rocker, wittlin' again. I came for shirs', but I was leaving with a bloom, an experience, and the very real loss of two thousand dollars. *I must be a fool.*

I could have easily and cynically discarded the day as a waste of time at the least, or a rip-off at most; but deep inside I knew I couldn't seriously consider either perspective. For some reason, I felt the day had some kind of intrinsic value, but I was struggling to identify it.

I stood there next to the open car door, almost in a trance. I turned and searched her face. She paid me no attention but was swooshing the last cold drops of coffee in her dingy mug. After a last swish and a gulp, her rocking began once more. Within seconds she was hunkered down in her rocking stance, wittlin' in hand. She hadn't looked up at me since I turned to look at her.

I climbed into the Durango and started the engine. I adjusted the AC to max cool, and put the transmission into reverse. I looked once more at Mothe' Moses. I simply couldn't understand my swirling emotions. I felt love, disappointment, anger, and hope all at once. All my emotions, good, bad, and everything in between were mashed together into one feeling: I felt like Mothe' Moses had been good to me, but in what way? I could not identify it.

I pressed down on the accelerator. Just as the Durango started to move she raised her head and looked in my direction. She quickly raised her hand as if to wave but held it motionless. It hung in the air for a few seconds then dropped. She nodded her head, and I heard words in my mind, "*Yuh be a good man, a humble man.*"

With that thought, the moment and the bond were broken. The Durango noisily tracked back, over the gravel, then onto the paved but broken road. I put the transmission into drive and set my course back to New Orleans. I purposely drove slowly past the gas station. I noticed Mothe' Moses's hulking son, sporting his curly and unruly hair, and dressed in dirty mechanic's coveralls. He had a dirty cloth in his hand, making another wasted attempt to clean something from his oil-stained hands. As I drove past, his eyes followed me until I escaped their reach.

When I got back to my hotel room, it was late. I didn't call Jensen, and I hoped that he wouldn't call me. I didn't want to interrupt my state of mind, which was full of questions. In some way I didn't understand, a level of peace had befallen me. It was something that I had never experienced before, and I didn't want to break the spell, so I slowly removed my dirty clothes, cleaned up, and got into bed. The sounds of the night were banished from my mind as I thought of the words of Mothe' Moses. "Yuh be a good man; a humble man."

— CHAPTER FIVE —
THURSDAY MORNING: AT THE CONVENTION

Bob's Report

I WAS VERY BUSY on Thursday morning. As exhibitors, we were scrambling, working hard to finalize our product displays. The crowds wouldn't arrive until five o'clock when, during happy hour, they could wander through the exhibition hall. I liked this format better than standing in an otherwise empty room making happy talk with attendees. Besides, I didn't drink, and I always felt foolish carrying around a glass of ginger ale.

At two o'clock I decided it was time for a break and took a taxi back to the hotel. I rested up, took a shower, and put on my business attire. Around 4:00 p.m., I went to the common door that adjoined Jensen's room and knocked. We hadn't seen each other due to our long to-do lists. I was sure Jensen would want to know about my trip to see Mothe' Moses, but wasn't sure what to tell him. I had a clear memory of the entire day, but a cloudy understanding of what really took place. The door swung open.

"Hey, Bob," he greeted me. "I noticed you made it back yesterday. I'm sorry I didn't call you. Things have been crazy."

"Yup. Safe and sound," I replied. A myriad of thoughts traversed my mind, the story being much more intricate than my answer.

He motioned me in and asked, "So, did you get any shirs'?"

"No, I didn't get any shirs'."

He turned to face me, looking a little surprised and asked, "Well, what did you do all day? You were gone a long time."

I put on a wan smile. "Well, I took a swamp tour with the o-wom'n, and, well, I like the lady, so she's become Mothe' Moses to me."

He took on a look of incredulity. "You took a swamp tour with Mothe' Moses?"

I added, "Yup, and I paid your debt. At least that's what I think I did."

That stopped the smile on Jensen's face.

"Oh—you—got caught in my—ah—financial adjustment."

"You mean, your theft, you cheap S.O.B!"

Jensen's demeanor immediately switched to an air of defensiveness. "Come on, Bob, you know she ripped me off. There's no way she made these shirts, and you're probably lucky you're not gata bait at the bottom of the swamp. That's probably what happened to the guy who originally owned the shirs'."

I put a *you-should-feel-guilty* look on my face and returned his sarcasm, "Spin it anyway you want, Jensen, but you stole money from Mothe' Moses, and I bailed you out of hot water!"

Jensen turned, walked to the wet bar, and poured his self-prescribed treatment. "Okay, okay, simmer down. Look, after the convention is over, and I get back to the office, I'll send you a check. Feel better now?"

I stood in my place wanting him to feel the heat. "Not really. I spent an entire day of my life out there in the swamp, and I'm not sure for what purpose, other than to keep your skinny ass out of jail. Do you know when I got there, she had apparently just returned from the bank? She saw your rental and came at me like I was the devil. I didn't know who to fear most, Mothe' Moses, or that two-ton hulk she calls her son. She was mad and, buddy, if you had been there, you'd have paid for it in blood. In the end, I decided she was more dangerous than her massive son."

Jensen shrugged his shoulders as if to concede. "Okay, okay. I get it. Let's go to the Convention Center. When happy hour is over, I'll buy you that steak dinner I promised and, I tell you what, I'll write you that check right now. I don't want your blood pressure to blow a hole in that bleeding heart of yours." He stopped, looked at me solemnly, and asked, "But would you hang onto it for a week?"

I think he expected me to smile as he tried to hold me with his eyes and one raised eyebrow. I was annoyed at Jensen. "Will it be good in a week?" There was no smile on my face.

He stood as still as could be, as though he'd been trapped.

Undeterred, I continued. "Look, Jensen, we've been friends for a long time, and you've always been square, but this little stunt was pretty rotten. You sent me out there knowing I'd catch hell for it."

He took a step toward me. "Now, Bob, I didn't have any idea that would happen. That was just bad timing. I had no idea the woman would drive all the way to a branch of my bank to cash that check. You have to admit that's a little amazing."

Still standing my ground, I couldn't help but rub it in a bit, although I was beginning to feel sorry for his discomfort. I put on a most serious face. "Maybe she's been ripped off before."

He took another step toward me. "Okay. I'm sorry; I didn't mean to get you into trouble."

I finally softened my look, and stepped toward him, attempting to fill in the gap of a now-strained friendship. I reached out and put my hand on his shoulder to re-establish our long-term friendship. "I forgive you, and I appreciate the check. Look, it's been a long day for both of us. Let's get over to the hall. It's nearly time for happy hour."

Jensen nodded, shook my hand and said, "I really am sorry."

"I believe you," I said, even though I was still slightly annoyed.

But the moment passed, and Jensen quickly jumped into business mode, a flash of thought covering his face. "There are a couple of people I'd like to give these shirs' to. I think it would be cool to see them walking around wearing them tonight."

Putting on a smile, I asked, "Are you going to wear one?"

Jensen had started walking toward the bedroom where the shirs' were stored. He stopped, turned to look at me, and said, "Wow, do you think I should? This isn't the only line I'm pushing. I've got a lot of money at risk, and I don't want to scramble after a few dollars while chasing off thousands."

"Suit yourself, but if you won't wear one of them, why should they?"

Jensen put on a devious smile, "Maybe I'll wait until they've had a couple of drinks. Besides, I know at least one guy who will wear one just to make an outlandish statement. He'll be my guinea pig."

I shook my head and smiled at him. "So, you're going to stand up in the Jensen?"

He laughed too and asked, "Are you willing to drive?"

I looked intently at him, the words of Mothe' Moses ringing through my mind.

"No, not this time. You'll have to play the gag alone."

He displayed a look akin to disappointment and turned to walk through the bedroom door. However, as he got to the door, he slowed his pace. I followed, wanting to see him pull a shir' from the box. The closer he got to them, the slower he moved. He stopped when he stood next to a box and simply stood there.

I laughed and said, "You can't even pick one up, let alone wear one."

My teasing spurred him to action, albeit slow, deliberate action. I watched Jensen tepidly reach out to the top box of shirs'. As though handling a dangerous explosive, he carefully opened the lid. Very slowly, he reached into the box, gingerly picked up a shir', and began to lift it out. He reminded me of a demolitions expert disarming a bomb. As he pulled it out, I wondered if he was hearing rattling sounds. I have to admit; I felt the hair on the back of my own neck rise and almost imagined I heard rattlers, too. I quickly shook off the feeling. *Maybe the herbs are still at work.*

Jensen suddenly looked around the room. I saw him eye a small box, which he headed for. He picked up the box and unceremoniously dumped the shirt into it. He securely folded over the flaps and looked up at me. With a smile, he said, "Okay, let's go."

At the front door of the hotel, we asked the doorman to get us a cab. Within a few minutes, we were on our way—Jensen, his hidden snake shirt, and me.

In less than ten minutes, the cabbie pulled up to the curb. Jensen was quick to open his wallet and pay the driver. "Don't worry, I got it," he said with a sheepish smile.

"Thanks," was all I mustered, pleased that he knew he owed me.

Through the doors we went and off to our displays. We'd requested spaces next to each other since our customers would be seeing both our products in the hospitality suites. Our products were not competitive, but complementary in nature. We might be battling for someone's budget resources, but we hoped they would like our lines of clothing.

As five o'clock passed, we began to see a number of hostesses carrying trays of drinks. Like carrion to spoiling flesh, the room was soon full of people milling around the hall, happy, relaxed, and willing to talk about most anything. As exhibitors, we stood in front of our displays, meeting, greeting, and chatting with friends, customers, and future types in both categories. I decided to leave the ginger ale at my display. I felt a little out of place, but decided I didn't care. If my throat got parched, the soft drink was nearby.

Jensen was having a good time. His attitude seemed to adjust, and he happily glad-handed everyone that went by. I noticed that he kept looking back at his display. I began to realize that he might be trying to drum up the courage to bring out the shirt. At last, during a slight lull in activity, he went to his display and grabbed the box.

I purposefully watched him pull the shirt out of the box and nearly gut-laughed as I saw him fold the shirt over his arm. I imagined and could almost feel the hair standing up on the back of his neck. It looked like he braced himself, then walked out into the middle of an aisle. I noticed he had his eyes on a man about fifty feet down the hall. I disengaged with someone I had been talking to, using my ginger ale as an excuse, but my real purpose was to watch Jensen.

Jensen walked like he was full of courage. He was bold, positive, and assertive as he presented the shirt to his target—one of his favorite and most important customers.

Jensen Gives Away a Shir'

"Hey Marshal, how you doing?"

I managed to reach out and take my customer's hand as he held it out in greeting, without upsetting the shirt. It was folded over my left arm, and the snake head was hidden. As I had walked toward Marshal, I thought of the fangs that were so near to the flesh of my forearm. It was all I could do to keep from screaming and throwing the shir' into the air.

Marshal was always effusive in his southern cheer. "Jensen! It's been a few months. Good to see you. How yuh doin?"

I puffed up my smile up to match his larger-than-life Texas grin. "I'm doin' great, and I've been looking for you. I want you to see an item in my new clothing line. I think you'll love it."

Marshal responded in his Texas way, "Shoot, we got plenty a time for that. Come on, have a drink. Tonight's for fun! We'll get to business tomorrow."

With that, he raised his plastic cup of some kind of booze, and I raised mine to his.

After a sip and a laugh, I nearly shouted, "But I've got something to show you right now!"

I think my approach was unexpected. Rarely did happy hour include showing samples. I hurried to fill the gap between words.

"I know, I know, this is party time, but I have to show you this now!"

"It better be worth it. I've got booze wait'n for me."

"You decide."

With that I took the shirt off my arm and thrust the fanged snake head close to his face. Rather than jump, he gave a big Texas holler.

"Yee haw! Look at that damned thing!" Delight washed over his face. Marshal grabbed the shirt from my hands to take a closer look. "Shoot, this is like the ones on my own spread, just smaller."

Marshal was a good client, and although he owned a large retail chain in Houston, he had a ranch in east Texas, near Beaumont. He loved his ranch, and it was where he spent most of his time. His office was at the ranch, and he conducted as much of his business from there as he could. He had even built a home for his administrative assistant. The job requirement was that the assistant would be willing to live and work on the ranch. When it came time to leave the ranch, Marshal would simply walk out the back door where his Bell Twin Ranger light duty helicopter was waiting. Of course, his valet had already moved it out of the hanger and warmed it up. Marshal was a busy man and time was money. He loved flying his helicopter. He could easily afford his own pilot, but he never gave up an opportunity to fly his favorite toy to his personal helipad on the building he owned. If needed, a limousine and a chauffeur would take him to his next deal.

Marshal kept eying the shirt with the bold image of the rattler.

"Shoot, this is just a wee one. Damn, this would be a small breakfast for the monsters I've got on my ranch." With that he let out a belly roar that could be heard around the hall. Those nearby joined him, and everyone in earshot turned to see what had caused such laughter.

Marshal was a big man, and I was glad that I'd found a 3XL in the box. It had been difficult for me to sift through the shirs', not knowing if the box contained his size. If anyone could boldly display my shirt, it would be Marshal. His bravado was second to none, and his money drew even more attention.

"Put it on, Marshal. Let's see if it fits. You'll be the life of the party wearing that little trophy."

Without a blink, Marshal stripped his own shirt and had the rattler shirt on in seconds. From that moment on, the atmosphere around him changed. He became both feared and loved. People still loved his money and wit, but their skin crawled as they got near the dangerously fanged snake head. Shaking hands became an act suited in terror. Marshal began to enjoy the panic he was causing and decided to take it one step further. From that moment forward, every female had to get a hug from Marshal, a hug that put the fangs of the monster into the bosom of a terrified woman. Of course after the horrid hug, it was all fun and games, and those who'd been hugged stood around, watching for the hugging of the next victim. Though a tally hadn't been kept, it was likely that every willing woman had been hugged, plus a few unwilling victims. Only a few escaped the high-spirited hug of Marshal, the good-hearted, wealthy Texan, with just a li'l ole snake on his shirt.

As the night went on, I made sure I stayed close to Marshal. He was more than willing to make sure everyone knew where the shir' had come from, pointing often to me. Of course, I knew that he'd be expecting some kind of discount for displaying my shir' in such a public and effective manner, and I knew I'd be happy to oblige him. My face and name had been spread across a larger audience than I could have arranged on my own. Even more exciting was the considerable number of buyers who asked about the snake line, and many of them wanted a sample of their own.

Marshal Takes a Break

As the party wore on, I decided to break away from the reverie, making my way to the restroom. I'd already put it off longer than I should have, and I felt like my bladder was about to burst. I was as proud as a Texas sunrise. I'd hugged every woman in the hall by the time I'd finished up; and there were some lookers in there, too. I was overjoyed at the screams and laughter that my hugging antics had created. Heck, I could barely remember a night when I'd had so much fun. That Jensen feller had given me a shirt that was, by *dang*, a damned cool shirt, at that.

The noise from the hall was but a din, and I couldn't help but burst into the Texas Longhorn fight song.

"Yea Orange! Yea White!

"Yea Texas! Fight! Fight! Fight!

"Texas Fight! Texas Fight!

"Yea Texas Fight!

"Texas Fight! Texas Fight!

"Yea Texas Fight!"

I finished up with two lines from the first verse.

"Hail! Hail! The gangs all here

"And it's good-bye to all the rest!"

After singing several parts of the song a few more times, I turned and walked to the restroom sink. I was a little tipsy and kept my eyes on the dark, infrared emitter of the spigot to make sure I was focused, and that I wouldn't fall to the ground. The few moments of relaxation made me realize I was tipsier than I realized. I rinsed my hands and reached for a nearby towel. While drying my hands, I looked up into the mirror to make sure my hair was in place. It's one thing I'm vain about. I am very proud of my thick head of graying hair.

I'd nearly forgotten about my fanged companion. As I stared at my reflection in the mirror and that of my snake head, I began to feel odd. My vision was becoming blurred, and I felt flushed. I wondered if my ability to hold my liquor had diminished. Then my chest began to feel heavy, and I speculated about an impending heart attack, the one my doctor had been warning me about. I became more and more dizzy and highly disoriented. My eyes were now seeing the world as through a tunnel. I shook my head in disbelief, trying to clear my senses. In my alcohol-flooded mind, I began to wonder if I might be hallucinating, because a vision was opening before me that made no sense and could not be reality.

I could see it in the mirror. In slow motion, it seemed that the giant snake head had detached itself from my shirt, although the body appeared to stay connected. There came to my ears the buzzing of the rattles at the tip of a rattlesnake tail, which sounded again and again, becoming almost incessant. It was a sound I knew well. There was no mistake. The snake head weaved back and forth as though charming a bird. In my rapidly diminishing state, I became aware of the snake's eyes. They were eyes of malevolence. It looked to be a hateful creature with only one thing on its mind. Death.

As the orange eyes grew terrifyingly larger and more malicious, the mouth began to open. The red tongue flicked in and out as if sizing up its prey—*me!* The vision was over in seconds, but in the last instant, the snake body coiled and made a strike. My mind slowed the millisecond-strike down to a mere crawl. I saw the mouth open wide, the fangs extended. But the fangs were unlike any rattler fangs I had ever seen. This monster had fangs on both the top and bottom of its mouth. Venom was already oozing and dripping from them as if it was salivating for a kill. In that long instant, the head snapped toward me, the mouth opened revealing the black hole of its throat. It took my entire head in its jaws. I didn't feel the puncture, and my mind wondered, *why not?* The mouth and fangs held me for a long moment while I tried to scream in terror, but nothing came from my mouth but a silent loathing of the snake that held me in its grasp. And then I felt it. It was as though an injection of hot lead was flowing from the fangs into my head and through my vascular system. As the venom flowed, I imagined the hemorrhaging of my tissues and the misfiring of the neurons in my nervous system.

Is this the feel of death? I wondered as I slipped to the floor, my strength failing and confusion reigning. I began to assume that my doctor's warning to eat less Texas beef had become the reality of a heart attack, and that my hallucination was the feeble wanderings of an oxygen-deprived mind. I knew about hypoxia and reasoned that I was probably short on it. My vision faded from gray to black, and for some odd reason, I could hear my heartbeat. The rate was slowing and pumping too little blood to my inebriated brain. Surely, the snakebite was a feeble attempt to explain the unexplainable. I suddenly felt incredibly cold. And then I felt nothing at all except the darkest black of a blackened night. Soon, even the blackness was gone.

Jensen Joins the Crowd

MOST OF THE BUYERS had been enjoying the boisterous gathering. Only those near the front doors had heard the first blaring of the sirens as the EMTs pulled up to the Convention Center doors. I was one of them and turned to see four EMTs running through the front doors. They appeared to know where they were going. I watched them race toward the main restroom complex. Faces turned and eyes, including mine, followed the four men as they rushed through the hall. As we watched them, we could see a group of people at the entrance to the restrooms. Some were trying to see inside, but most had just gathered to talk about the interruption. The crowd parted, like the sea before Moses, when the paramedics arrived.

I had no particular reason for being there, but I followed the EMTs and pushed into the restroom. To my shock, Marshal was lying on the floor with a terror-stricken expression on his face.

The EMTs shined a light into both his eyes.

"His pupils are barely reactive," one said.

With his hand on Marshal's wrist, another said, "I don't feel a pulse."

"Get him on oxygen and get an IV running," came the command from the lead EMT, who was standing over Marshal. "He'll be gone soon if we don't bring him around. Stand by with the defibrillator."

Marshal's shirt was cut open in one swift stroke. I barely noticed the malicious snake head on the left breast side of Marshal's shirt. The EMTs appeared to have given it no notice. The tragic event kept serious thoughts of the shir' out of my mind.

The EMT was now checking the carotid artery, "I've got no pulse at all!"

The other EMT started CPR and called out, "Charge the paddles."

"Ready!"

"Clear!"

The EMT had started with a 400-volt charge from the paddles to the heart. Marshal's body convulsed from the electrical assault. One EMT checked his pulse while another gave him external heart massage.

"Still no pulse."

"Set it for 600."

"Charged!"

"Clear!"

Once more voltage surged through Marshal's body. Once more his nerves and muscles convulsed from this instant jolt of electricity.

For ten more minutes, the EMTs worked over Marshal. It was excruciating. He was my friend, and the treatment seemed almost abusive. The crowd had thinned and news of a heart attack spread through the hall. At first, unaware, I now noticed that Bob had moved up to stand beside me.

"How is he?" Bob asked, putting a hand on my shoulder.

Without turning, I responded, "It doesn't look good."

Frustration began to show on the face of the EMTs. They hated losing someone at the scene. Their goal was to get their patients to the hospital while still breathing and alive; but it appeared that Marshal might not make it to the hospital with his life-blood still flowing.

After one last jolt of nearly 1,000 volts, an EMT screamed, "I've got a pulse! It's weak but it's a pulse."

Marshal was quickly rushed out of the hall and into the ambulance. The lights flashed, the siren blared, and the vehicle hurtled toward the emergency room. Maybe they can save him. *I hope so.*

Jensen's Consideration

I PLOPPED DOWN IN a chair at Bob's display. The crowd was subdued, some had left, but many were still in the hall. Though the tragedy was sobering, the crowd was pragmatic. Marshal's apparent heart attack wouldn't stop the world. They all had customers, of one sort or another, and life would go on. Almost as a group, the crowd concluded that Marshal would want them to continue.

As for me, I felt a great loss. I was obviously concerned about Marshal's welfare, but his promotional efforts had been thwarted. Taking me out of a near trance, I felt more than saw Bob sit down beside me. We just sat there. Neither of us could find words that seemed right.

Turning toward me and speaking in a kind voice, Bob finally said, "Look, I know this is a tough blow but he'll be all right. And check it out, the party animals are still hanging around. Let's get as many of them as we can to our hospitality suite. Surely they're interested in more free booze and food before they take in Bourbon Street. Many will believe that the booze will numb their pain."

I'd been sitting with my head down. I raised it to look at Bob. For a long moment, I searched for an appropriate response. At last, I said, "You're right. The night, *and life*, must go on. He'll probably be good as new in a few days. It's nearly closing time." Nodding toward the crowd, I added, "Let's remind them about our party and the debauchery on Bourbon Street."

"Let's do it," said Bob with a feeble smile.

Over the next few minutes Bob and I mingled with the crowd in the exhibition hall. I passed out the reminder cards and entry tickets for those who were invited to my hospitality suite. Most looked forward to continuing the celebration, and many looked forward to food more substantial than they had been offered at the Convention hall. At length, I asked Bob to go to the hotel to make sure everything was ready. I stayed to urge buyers to attend our after happy hour reception, promising booze, food, and fun, in that order.

— CHAPTER SIX —
THURSDAY NIGHT: HOSPITALITY

Jensen's Big Tip

AS THE CABBIE DROVE onto Bourbon Street, I could see that the street was waking up. It was approaching dusk, and the lights were beginning to reveal themselves. The cabbie dropped me off at the Royal Sonesta, and I immediately thought of the shirs' up in my room. I paid the fare plus another tip, but my tips were getting skimpy. Another cringe swept over me as I put the wallet back into my pocket. The cash was going fast, and it was just the first day. I stopped to talk to the doorman before entering the hotel. After a short query, I learned that he was working until midnight. I opened my wallet once more and pulled out a hundred-dollar bill. I handed it to the doorman whose job it was to make sure any who had either my card or Bob's card would be directed to our hospitality suite. I had made it clear. I simply didn't want anyone to get lost on the way to our rooms.

I opened the door of the suite. It was clear that Bob had already been here, but I could see the room needed one last minute change. I grabbed the sign announcing party central and attached it carefully to the door. It had to be straight and appealing. No detail could be left undone. A quick perusal of the room assured me that everything was in place. While checking the time, I looked down the hall just as the elevator door opened. The bartender and two lovely hostesses emerged from the elevator and began walking toward me. *Right on time,* I thought. Rushing through the suite and through the adjoining door into Bob's room, I located the other sign and quickly attached it to Bob's door.

The room was elegant, painted in warm colors with rich accents. The two suites, one a center suite and the other a corner suite, looked out over Bourbon Street. A set of French doors, one from each suite, gave entry to the balcony. I opened them, stepped out, and took in a deep breath of the night air. It was savory, filled with spices and the aroma of Cajun cooking. In my mind, I visualized crab and shrimp and steaming bowls of jambalaya. I could smell the garlic, onions, and butter in dishes of crawfish étouffée. Bob had been standing on the balcony outside his suite, taking in the sights. "It's going to be a great night," I said, as he turned to me.

As if on cue, the first of our visitors came through the door. Set before them was a feast of crab meat, crawfish, oysters, shrimp, and smoked mushrooms. Gumbo and jambalaya steamed in big pots. Exotic salads were on small plates and, of course, there was the bar with drinks both soft and hard. Beautiful women served the food and kept empty plates picked up. A variety of chairs had been placed in the suite to rest tired feet and sore backs.

The music of the Bourbon Street nightlife began to permeate the suites through the open French doors. Music from the cabaret across the street competed with various strains of jazz from other quarters. Soon the chairs had all been taken, the room was near capacity, and the balcony sported those who wanted to enjoy the night air. It was at this point that I saw a specific customer arrive. I caught him just after he entered the door.

"What do you think?" I called out over the din of the party.

"Looks great!" he replied.

"I'm glad you're here! Help yourself, chat with your friends, and have a good time."

The customer gave me the thumbs up, and I had renewed hope for a big order from him.

Bob and I both set out to talk and laugh with everyone we met. Spirits were high, the talk was loud and nearly every face wore a smile. As the evening progressed, visitors came and went, enjoying the free and exotic flavors of this very special open house.

Jensen: More Shirs'

AT LENGTH, MY MIND went to the shirs'. Since the emergency with Marshal, I was wondering if the shir' had anything to do with his apparent heart attack; so I was a little leery of giving them out. I wondered if their presence would dampen the party. After serious contemplation, I went into the bedroom and grabbed a shir'. I decided to give them away one at a time, and over the next hour I gave away ten shirs'. The reception was mixed. There were some who simply didn't want one. I became more careful about the people to whom I offered the shirs'. As I gave out the last one, I wondered how many would be worn tonight, and how many would be worn at the show tomorrow.

One man, who'd had quite a bit to drink, decided to wear his shir'. The reaction was immediate. Some cringed and moved away from him. Others laughed and thought he was the funniest man alive. All I knew was that I didn't want a hug from him. Gratefully, he didn't follow the example of Marshal, so there were no screaming and cringing women trying to avoid the fanged comedian.

Eventually, the funny snake-shirted man left the hospitality suite. Coincidently, I moved to the balcony as he walked across the street. I was secretly glad he was gone and glad that nobody else had put on their shir'. But I had to ask myself a question. *The shirs' are promotional, so, why do I fear the idea of people wearing them?* I reminded myself that the shirs' could mean orders. Orders meant deposits, and deposits meant payment upon delivery. I decided that I had to rethink my priorities and get back into the game full stride.

Enthused with the possibility of a new sale, I was still standing on the balcony, talking to a new client about a potentially large order. Once more, I heard the piercing sound of sirens. I could tell they were getting closer, but was surprised when they turned onto Bourbon Street. The lights flashed, the siren screamed, and the horn blared, shooing people out of the way. The ambulance pulled up across the street from our hotel. Two men rushed out with paramedic bags in hand. They entered a bar filled with jazz and more booze. I watched for a while, my curiosity getting the best of me. Soon another group of EMTs arrived. After thirty minutes, two of the EMTs came out of the building to retrieve a gurney. Within ten minutes the gurney was wheeled out through the doors. To my surprise, whoever was on the gurney was covered with a blanket.

"I guess the guy didn't make it," said my client friend.

I thought of the party atmosphere. "It's too bad they checked out while having so much fun."

Bob had joined us on the balcony as we watched. "I wonder who the guy was."

I shook my head. "I don't know."

Bob waxed philosophical. "I wonder if he had a family? Did he have friends here tonight?"

"You're assuming it was a guy. It could have been a woman."

Bob nodded, "Yes, it could have been."

We let Bob's statement hang. Whoever it was, had gone on to something else. I was not necessarily a believer, but could not completely divorce myself from belief in some sort of life after death. *Now this person knows,* I thought. *Too bad I can't ask him—or her.*

There were only about ten of us on the balcony. A few people were eating the last of the food inside the suite. Bob moved close and whispered, "Should we invite people to leave now? I think I've had all the partying I can take for one night."

I looked at him and said with a smile, "Bob, I know you don't drink, and you don't carouse; I can't even imagine how you tolerate being in a place like this with all these drunks and their shenanigans."

Bob looked back and said as calmly as summer morning, "True, it's not my thing, but I know it's important to them. If I want to do business with them, I have to allow them to have their fun."

"You're a good man, Bob. Better than me, I think."

I patted Bob on the back, and he responded with, "Thanks. Let's close it down. I'm bushed."

With all the grace we could muster, we moved the last of the crowd out of the suite. We did this by announcing that the bar was closing, and the food was all gone. It wasn't long before we were alone. The doors were closed, our shoes were off, and our feet were up. The quiet was intoxicating.

— CHAPTER SEVEN —

FRIDAY: CONFUSION

Dr. Whitely

I HAD JUST FINISHED my rounds at the Tulane University Medical Center, School of Medicine. I had dismissed a new team of medical residents and was walking the halls that would take me over the sky bridge and back to my office in the Tulane Medical Center, when my cell phone rang.

"Dr. Whitely, this is Wilson Parsons, the medical examiner from the city morgue. I'm a forensic pathologist, and I'm investigating some recent deaths in the city."

I continued walking, "Hello, Mr. Parsons, or is it Dr. Parsons? I've heard your name before."

"I'm not a doctor," he said. "The city doesn't like to spend that kind of money."

Then Parsons quickly explained that he was standing in the New Orleans City Morgue.

"I've got two tables in front of me, and two bodies lay covered on the tables, except for their heads." After giving me that information he simply said, "I need your help."

"What is it?" I asked.

"Well, doctor, it's complicated, and I'd rather not talk about it over the phone, but I really need your help. It's important to our community. Please, can you come to the morgue right now?"

"Right now?" I asked, looking at my watch and knowing I had a busy day scheduled. "That will be tough; I have responsibilities at the hospital."

There was a note of gravity in Parson's voice, "I'm sorry, but this is extremely important. I've been told you're the best doctor in town and—well—like I said, I could use your help. It will take someone like you to help me figure out my—our—problem, and—um—it is a matter of life or death. I really need your expertise."

I disconnected the call. There were also many people in the hospital who were depending on me. I opened the calendar on my smart phone. I knew I had no surgeries scheduled, but what else was on the calendar? To my relief the list was full, but manageable. I dialed the number of the hospital administrator.

"Dr. Vincent, this is Dr. Whitely. The medical examiner just called from the city morgue. He wants me to meet with him right away. He won't say why, only that it's important, and some kind of life or death matter. I feel I should go, and I need someone to fill in for me. Can you make those arrangements?"

There was silence for a moment.

"Dr. Whitely, are you telling me or asking?"

"I'm sorry, Dr. Vincent. I really am asking, but at the same time Mr. Wilson seemed very concerned. I'm just trying to meet his needs, as well. He did say it was a crucial matter." I switched the phone screen back to my calendar. I scanned through the calendar once more to confirm that there were no critical medical problems on the schedule. I decided to press the administrator a little more. "I feel I need to go to the morgue, as requested. Will you help?"

The hospital administrator didn't answer right away, but at last he sighed and said, "Okay, Dr. Whitely. I'll find someone to fill in for you. You'll owe them, though. You know, they'll either be exhausted from working long hours or called in on their day off."

"That's fine. I'll owe them," I said as I opened the door to my office. I disconnected the call and ditched my white lab coat. I pulled my keys from my pocket and then stopped. *It's a short drive to the morgue and parking is a hassle. I'll take a cab.*

I stuffed the keys back into my pocket and rushed out of the hospital. In minutes, I'd hailed a cab, paid the fare, and dashed into the morgue. I trotted down a hallway and crashed into the double doors that served as the entryway to the morgue. They were locked!

In an instant I saw the large red sign that read, "Ring for Entry." I pressed the big red button, and shortly, the wide doors swung open. I scurried through, continued on through one more door and into the room where I'd been told to meet the medical examiner.

Upon entering the room, the sight of the medical examiner leaning nonchalantly against the counter immediately annoyed me. His attitude suggested anything but an emergency. Two more people, a man and a woman were standing with him. They acted like they had all the time in the world. I began to wonder why I had rushed to their aid. In the seconds that passed, since entering the room, I processed the visible data. There was no apparent emergency, but they all looked like they'd seen a ghost. They were subdued and pensive, and it was clear they were pondering a very serious matter.

The M.E. looked up, recognized me, and stepped quickly toward me. I barely noticed the cold, stainless steel sterility of the room, but I did notice that he was visibly shaken.

"Thank you for coming, Dr. Whitely. We have a very strange situation here. I don't want it to get out just yet."

He pointed toward one of the bodies and said, "Go ahead, Mr. Parsons."

Mr. Parsons stepped up to one of the dead men, a man whose head was uncovered but his body was not.

"This man was brought in yesterday afternoon. He came from your hospital E.R. where he had been pronounced DOA. The paramedics said they tried but were unable to keep him alive. We processed him and stored him overnight, intending to perform an autopsy this morning."

Mr. Parsons then pulled down the sheet covering the man.

"You can see we started the autopsy."

I noted that gauze had been placed over what appeared to be a six-inch cut. I also saw blood seeping through the gauze. *That can't be.* My eyes flicked back to Parsons. "Tell me more."

"Well, you can obviously see the blood. When we started the incision, blood began to ooze from the body. At first it was puzzling, but as the incision grew, more blood oozed out. We stopped cutting and began to believe that somehow this man has blood pressure. A corpse simply doesn't have blood pressure."

I now knew why Parsons was spooked and spoke up. "That surely cannot be. If he died yesterday, his blood would have coagulated, and it certainly wouldn't ooze from the incision."

"That's how I see it," replied Parsons.

I looked at him with widening eyes. "What are you saying, Mr. Parsons? Is it possible this man is still alive?"

"He appears to be dead in every way, but we believe we've heard a heartbeat so faint that it could never have been heard without very carefully searching for it."

I reached out and touched the body.

"This body is cold as ice!"

"Yes, and now you see why I wanted you here. We need to figure out if this guy is dead or alive. Right now, I'm not sure which it is, and I hoped you could help us verify his status."

I let out a long sigh. I looked around the room. There was no evidence of any kind of medical monitoring device.

"Do you have a stethoscope?"

Parsons pulled one out of his lab coat pocket and handed it to me. "Go ahead, check for yourself," he said.

I put on the scope and placed the diaphragm on his chest without warming it up. I moved it from one place and to another, listening carefully for a heartbeat. After moving the diaphragm to several locations I found something unusual for a dead man. I listened for nearly a minute. A long, soft, barely audible whistle escaped my lips. Then I placed the shiny, backside of the diaphragm under the man's nose for another minute. There was no sign of water vapor appearing to fog up the device. I pulled out my pen light, forced the man's eyelids opened and shined the light into the man's pupils. They were dilated and there was no reaction. I turned to Wilson Parsons.

"Mr. Parsons, I don't know what to think. He could be dead, but I heard what I thought were a couple of heartbeats. His pupils are, however, non-reactive, and I can't detect any breathing. If he is alive, I don't know how he can remain alive. His body temperature is very low; a living person would be hypothermic."

Folding his arms across his chest, Parsons simply said, "I agree."

I felt frozen in place, but my brain was racing beyond its normal capacity.

"Have you got a vehicle we could use to transfer him to the hospital?"

Parsons nodded his head toward the door. "Yes, we've got something akin to a hearse out here."

"Get it ready," I demanded. "I want him in the hospital, stat!"

Parsons hesitated and looked me square in the eyes. The look was so piercing that I stopped and felt the chill of the room. "Is there more?"

Parson's pointed to the second table. There was another man whose head was bare but his body was also covered. He nodded to the woman standing by the other body. She pulled down the cover.

I gasped as my eyes turned back to Parsons. Parsons nodded his head up and down then finally said, "Yes, this man is in the same condition."

I walked over to the other man. It was then that I noticed they both looked somewhat gray.

"Have you ever seen this before?" I asked the M.E.

"No. This is a reaction to death that I've never seen before."

I noted similar gauze on his chest. It had the same dark seepage as the first. "You started the autopsy on this man too?"

The M.E. picked up the scalpel from a nearby stainless steel cart. "With this very scalpel."

Just then a phone rang, shocking me into a twitch. One of the assistants walked over, picked it up, and answered it. After just a moment she put the phone down. "We have another DOA at the hospital. They want us to come and pick up the body. It's a woman."

The M.E. asked, "Have they determined a cause of death?"

"No."

Looking intently at me, the M.E. asked, "Do you want us to send both men back to the hospital?"

This is crazy! I screamed inside, but calmly answered, "Yes, let's get them both to the hospital. I don't know the best place to put them, but let's get them on their way. I'll make some kind of arrangements."

"Shall we use an ambulance or send them in our own vehicle. It doesn't have any medical support."

Once again, I had to ponder a new experience. "Zip them up in body bags, load them with ice, and cover them. I'd like to keep them as cold as possible. Go ahead and use your vehicle. I'll call the hospital and ask them to arrange a means of keeping the bodies cold. I don't know if it will make a difference, but I think we should keep them in their cold state. Just in case."

I drove back to the hospital, knowing the two bodies would soon follow. I simply wasn't sure where to put them. After giving it much thought, I decided to use an operating room that was being re-equipped. Though not functional, it could be cooled to 60 degrees and, at the same time, we could watch their progress. It seemed the most prudent thing to do, and there was plenty of room for both bodies.

The arrangements were well underway when I opened the doors to the out-of-service O.R. The room wasn't sterile, but I wasn't sure that was necessary. *They can clean it up while we are working.* The main thing I wanted to get into the room was a set of monitors. I preferred the type in the ICU, but decided I would take whatever I could get. *I need to determine if the nearly undetectable, slow, and erratic heartbeats were truly present or if it was merely my imagination.*

Another Body

THE EXHIBITION HALL WAS scheduled to open at 10:00 a.m. I had been hustling to get my display ready when Jensen showed up. He looked like he'd had a little too much to drink and had little dark smudges under his eyes. Looking around, I realized that it was common amongst nearly everyone in the hall.

"Hey!"

"Hey."

With a slight smirk I suggested, "A little hung over this morning?"

Jensen rubbed both temples. "Yes, I'm afraid I am. I should know better. Maybe I need to take up your lifestyle. No booze and a marriage."

"I'm happy," I assured him.

Barely looking at me, Jensen remarked, "Yes, I think you are. I feel like crap today."

Without saying anything more he walked over to his display. It was time to go to work; the first buyers would soon be coming through the doors, at least the ones that were awake. Many of them would probably still be coping with morning-after effects of partying hard the night before. I noticed Jensen was carrying a lone box. It was old and a little battered. It was one of the snake boxes. I shook my head and wondered what kind of trouble we might see today. I didn't know anyone else as flamboyant as the Texan and felt like we'd probably not see that again. I still wondered . . . *would these shirts cause the same stir today as they did last night?*

At 1:00 p.m. the hostess brought us some expensive, although typically poor, concession food. We ate a mouthful here and a mouthful there, in between discussions with existing and, hopefully, future customers. The food was tasteless and soon turned cold, but it didn't matter. The traffic picked up, and Jensen looked like he was feeling better. He seemed to be his old self as he met and greeted old and now new friends. In some ways I envied him. I didn't have quite the same panache as Jensen. He was such a natural, and people genuinely liked him.

I had been refolding some merchandise when a shadow interrupted my thoughts and work. I looked up and nearly choked. He was an old customer, and he was wearing one of Jensen's snake shirts. I tried to hide my startled look, but the customer noticed it.

"What's the matter, Bob? Are you freaked out over this shirt?"

I burst into a smile. "You know; they do creep me out. I came across a few small rattlesnakes, growing up in Arizona, but this monster is bigger and more malicious than anything I ever saw."

The customer did a pirouette. "Am I ready for the runway?"

Laughing I said, "Yes, I think you are, and with that shirt the whole crowd will be watching you—carefully."

We had a good laugh and he said to call him; he had an order he wanted to place. Then he was on his way, snake shirt and all.

It was nearly half an hour later when I heard sirens again. Once more, EMTs were hustling through the hall and into a men's restroom. I was with a customer, and we both stopped to watch the disturbance.

"What the heck?" commented the customer. "Didn't we have someone wheeled from the restroom yesterday?"

I remained quiet.

Soon two more EMTs arrived with a gurney.

The customer said, "You know, I heard on the news this morning that someone taken from the Convention Center died at the hospital last night. Could it have been that loud-mouthed Texan?"

A shudder went both up and down my spine. *I wonder.* The Texan was also my friend and a good customer. I prayed it wasn't him. I was irritated that he'd been referred to in such a way, especially if he had died. I said nothing for a few seconds, but finally managed to say, "I hope not."

We continued to watch. It was getting freaky. No one moved, they just stood as though in a trance. Ten minutes later, the gurney was wheeled out by the four EMTs. A body was covered with a blanket. There were a few audible gasps and some quiet murmuring. Two people in two days had succumbed to some illness, both in the men's restroom. It was weird. In all my years, I'd only seen one episode at a convention, a man who had stumbled and fallen into a diabetic coma. This was far different than that episode and felt much worse.

I walked over to Jensen's display and asked in a subdued voice, "Do you know who that was?"

Jensen simply shook his head in the negative.

Fewer people had crowded around the bathroom door this time, but those few had a little news to share. From them we learned that the man was the one who promised to place a larger order with me. I know I shouldn't have thought it, but the words ran through my mind. *I can kiss that order goodbye.*

The Hospitality Suite

THE DAY PASSED, THE crowds left, and Jensen and I were back in our hospitality suites. Our own open house was scheduled to begin in a few minutes.

Jensen looked at me and remarked, "Well, old friend, here we go again. After the open house, tie me to the bed and don't let me leave."

"I'd be happy to, but remember, my wife is coming in tonight. She'll take a hotel shuttle and should arrive around ten, just after our guests have gone."

A faint smile crossed Jensen's face. "I forgot about your wife. I guess I'll have to party without you. Actually, I was going to buy you that steak tonight."

I smiled broadly, "I'll tell you what. Let's skip the parties, and we'll go Dutch tonight. You can buy me that steak another time."

"I like your way of thinking," Jensen chuckled.

As the evening progressed, more of our expensive food and drink was consumed. As before, both suites were filled with people, and booze and food flowed freely. Some well-positioned clothing hangers were placed around the rooms. It appeared to be worth it. I had met a number of potential new customers and got phone numbers or a method of contact from most of them. Jensen passed out a couple more shirts. One loud woman, who I didn't know, put one on. She reminded me a little of Marshall but was from the northeast. Judging by her accent and demeanor, probably New Jersey.

Everyone was having a good time, and then I noticed through the adjoining doors that there seemed to be a line up by the entrance to Jensen's bathroom. I could see that some of the people were in distress. Since the line was in Jensen's suite, I went to him.

"You might have a problem over there," I said, nodding toward the bathroom.

Jensen took a look, spit out a sarcastic, "Oh, brother," and headed for the bathroom door. "Hey folks, we've got more than one bathroom. Go through the adjoining doors, there's a bathroom and more food and drink in that suite."

The more uncomfortable rushed away. A few stayed behind saying they could wait.

"How long has the door been closed?" Jensen asked a woman standing nearby.

Before she could answer a man spoke up and said, "It's been fifteen minutes, maybe more."

I joined the group and suggested, "Maybe we should knock on the door."

Jensen looked at me, shaking his head negatively, and said, "I hate to, but here goes."

He knocked tentatively on the door. There was no answer. He knocked once more, a little louder. There was still no answer.

My skin began to crawl, the nerves in my spine sent a shudder up and down my back, and adrenaline shot through my system. I heard a sound that carried me back to the time I was walking a trail in the mountains of Arizona and heard my first rattlesnake. While contemplating that thought, Jensen turned to look at me.

Barely out loud, he said, "Did you hear that?

I nodded, "Yes."

Jensen stepped back from the door as if it was the face of danger. I didn't know if any of our guests heard the sound. No one had screamed, or spoken up, so I assumed they hadn't. I looked around, saw no fear, and assumed that only Jensen and I had heard it.

"What should we do?" Jensen whispered.

I knew what we should do, but couldn't speak the words.

Jensen looked nervously around the room. I only assumed what went through his mind because I knew what was going through my own. I didn't want our guests to be spooked. It was only 9:00 p.m., but there was no way we could get them out of the room.

Finally, Jensen reached out to touch the door handle. He began to turn it. It resisted. He twisted a little harder. "It's locked," he said.

More of the guests were developing an interest in the long-locked bathroom door.

"Who's in there," one man asked.

"I saw the woman from New Jersey go in there quite a while ago," another said. "She was wearing one of those freaky snake shirts."

Another cold shiver ran the length of my spine. I looked at Jensen and said, "You'd better call the hotel and have them open the door." I was glad it was his room and not mine.

Jensen nodded his head in affirmation. He walked to the phone, picked it up, and made the call. It was only a few minutes before a man in a hotel uniform rushed through the door. The key was already in his hand.

"Is there someone in there?" he asked.

"We think so," Jensen replied. "It might be a woman, about thirty years old."

The hotel manager knocked loudly on the door, "Ma'am?"

There was no response. He knocked again and called out even louder, "Ma'am? Are you alright?"

Everyone in the suite was intently watching.

There was still no response. He took the key in his hand and inserted it into the door handle. He twisted it, the lock clicked, and he pushed the door open.

There was really no logical reason to do so, but Jensen and I both stepped back. The sound had been clear and completely identifiable to me. *But it can't be,* I thought. I was relieved that no monster rattlesnake had come slithering through the door. Unaware of what Jensen and I were feeling, the manager rushed in.

"Quick!" he called out, "Someone call 911!"

Several cell phones popped out of pockets and within seconds a connection was made and a rescue requested.

"They're on their way," a voice called out.

The manager shouted, "Someone help me! Let's move her to the couch."

It was Jensen's suite, and he would have been the logical assistant, but he was frozen where he stood. Another man pushed by him. In seconds the woman was on the couch. The manager bent over with the intent of listening to her heart, but he stopped cold. The orange, malicious eyes of the rattler met his. The hesitance lasted only a few moments, but it was noticeable to everyone. He picked up her arm and started feeling for a pulse.

He said nothing, but I read fear in his eyes. His finger kept moving around the wrist. In what looked like desperation, he placed his middle finger on her throat, trying to identify a pulse. He looked at Jensen, who had finally moved to a nearby couch.

"I can't feel a pulse," the hotel manager said.

Gasps came from the small crowd. The manager looked at his watch. It had been less than ten minutes since the 911 call. He was clearly worried.

"Someone give her CPR!" came a voice from the back of the room.

The manager hesitated.

"Here, I'll do it," and a woman pushed forward from the back of the room. When she saw the snake shirt, she hesitated, but only for an instant. She went to work, clearly experienced in CPR.

It seemed like forever, but we finally heard the siren. The balcony door was open, and it was obvious when the paramedics pulled up to the hotel. Several guests poked their heads in and shouted, "The ambulance is here!"

The crowd simultaneously breathed a sigh of relief. Within a few minutes, a hotel staff member burst through the door with two paramedics following behind.

In seconds they determined she had no heartbeat. The snake shirt was cut open and the defibrillator was used several times. After ten minutes of work and several phone calls to medical support, they stopped. Her shirt was pulled back to cover her. It was then that one of the paramedics said, "Hell, she's wearing that same shirt!"

The paramedics looked at each other, but said nothing more. After another phone call and some heated discussions with the hotel manager, they loaded the deceased woman onto another gurney. She was transported out of the hotel and into the ambulance. The paramedics wanted to wait for the Medical Examiner, but the hotel manager wanted the body out right away. The manager won the discussion.

Down in the Dumps

JENSEN AND I WATCHED from the balcony as the body was loaded into the emergency vehicle. After it pulled from the curb, a few of us turned around and walked into the suite. It was nearly empty, making it clear that the party was over. The only remaining guests were existing customers who were also close friends. We all gathered together, but very few words were spoken. Finally, one of them spoke up, making an obvious statement, "I'm sorry Jensen. This is really bad luck for you. I'll see you tomorrow."

The customer turned and walked out the door. Others followed him and within in a minute, Jensen and I were left alone in the suite.

"What the hell just happened?" asked Jensen.

I had no answer. I walked over to a comfortable chair and plopped into it. I knew I had to say something, even if it was a trifle, "I don't know."

Jensen sat across the room. After a long period of silence, he quietly said, "You know, I thought I'd heard rattler buzzes a number of times since I loaded those boxes into the rental car. I passed it off as my own crazy fears—but you heard them too, didn't you?"

I didn't want to admit it, but I had. "Between you and me, yes, I heard rattler buzzing, but to anyone else, I don't know what I heard. I just know it scared me, and when he opened that door, I expected to see a rattlesnake."

"Me, too."

We sat in silence for an even longer time.

"I'd sure like to get those boxes out of the suite tonight."

I looked at him and with total and complete seriousness said, "I would too, if I were you."

Again, we sat in silence. I figured the events would hurt my business, but knew it might be devastating to Jensen's business. I wasn't sure anyone would come back to the suites on the next and final night of the convention. The minutes ticked away. The only interruption was the hotel staff crew that came to the door. They meekly asked if they should clean up, and we conceded. They went about their business, and we only half watched, not saying a word.

At last, a chiming clock in the room announced that it was 10:00 p.m. I was surprised. Jensen didn't move his head, even though I knew he was awake.

"My wife should be here any minute," I said. "Her plane landed forty minutes ago. I'd better go back and clean up the suite a bit. I need to straighten up the bedroom."

Jensen didn't respond. I got up from the couch and moved toward the adjoining door. Before leaving, I turned to Jensen. "I'll see you tomorrow."

He barely raised his hand in a gesture of goodbye. He didn't say a thing.

Detective Chavanet's Visit

I CLOSED THE ADJOINING door and locked our side. The episode had cast a pall of gloom over the convention. Even worse, I suspected that Jensen felt doom. I was washing up when a knock came at the door. I was sure it would be Anne, so I opened it wearing a big smile. I was surprised to see the hotel manager and a man in a worn and wrinkled suit.

The manager spoke first, "Mr. Preston, I'm sorry to disturb you. This is Detective Chavanet."

The detective dipped his head in greeting, "Hello, Mr. Preston."

I stammered, "H-hello?"

"Mr. Preston, I need to talk to you for a few minutes."

"What about?" I asked, my eyes flicking back and forth between the two men.

"About the events of this evening."

Another cold chill ran down my spine. Add the fact that policemen always intimidate me, and I became weak in the knees.

"Okay, come on in," I said as I turned to walk to an overstuffed chair, plopping into it before I fell.

The detective turned to the hotel manager. "You may go now. I'll have a chat with Mr. Preston. I assure you, he will be treated with respect."

The manager said, "Thank you," but looked at me for a long moment. I wasn't completely sure what message his eyes conveyed. The part of me that felt guilty, also felt accused; but another part of me suggested the manager was only looking out for my welfare. He quickly turned, and I heard his heavy footsteps as he walked down the hall. The footsteps stopped suddenly. The detective turned his head to watch the hotel manager. I couldn't see what was going on and could only imagine the manager's concern. I realized that his hotel would have a lot at stake in this crazy situation, and concluded that he must have wanted to stay, ensuring a proper handling of the interview. He apparently made another decision, and I heard the heavy footsteps continue down the hall.

The detective asked, "So, may I come in?"

I nodded my head but didn't rise from the easy chair, feeling a little sick to my stomach.

He entered the room casually. He seemed to be trying not to alarm me, as if he knew my internal alarms were in full shriek mode, and he didn't want to set them off. He started by saying, "Mr. Preston, I'm talking to you first, but I already stopped at Mr. Jensen's. I told him I wanted to chat, and he is waiting for me."

The detective asked a few questions about me, about Jensen, our relationship, and our businesses. He asked me to repeat the events of the evening. I told him everything, except I didn't tell him about hearing, or sensing, that rattle. I wasn't sure it was even real, and I didn't want to be accused of losing my mind. I was beginning to have doubts about my own sanity, anyway. It crossed my mind that if I were to report the events of the last several days, I would likely be committed. No one would ever believe me—not even my wife. I decided right then and there, that I wouldn't tell her until I absolutely had to about the buzzing sounds.

The detective continued to ask questions, some of them twice. For some reason, I felt guilt but didn't know why. Neither Jensen nor I had done anything wrong. The poor woman just happened to die in our bathroom. I now suspected that the food and booze had been taken in as evidence to be checked for toxins. *Maybe she was allergic to shellfish,* I thought. The detective voiced no suspicions of any kind, but the questions seemed unending.

Where is Anne? I wondered, as the questions slogged on. I longed to see her. I wanted her company, not necessarily for strength, but just to have someone with whom to share this amazing week. Then I remembered I wasn't going to tell her about the buzzing. Suddenly there was a knock at the door. *It has to be her.*

"Excuse me, Detective Chavanet."

I opened the door and was immediately relieved. It *was* Anne. I stepped into the hall and gave her a big hug. She responded, but then pulled back. "What's up?" A smile spread over her face. "Have you missed me that much?"

"Yes," I said desperately.

I hugged her again, and it seemed that she really appreciated it. She gave me an extra tight squeeze and whispered in my ear, "Let's go inside."

I whispered in her ear, "There's a man inside." Her smile diminished. "He's from the police department." Her smile disappeared. "Something's happened, but I'm not in trouble." Her face became stone cold serious. "I was a witness, and he's asking some questions."

I turned toward the detective, her hand in mine, and led her into the room.

"Detective Chavanet, this is my wife, Anne. She just flew in from New York and knows nothing about this evening's events.

"Good evening, Mrs. Preston. Actually, I think I'm finished. You must be tired and, well, I think we're all tired."

The detective turned to leave the hotel room but stopped in the doorway, swung back around and remarked, "That is quite a shirt that the woman was wearing."

I gave a positive nod but said nothing.

He held my gaze with his eyes for a moment, never flinching, then he turned and was gone. I closed the door and fell into the couch.

Still standing, Anne asked, "What's this all about?"

"We had a woman die at our party tonight. She went into the bathroom and just—died."

"Oh, Bob, that's awful!"

"Yeah. It was bad enough that she died here at our party, but our suite was also full of guests at the time. I don't know what the fallout is going to be."

For the next few minutes I told her bits and pieces of the story, but it became so confusing that I had to go back to the beginning. I also decided it was best to tell her everything. The marriage counselor said we should have no secrets from one another, so I related every event that seemed pertinent, including the buzzing. She listened quietly, asking a question now and then. She expressed amazement when told about Mothe' Moses and was saddened to learn that the pastry shop had closed. She remembered the shop, too. She was also intrigued with the Voodoo Shop, but laughed at the idea of the snake shirs'. She had quickly picked up our slang reference to Mothe' Moses's crazy creations. By the time we had finished talking, it was very late and whatever romance I'd previously planned was now a second-hand notion to the drama of the death at our party.

At length, I thought about Jensen and wondered how he was doing. I went to the adjoining door and listened. All seemed quiet. I thought of knocking but decided against it. I joined Anne in the bedroom only to toss and turn in a fitful night's sleep. I can't call it rest, because I don't think I rested. I remembered too many visions of snakes, swampland, a white flower, Jonah, and the dead woman in our bathroom.

When morning came, I didn't want to get up but was grateful the restless night was over. I was tired of the horrid dreams inspired by the crazy events of the last few days. The convention had almost become an afterthought. I thought a shower might take my mind off the drama.

It didn't.

Detective Chavanet: The Police Investigator

INVESTIGATING DEATH. I SHOULD be used to it by now. During my career, New Orleans has consistently been a city of death, although it's no longer the murder capital of the United States, as it once was.

As I walked from my car to the door, I looked up and down the street and then back at the door. This bar was no different than any other jazz bar on Bourbon Street. It was just another day of death. But, I reasoned, there is something different with these deaths. I greeted Officer Abellard, who was guarding the entrance.

"Good morning, Detective Chavanet," he responded.

I looked at my watch. It was nearly 5:00 a.m. I muttered, "I thought it was still night, but you're right, I should now think of it as morning." I walked through the door.

The investigating officers had declared the bar a crime scene, although they weren't sure why. In every way, the incident seemed like another heart attack, but the coincidences were piling up, and they couldn't be overlooked. The bar reeked of beer, sweat, and cleanser. The humidity had magnified the odor to the point of revulsion. I should have been used to the smell by now, but I'm not. It always turns my stomach. The customers hadn't been allowed to leave, but they were served no booze. Their eyes followed me as I walked past the tables where they lounged. There was a lot of coffee on those tables, and the jazz band continued to play, but with subdued enthusiasm.

The man lay flat on the bathroom floor. He looked normal in every way except for his face that, in its death mask, was transfixed in a look of terror. *What was this guy so afraid of?* I asked myself.

There really wasn't much to see. The man was lying on the floor. There were no signs of a struggle; there was no blood and no weapon. There was, however, a witness, but he gave no evidence of anything unusual. The witness said the guy suddenly became terrified and dropped to the ground, as though he were scared to death. It is a very unusual thing for a person to be scared to death. I had never seen it before, but I doubted the cause of death was a scare.

The dead man was lying on his back where the EMTs had left him after trying to save his life. I saw one glaring fact that sent chills down my spine. The man was dressed in a pullover, collared shirt with a life-like image of a rattlesnake on it. The two other dead people were dressed in the same shirt. *Can this be a coincidence, or do I need to look into these shirts?*

After a cursory look at the body, I went back out into the bar. Another officer was sitting by a man who sat alone at a table. He looked like a tourist and in a quick glance to a table nearby, I identified the woman who had been with him, or at least that's what I thought.

I sat down across the table from the man. The cheap table wobbled as I leaned on it.

"I'm Detective Chavanet. I understand you were in the bathroom when this man collapsed."

The tourist wasn't a suspect, but I could see that he was uncomfortable, so much so that I wondered if he was guilty of other crimes. New Orleans seemed to bring both the best and the worst into its bawdy grasp.

"Yes, sir."

Too polite, I thought. *He's been here before.* "Tell me in your own words what you saw."

I watched him closely. Observation was one of my most important tools. The man was clearly in distress; he swallowed hard and struggled to begin. At last he said, "I was washing up when this man walked into the lavatory. He was pretty wasted. He looked at me and said, "What do you think of this cool shirt?" I had barely started looking at it when he turned to look at himself in the mirror in an admiring way. You would have thought he was the center of the world. All of a sudden his face took on the look of terror, like he'd just seen the devil. He didn't scream at first, except a muffled groan rose from deep in his throat. I saw him raise his hands up to cover his face, as though he thought he was about to be hit in the face."

The man stopped. He seemed to search for the courage to make this next statement. After years as an investigator, I pretty much knew when people were lying. This man was not. Whatever else he might be guilty of, he was telling a story that to him was the truth. In a moment he began again.

"Detective, I don't know what happened next, but he covered his face with his hands and shrieked in a manner that still curdles my blood. Whatever he experienced must have been the most horrible moment of his life. After the shriek, he stood for just an instant. He was quiet but still covering his face. Then he just crumpled to the floor. It all happened so quickly. I was barely finished washing my hands. They were still wet."

The man had already told the story, twice. Two different officers had also questioned him, and he had not mixed up his statement. He had told the story three times, to three different people, and each story agreed with the other. Normally, we'd have thanked him and sent him on his way, but the events of the evening demanded other actions.

"Thank you," I said. "Are you planning on leaving town today?"

"No," the man replied.

"Good. Stick around. I may want to talk to you again."

I gave him two cards and a pen. I asked him to write his name and local phone number on one of the cards. When he was finished, I slipped it into my shirt pocket.

Holding his gaze with my own, I said, "The second card is for you. Call me if you think of anything that I should know."

The man slowly shook his head up and down.

I looked over at the woman, who was obviously concerned, and nodded toward her, "Is she with you?"

"Yes."

"Have you told her what happened?"

"Not in detail, but yes, I did while waiting for the police to arrive."

"I'll want to talk her, too. Go back to your hotel, stay there, and wait for my call. I shouldn't be long."

As I got up to leave, he reached out, grabbed my wrist, and stopped me. "Detective, it was the most awful thing I've ever seen. It was like the man died of sheer terror. I don't know what happened, but I don't think it was a heart attack. Whatever it was, I think the man was literally scared to death."

I watched the witness leave the bar. He didn't even look back at this girlfriend. He was visibly shaken. Maybe he was an innocent man after all, and this experience had been too much for him. I had seen other people lose their senses for a little while after witnessing a horrifying moment. Most of them recover. *He will too,* I thought.

I stepped over to the table where the girlfriend was seated. She was far too nervous, which made me suspicious all over again. Why, after all, should *she* be nervous? Some great guilt was weighing on her mind. Maybe they were lawbreakers, or maybe they were fidelity breakers. It didn't really matter to me. Right now, I just wanted the facts as best I could get them. And then I wanted to go to bed. Her story was as I expected. She really had nothing to add, and the little part she knew was similar to her boyfriend's story. I sent her on her way, but told her she and her boyfriend needed to stay in town. Whatever was on their minds besides this horrific bathroom death must have been serious. I figured I'd let them sweat for a day. Maybe it would change the course of their lives.

Questions for Jensen

THE NOISE AT THE door was loud, demanding, and disturbing my early morning sleep. After the detective left, I tried to sleep, but tossed and turned fitfully. At about four in the morning, when it looked like I might not get to sleep, I reached over and turned off the alarm. I knew I would be too tired to get up and didn't care if I overslept. Finally, I fell into an uncomfortable fit of slumber. At first, I wasn't sure it was a knock; I thought it might have been a continuation of the dreams thrashing through my mind. I shook my head trying to make sense of the torment in my foggy brain. But, the knock came again—even louder. I, at last, gained enough sense to realize that there really was someone knocking at the door. Bleary-eyed and hair uncombed, I opened the door. It was Detective Chavanet.

"Good morning, Mr. Jensen. Well, we actually already know that's not your name. What is it?"

Confused, I simply answered, "Alex McIntyre."

"I can see why you go by Jensen."

I didn't respond, but wondered why he had come back so early in the morning. Didn't the man ever sleep? I steeled myself against his questions. I wanted to tell him nothing more than he would require of me. My mind flashed to the shirs' and the stop payment. They could be considered stolen shirts. *Could that be it?*

"I won't be but a minute, Mr. McIntyre. Actually, is it okay if I call you Jensen? It just seems right."

I nodded and muttered, "Yes."

"I want to report to you that we had three more deaths last night, in addition to the woman who died here. You may wonder what this has to do with you, and I don't know the answer to that question, but I don't want you to leave town. I'm not going to arrest you, but stay in town where I can contact you when I want to."

"I plan on being at the Convention Center today," I told him, "and I had an open house scheduled here tonight, but I don't know if anyone will show up at this point."

Still standing in the doorway, the detective looked around the room.

"Nice digs," he said, leaning in a bit and panning his head from side to side. His eyes seemed to take in every detail, although he'd already seen it all.

"Look, I can't advise you about your open house, but there is something going on, and I don't know what it is. All I know is that, obviously, you are somehow involved. You and your shirts."

I shifted from one foot to the other. "Obviously?"

"Yes. Let me tell you why. All the deaths involved people who were wearing your shirts."

I nearly fell to the ground. Only the grip on door handle held me up. "Wearing my shirs'?" I asked, nearly whispering.

"Yes. They were wearing your shirts. At first, we didn't catch that, but as new reports came in, and we looked over what I am now considering as crime scenes, two things were clear. They were all wearing your shirts, and they all occurred in a restroom or a bathroom."

"A bathroom?"

"Yes, or a restroom," he answered.

"I'm sorry, I've got to sit down," I said as I dropped into a chair near the door.

The detective stepped into the room. "You say you've given away these shirts?" he asked.

"Yes. I'm in retail clothing, attending the convention. I'm considering making them a line in my shirt collection. I believed there to be a niche market for them."

"How many have you given away?" I looked toward bedroom where the boxes were still stored. I don't know, maybe fifty or so."

"That many?" he asked.

I nodded, looked at him and added, "Or so."

"Or so?" The detective let the words hang in mid-air, and the room was quiet. At last he spoke once more, "Can I have a look at them?"

"They are in that bedroom. In the old boxes."

The detective walked to the bedroom, and I followed him. He stepped up to the boxes, picked up the top one and shook it. I was sure it was my imagination, but I thought I heard the buzzing all over again. He pulled the flaps up. I expected to see a snake strike from the box. He must have, too, because he appeared cautious as the lid opened. For the longest time he just stood there looking into the box. Then he stood even longer, unmoving, unspeaking. At last he let out a long, low whistle. "That's the damnedest thing I've ever seen."

I agreed with him but said nothing. "Damned" was an appropriate word, I thought. I don't think it's the artwork of a good person.

"Can I take one?" He had already picked one up, and I admired his guts.

"Sure, go ahead."

"Actually, I'd like to take it with me?" He said.

"Be my guest," was my response.

Folding the shirt into a tight wad of fabric, he said, "Don't forget. Do not leave town. I'm sure to have more questions for you. Right now, we're considering this a mass murder case. I don't see you as a mass murderer, but—just don't leave town. If you do, I'll issue a warrant for your arrest. In your line of work, that wouldn't be a good thing."

"I'll stick around," I promised. It was all I could muster.

Detective Chavanet turned and walked out the door of the suite, closing the door behind him. I looked at my watch. It was 9:00 a.m. The convention hall opened in an hour. I was even less motivated since the feeling of being punched in the gut was in full effect.

Just then, another knock came from the door. I cursed under my breath, thinking it was the return of the detective. I opened the door.

"Jensen, I heard voices. What's going on?"

I was relieved to see Bob's face rather than a policeman.

"Detective Chavanet was back again. He just told me there were three other deaths last night, in addition to the woman who was here. He also said they were all wearing my snake shirts."

"Wearing your shirts?" I was incredulous; even Jensen sounded surprised.

I noted it was the first time in days he hadn't used the slang *shirs'*.

"Yes, and apparently every death either happened in a restroom or a bathroom."

"No kidding?" His head shook quickly back and forth.

"Yes, that's what he said."

Anne had followed Bob into my suite and heard the exchange. She stood still, silently taking in the scene and the conversation. "Are those the shirts?" she asked, nodding toward the old boxes visible through the bedroom door.

I nodded my head to confirm that the boxes held the shirts. To my surprise, Anne immediately walked into the bedroom, over to the boxes, and lifted out a shirt.

"Wow! Now I see why you were so taken by them," she remarked. "That is incredible artwork and the shirts are perfect. The snakes remind me of the ones I used to see in the Everglades. These are nasty snakes at the best of times, but I'll say this, rattlesnakes always warn you before they strike. It's the cottonmouths that always scared me. You never knew when you might step on one."

"You're familiar with these monsters," I asked, my eyes flicking to Bob and back to Anne.

"Yes," was all Anne said.

She leaned down into the box and rummaged through it until she found a shirt that was her size. She held it up and said, "Yes, this will do for me. Do you want to stay out of suspicion? If you do, then wear one of these today, at the convention. If you wear one, people will realize they're safe, and that you and the shirts aren't to blame. And—I'll wear this one." Her face spread into a big smile, and with her smile the gloom lifted. But then I became filled with anxiety.

I held my peace. Bob said nothing either. At last, breaking the silence, Anne asked, "May I have it?"

I looked at Bob, and he shook his head no.

I looked quickly back to Anne. I sensed her determination, and it looked like she had already made up her mind. Looking back to Bob, he seemed also to recognize that her mind was made up, too. Trying to be considerate of Bob, but feeling some hope in Anne's offer, I said, "Are you sure that's a good idea?"

Anne looked at Bob and then at me. She became very serious. "Jensen, based on what Bob said, you've only given away a few of these shirts. Not everyone died. You two are acting like the shirts are alive, or possessed, or something. I don't believe in that foolishness! It's just a painting of a snake on a shirt; a big mean one, I'll admit, but it's just a painting. That old woman's got you two shaking in your boots, and you're looking for every excuse in the world to be scared. Come on! Stand up! Be men!"

It actually hurt to have Anne insinuate that she considered us to be less macho than she, so the macho man inside of me shouted, *no way!* I stood up, walked over to the box of snake shirts and found one that was my size. "You're right; I'm going to wear this today."

Anne smiled, turned to Bob and asked, "What about you?"

"Baby steps," he said. "Baby steps."

Putting the talk behind me, I ushered them out of my suite, showered, shaved, put on my snake shirt and headed for the Convention Center.

I have shirts to sell.

Dr. Whitley, Monitoring Room: 8:00 am

*BOY, THIS ROOM IS **cold**!* Of course that was what I'd wanted, but I wasn't enjoying the temperature. At my direction, the nurses had monitors connected to nine people. I noticed movement in front of me and looked up. Detective Chavanet was looking into the room and motioned his desire to enter. I nodded, giving him permission to enter.

Once he was close to where I was standing, he asked, "Well, Doc, whad' yuh think?"

"The truth?" I asked. "I don't know what to think."

"Are they alive?" he asked as he stood by my side.

I shook my head *no* but said, "They might be. I don't know, maybe they've become zombies."

The detective's mouth curled a bit at my crude humor. He placed his hands on the edge of one of the beds, "Have you figured out what happened to them?"

"No, I haven't. We've been analyzing blood samples. We've not detected anything unusual. Specifically, we found no snake venom in their blood. I know it sounds strange, but I was hoping to find snake venom. That could explain a lot."

In reality, I wasn't sure if I was disappointed or glad there was no snake venom in the patients. On the one hand, there would have been a clear treatment regimen. On the other hand, we would not have been able to explain its presence. No snakes had been found at any of the scenes, except for the snakes on the shirts.

Now yawning, the Detective rubbed his eyes, then his temples. "What *do* you know?"

Again I shook my head. "They all have heartbeats, but they are weak and very slow. It's hard to imagine that their hearts can be keeping them alive. They have no blood pressure. Brain waves exist but at a level so low that we can barely detect them. They are not breathing. They are unresponsive to every stimulant we've attempted. I hate to say it, but 'zombie' is the only thing that comes to mind."

Chavanet's face screwed up in an expression of distaste. "Not brain-eating zombies, I hope."

I shook my head again, and my chin fell to my chest. "No Detective, I don't think they are brain-eaters, but it *is* almost as if they are undead. They are alive and dead, both at the same time. I've called the CDC and sent them test results. They've got people on their way here. I think they'll order a quarantine, even though I don't think there are any infectious dangers here."

Chavanet looked surprised and annoyed. "That means I've lost control, and I may even be infected myself, if they are infectious."

"I think you're safe. I sent teams to question anyone who was near the incidents about the events that led to their deaths. Each of these nine people was near, or with, a lot of other people, some of them intimate. No one else has taken ill."

Tugging on his chin Chavanet responded, "I think I'd better confiscate those shirts."

The doctor stopped what he was doing and looked directly at the detective. "I don't know why, but I think that's a very good idea."

Jensen and His Shirts

I MANAGED TO GET to the convention hall early. Despite the crazy night and Detective Chavanet's visit, I decided it would be best to get an early start. Everyone who knew me was asking about the shirt and the incident the previous night. Rumors spread like an uphill wild fire fanned by brisk winds. News of the death in our hospitality suite was rampant. The fact that the victim been wearing one of my snake shirts was spreading just as fast. I was sure the entire weekend was going to be a disaster. My credibility could be ruined for life, and it might mean the death of my business. I no longer had any interest in selling the shirts. I just wanted to save my business. It was then that I had a brainstorm. Maybe I could make the whole snake shirt ordeal work for me, and it was in those minutes that I decided to make a dramatic offer.

It was just before 10:00 a.m. and my display was ready to go. I noticed that Bob hadn't made it in yet. I went to the business center at the convention hall and had some cheap fliers made up. On the flier, I offered a ten percent discount to anyone who would submit a photo of them wearing the snake shirt with their paid order.

I put some fliers and some shirts in a box and started to make my way around the hall. Lots of people just laughed at me, but the serious buyers knew this was an opportunity to cash in on my troubles. I gave away all of my shirts. There were a lot of cringes, and some people were unwilling to touch them. As I walked back to my display, I saw a lot of shirt waving as people made jokes of them. It was a disturbing sight, but I believed that the discount on paid orders, even though it cut into my profit, could save my business.

At last I was back at my display. I put on my game face and prepared to get back to work. I was relieved when the party atmosphere picked up again, and it seemed to be the shirts that had initiated the fresh atmosphere. I saw more and more people put the shirts on, get their picture taken, and then hurriedly take them off. It was like an Internet video going viral. The idea was sweeping the entire hall. In fact, the shirts were being passed around so much that I lost track of who had worn them. I'd been trying to write down the names of those who'd taken pictures, but it became impossible to do so.

All at once Bob was at my side and asked, "What have you done, Jensen?"

I looked him and laughed. "I may have just saved my business. I'm giving a ten percent discount to every paid order that comes in with a picture of the buyer in one of my snake shirts. I can't believe it! Everyone is taking pictures! It's almost like they are all possessed! Isn't it great?"

Anne's Instructions from Bob

JUST BEFORE 10:00 A.M. I watched Bob get ready for the convention. He gulped down his room service juice and roll and, after kissing me goodbye, hurried out the door. He was going to be late.

I sat down on the bed, and then lay back to relax a bit more. I had no commitments, hadn't slept so well, either, and could do whatever I wanted to do. I stretched out, enjoying the luxury of the very comfortable bed. As I lay there, I thought about the snake shirts. I was about to get up and put mine on, but that made me think about shopping, and I began to wonder which stores I might visit. Then another thought hit me. *I wonder how many other wives will be out shopping today?* I don't like shopping in crowds, so I decided to get moving. I went over a mental list of what I wanted. I thought I should write it down but decided that if I couldn't remember it, I didn't need it. I knew Bob would be happy about that.

After mentally reviewing my list, I rolled over, only to be greeted by the decidedly fierce-looking Eastern Diamondback Rattlesnake on the front of the shirt I had taken from Jensen. "You are a nasty one," I said out loud, making a face at the snake image.

I rolled past the shirt without a second thought and left it lying on the bed. I began to get ready for my day of shopping. It would be a great day. My credit card had been paid down, and there was lots of room for some glamorous new clothing from New Orleans—room on both my card and in my recently organized closet.

While dressing, I looked at the snake shirt, still lying on the bed, marveling at the in-your-face statement it made. I stopped abruptly and thought about wearing it during my shopping spree. I picked up the shirt and held it up to me. It looked like it would fit nicely. I looked around for a mirror, but there wasn't one in the bedroom. *I'll have to go into the bathroom*, I mused. With shirt in hand, I headed for the entrance to the bathroom. I had just entered the short hallway when the phone rang.

I turned back to the bedroom where I thought my phone had been charging. It rang again and I realized it was charging in the bathroom. I hustled into the bathroom, threw the shirt on the marble vanity, reached for the phone, and gave a breathless, "Hello."

"Hi, Anne, it's Bob."

"Hi, Bob," I said as I sat down on the padded seat next to the vanity. Is everything okay?" He hesitated and I was compelled to ask, "What's wrong?"

"It's those crazy shirts! Jensen made a point of giving them all away. In fact, he said he'd give a ten percent discount off on order taken and paid for at the convention, *if* they'd take a picture of themselves wearing the shirts today."

"Wow, that must be quite a sight!" Remembering the story of the Texan, I envisioned all the men going around hugging the women. I laughed to myself. "So what's the big deal?"

Bob clearly did not share my nonchalant attitude toward the shirts or he wouldn't have called in the first place. He didn't answer right away. His silence spoke volumes, and I knew he was planning his delivery.

"Anne, I do not want you wearing that shirt today. I know you said you would—but—please, don't wear it today."

I looked at the shirt crumpled up on the countertop. I thought it over for a minute and concluded that my determination wasn't worth a fight with Bob. "Okay, Bob, you got it. I won't wear it."

I could feel the relief on the other end of the line even though a mile of the city of New Orleans separated us. "Thank you, Anne," he said. "Thanks for doing this for me. I love you and—well—thanks."

"You owe me one, Bob." I laughed, "You know, I may max out my card *and* yours today."

There was a laugh on the other end of the phone, "If it means you'll be alive at the end of the day, have at it. I won't care."

I heard a commotion in the background over Bob's phone.

"Gotta' run, sweetheart! Thanks again."

Before I could say anything, Bob had hung up. I looked at the shirt lying on the countertop. *How can one little shirt cause so much trouble?* I picked up the shirt and held it up once more while standing in front of the mirror. Just as it fell into place, there came a knock at the door. "Just a minute," I called out.

I dropped the shirt in a pile again and went to the door. It was the maid wanting to clean the room. She said she'd come back, and I thanked her for that. I was wasting shopping time, and with my new leverage over Bob's credit card, I could feel the shops calling. But, first, I had to get to Jackson Square for a beignet. I simply had to start the day off properly in this amazing city of cities.

I walked out the front door of the hotel, turned right, and marched along a nearly deserted Bourbon Street, something I would never have done at night, but I wanted to start the day off with a brisk walk before it got too hot. The air was humid and warm and before long, I began to feel the stickiness that is big part of the humid climates of the world. *Maybe it's already too hot.*

Intervention at the Convention

As the morning proceeded, I kept an eye on both Jensen and the craziness in the convention hall. Neither Jensen nor I believed in the occult, or voodoo, or anything like that, but the near frenzy in the hall was unbelievable. I was amazed at the way people were tossing the shirts around, putting them on, taking pictures, and shedding them just as quickly. I had to say one thing; Jensen's harebrained idea just might work. Jensen might have saved us both from a serious financial setback. The din of voices filling the hall was suddenly broken by a ruckus at the main doors and by a bullhorn.

"This is the police! This is the police! Please give us your attention."

Standing behind the man with the bullhorn was a SWAT team. Similar disturbances had broken out all around the hall and, in an instant, there were SWAT team members at every entrance. Every door to the convention hall was blocked with armed men in riot gear and face protectors. Then we saw even more uniformed officers running toward the restrooms. In addition, we could see more armed officers rushing through the other rooms of the convention hall as though they were searching for something dangerous. I began to wonder if we were in the middle of a terrorist bomb threat.

The man holding the bullhorn hit a button, making an electronic noise that caused everyone to stop talking, giving him their full attention.

"Ladies and gentlemen, what I am about to ask you to do is precautionary. I can't give you a good reason, but I want everyone who is in possession of one of the shirts with the rattlesnake picture to drop it on the floor. Please, just drop it in place. Our officers are circulating, and they will pick them up."

The crowd became vocal again, but in subdued tones.

"Ladies and gentlemen, please! I'll say it again, remove the shirts with the snake pictures on them and drop them on the ground."

I saw shirts falling to the floor. They began hitting the carpet like rotten apples falling from fruit trees. As the shirts dropped, people started moving away from them. A few minutes ago I had felt euphoria, now I felt devastation and a sickening sensation that my business was doomed.

Anne Meets Jonah

MY WALK ALONG BOURBON Street was brisk. I turned right on St. Peter Street and headed for Jackson Square. As I walked, I noticed the Voodoo Shop that Bob had spoken about on my left. Neither Bob nor I believe in such things, but the story was alluring, so I decided I would check out the store after eating my beignet.

I hustled on to my favorite beignet shop, the Café Du Monde, but settled into relaxed enjoyment while I was served three of the puffy little pastries, each dusted with powdered sugar. As I enjoyed the sweet delight, a question came to mind that I had never before considered. *Is a beignet a pastry, a fritter, or a something else?* It is made from a square-shaped piece of dough that is deep-fried, so it really isn't a pastry. Fritters are deep-fried, but usually have fruit in them. After some consideration, I decided it didn't matter. This location, and this powdered, deep-fried treat was in a class all its own. I enjoyed every last bite of the three beignets I'd been served, but the day was growing warmer, and I was terribly behind schedule.

I rose from my table, left a tip, and started walking around Jackson Square. I moved along the Northeast side of the square, since there was less traffic, then made a left and walked between the Square and St. Louis Cathedral. A few street performers were preparing to entertain the public, hoping for donations. I hurried past them, wanting to check out the Voodoo Shop. I rounded the corner to my right and started up St. Peter Street. There was the sign just ahead. I was at the door in minutes. I hesitated for just a moment before opening it. I don't believe in voodoo and don't like the idea behind it, so entering a voodoo shop is something I would not normally have done. Then again, this had not been a normal week by any plausible definition. I opened the door and stepped inside.

The shop was just as Bob had said and, within moments, there she was—the now infamous, at least in my mind, Jonah. She appeared just as she had been described in Bob's story. When he told me about her, I knew she had made a big impression on him. Her beauty was more than physical; it was as much in her demeanor as it was in her looks. Nonetheless, she was gorgeous, and I began to feel a little jealous.

"Good morning," she said in beautiful English, but with an accent that seemed to put the language on a higher plane—like a romanticized version of the language.

"Good morning," I replied with a smile that was truly genuine. I was intrigued, although still jealous of her beauty.

"May I help you?" she asked.

"My husband was in your store a few days ago, and I wanted to take a look for myself. He said your store was a study in retail marketing that I simply had to experience."

She looked around the store with her eyes, which eventually shifted back to look into my eyes. "Do you also like it?"

"Yes, it's beautiful. You have captured and conveyed a feeling that is . . ." I searched for the right word and all I could think of was, " . . . impressive."

"Thank you," was all she said, with the most pleasant of smiles.

I poked around her shop for the next fifteen minutes. Occasionally, I would ask a question. Her answers were polite and factual. When finished, I walked to a rack where she had been dusting.

"Do you believe in voodoo?" I asked.

The question surprised her, and she gave me a smile that I could not interpret. She simply said, "It is not for me to say. People believe what they believe. I am here to serve them."

I, at once, thought of crafty politicians with the skill to precisely deflect leading questions. She had that same skill. But there was something very different about this woman, and I wanted to get to know her. I asked questions about this trinket, and that skull, and on, and on. At length we began to have a conversation that felt real. Her personal walls seemed to have come down, and we began to converse in an air of friendship. I was amazed at the change from polite and perfect business etiquette to the open and friendly treatment. We spent a pleasant hour talking about this and that. It was a delightful hour, one that I didn't want to end, but the other stores of New Orleans were calling. I eventually had to end the conversation. I bought a keepsake that wouldn't be linked to voodoo, left the store, and looked for a taxi to take me to the Fleur de Paris, the first planned stop on my shopping spree.

— CHAPTER NINE —

SATURDAY MORNING: SHIRTS AT THE CONVENTION CENTER

Questions from the FBI

I HAD MY ORDERS, but they didn't make sense.

The badge hanging from a lanyard around my neck stated, Agent Thomas, FBI, to prove my jurisdiction. I had walked up to the man they called "Jensen" just as he was secured by two armed officers. They were about to throw him to the ground and his friend, too.

"Stop!" I bellowed. My overpowering shout brought the noise around us to a halt. In a state of surprise at the results, I said calmly, "Just handcuff them. There's no need to put them on the ground."

Then, looking at the two men in question, I calmly instructed, "Please let my men handcuff you. You won't be harmed, and you'll be given every right to which all citizens of our country are entitled."

I looked at the printouts in my hand. I identified Jensen and walked up to him. "Are you Alex McIntyre?"

"Yes."

"Read him his rights."

An officer began reciting the Miranda Rights to Mr. McIntyre.

I turned to the other man, "Are you Bob Preston?"

He nodded, "Yes."

"Read him his rights."

Another officer began reading Bob his Miranda Rights.

When both officers had finished, I spoke up. "I'm Senior Agent Thomas, FBI. Joining me are FBI agents, and SWAT members from the New Orleans Police department, and local CDC employees. We believe it is a possibility that those shirts, the ones with the snake pictures on them, may be contaminated with something that is harming people."

As soon as I spoke the words, I knew I'd made a mistake. It's not that the people weren't secured, and our teams had already gathered up the shirts, depositing them into biohazard bags, but it was the sheer terror that the words seemed to invoke. Wails of fear grew to a crescendo, along with shouts of concern and demands for medical treatment. The crowd was becoming frenzied, and I feared we might lose control of the situation. I could not risk a breakout to the streets of New Orleans. The city had already seen one too many disasters, and I wouldn't let another happen if I could stop it.

I pressed on the siren button on the bullhorn once more. It screeched a violent ear-splitting shriek screech that could not be ignored. After a few seconds I stopped, and with all the composure I could muster, called out to the people.

"Ladies and gentlemen, we believe you are safe. There are circumstances surrounding the affected people that you haven't experienced. Please, be calm and listen to my instructions. We have medical personnel standing by. Each of you will be examined. We will take care of each and every one of you. I truly believe that, as of this moment, you are in no danger. However, we want to make sure and verify that by conducting a physical examination of every person in this hall."

I had been monitoring the deployment of medical personnel through the hallways around the Convention Center. I noted that everyone was in their place.

"Ladies and gentlemen, please sit down on the floor right where you are. In a moment, medical personnel will enter the hall. We will do this in an organized manner that will ensure there are no accidents and injuries. Please take a moment to calm down and sit down."

My mind went to my orders. If anyone broke out of the group in an effort to escape, they were to be subdued, by force if necessary. I was not going to allow the development of any situation that might put anyone in harm's way.

I watched the crowd as we began. It was clear the process would be long and tedious, and they realized it, too. The city council had asked for a news blackout, which would not succeed. There were too many cell phones that had probably already been used to send word of one kind or another to friends and family.

There was a commotion at the doors and one was ajar. I saw National Guard troops through the opening. I'd been expecting them. With the guardsmen standing by, another army of people in white lab coats opened the doors and filed into the hall. More unarmed guardsmen began carrying in tables, chairs, and cots. Before long, it looked like an oversized MASH unit had been set up.

I turned to my second in command. "Dawson, I think things are under control here. I'm turning this over to you. I'm going ask these two gentlemen some questions."

Dawson nodded in agreement.

"Oh, and Dawson, I don't want anyone hurt or terrorized. Also, a team of psychologists will be arriving soon. Use them if you spot someone who looks like they could become a danger to themselves or anyone else.

After giving instructions to a few other policemen, I motioned to Jensen and Bob, "Okay, boys, let's go. I have some questions for you." With that, Special Agent Thomas led a team of four FBI agents and the two men toward two special rooms that had been prepared for the purpose of questioning these probably innocent suspects.

Anne's Disappointing Shopping Spree

"I HATE THIS HUMIDITY," I groused to myself after walking from the taxi to the hotel entrance at the conclusion of my shortened shopping spree. The doorman was there, offering a cheerful greeting and opening the door. After walking through the hotel lobby door, I added, "And thank goodness for air conditioning." The beautiful architectural feature again greeted me. It looked like an old New Orleans-style fountain that had been turned into a giant vase. It was as though it called to me with aromas and colors that freshened my mood and drove the disappointing shopping spree from my mind.

Yes, it was disappointing. My visit with Jonah had been charming. The shopping spree, however, had been a bust. I didn't buy anything. After two hours of shopping, I had found little to like, and even less to buy, hence, the need for rejuvenation.

After a close look at the lobby centerpiece, I turned down the hallway. The ambiance was peaceful; the colors were warm and welcoming. The tile was bright and spotlessly clean. I walked by some shops that attracted my attention, surprised that their delights had previously evaded me. My shopping enthusiasm was rejuvenated and with great excitement, I searched the racks for fashions that suited my current tastes. There wasn't enough variety to completely replenish my wardrobe, but I made enough purchases for a suitable start. I felt good as I walked through the door to my room with the bellman pulling a cart full of goods. In moments, he'd unloaded the boxes, accepted my tip, and was out the door.

As soon as the bellman left, I closed the doors, removed my shoes, washed my face, and flopped onto the bed. The room was cool, dry, and void of the musty smell of so many of the older hotels. I relaxed in the luxury of our room and soon nodded off.

After an hour's nap, my cell phone awakened me. *That's odd*, I thought as I checked the display screen, *the call isn't from Bob*. It looked like one of those numbers from a large organization, an outbound number only. I was sure it was a solicitor so I ignored it, knowing I could listen to the message later, if they left one. I decided to get an early start on the preparations for the evening's open house.

As I struggled to wake up, my mind went to the snake shirt, and I remembered that it was still lying where I had left it, crumpled up on the countertop in the bathroom. I got up, went into the bathroom, and picked up the shirt. The massive head and fangs were majestic in their own way, but admittedly vicious-looking. I'd seen plenty of them in my forays into the Everglades of Florida. They were never in the water like the cottonmouths, but they hung out in the grasses, on dry land. The snakes were big, like this one, and they didn't move terribly fast over the terrain, but their strike was quick and deadly. They were more of an ambush predator, and any prey within striking distance had no hope of escape.

I wanted to put the shirt on, but remembered my promise to Bob. I thought about it quite seriously, but rationalized that the promise surely was limited to wearing the shirt in public, not in our room. At first resisting, I carried the shirt back into the bedroom and considered what to wear after my bath. Nothing seemed interesting so I carried it back into the bathroom, along with the beautiful robe that had been hanging in the closet. *The robe will due for now*, I thought.

The bathroom was elegant, and the bath salts were perfect for soaking. I had nearly drifted off again when I heard the phone ring. I knew I could never reach the phone before it went to voice mail *so why hurry?* I would dutifully check the messages after my bath.

The hotel towels were pure white, fluffy, and soft. I mentally commended Bob for picking such an exquisite hotel. After toweling off, I looked at the robe. It, too, was soft and elegant, but it also looked thick, and I wanted something less bulky. Then I saw it again: the snake shirt.

I stepped over to the mirror and held up the shirt again, but just for a moment. I realized that if I looked at it too long, I just might chicken out. In spite of all my bravado, it was a freaky-looking snake. Its eyes seemed to bore into me, and the fangs had the crazy illusion of dripping venom. It was as though I could feel its malice. Unlike the snakes I had seen in the wilds that really would have preferred to slither off into the undergrowth, this one looked offensive in its nature, like it might actually attack, and chase a hapless victim through the glades. I knew if I didn't put it on soon, I would chicken out.

It truly was a nice shirt. Years of marriage to a clothing retailer had taught me the look and feel of quality. The thread-count of the cotton, the perfection in the seams, and the flawless hems made the shirt a thing of beauty. And despite the horrid head of a nasty snake, the cloth was soft and supple. I knew it would be a very comfortable shirt to wear, and comfort was just what I was looking for.

Agent Thomas Interrogates Jensen

My shirs' had clearly caused a stir. They had become the center of attention at the convention, and I reminded myself that, sometimes, bad news was good news. I had little hope, however, that the principle would apply to me, at least not for this incident. As I waited for Special Agent Thomas to re-enter the room, I wondered what more I could say to him. I'd already been questioned twice, once by Detective Chavanet and once by another FBI agent. Nevertheless, I was waiting for Special Agent Thomas who, according the previous agent, had more questions for me. I just wanted the day and the week to pass so the nightmare could end.

He seemed pleasant as he entered the door. I was glad his demeanor didn't suggest I would soon be on their most wanted list.

"Good afternoon, Mr. McIntyre."

I fidgeted slightly and offered a tentative, "Hi." I didn't want to say much more.

"Tell me again where you got the shirts."

Once more, I went through the story, which now felt like a never-ending one.

"I bought them from an old woman who lives in the swamps who said her name was Mother Moses."

His eyes never left mine.

"How did you meet her?"

"I simply went for a drive in the swamps. I needed some gas and wanted a cold drink. I stopped at a rundown service station and she was there. I bought a soda from her, and we talked. I told her that I sold shirts, and she said she had shirts. As you can see, I bought them."

His piercing eyes made me nervous, and I thought that, if nervousness is an indicator of guilt, he'd believe I am guilty. *But guilty of what?* I wondered.

"And this is all pure coincidence?" the agent asked.

I steeled myself and simply said, "Yes, it is a complete coincidence."

"We've had the shirts analyzed."

Good, I thought. "What did you find?"

At last he broke contact with my eyes.

"We found nothing out of the ordinary."

I breathed a little more easily and said, "Then can I go?" I was hopeful.

"I have just a couple more questions."

My heart sank, and I dreaded the continuing interrogation.

"Did you see any of the incidents take place?"

I was sure that he already knew the answer to the question, but I had no choice but to go along.

"I was in the hall when Marshal was found in the restroom and saw nothing of that incident. I was standing on the balcony when the second man went into the bar across the street, but unaware of his predicament until he was removed on a gurney. Even then, I didn't know who it was, or anything about the circumstances. I was in the suite when the woman collapsed in the bathroom, but the door was closed."

The questions went on for thirty more minutes. He asked me about Mothe' Moses, and shortly, the information about my stop payment came out. That seemed to interest him and he showed surprise when he learned that Bob had paid for the shirts. Oddly enough, he asked me if I thought that the stop payment and the snake shirt problems had any connection.

I had actually thought about a possible connection, but didn't dare say anything. If I told him my thoughts, I would likely be put in a mental health ward. I had thought over and over about her intense desire to know if I was honest. I felt bad when I had to admit that I hadn't been honest. Was there some relationship to my dishonesty and the snakes? Thoughts of voodoo spells ran through my mind. I dismissed them, never having believed in such things. Yet, the idea kept coming back.

I thought of Jonah in the Voodoo Shop and some of what she said, "I would not tell you if I could, and I cannot tell you because I am unable to speak the words."

Though my mind would not admit it, my gut told me there was some kind of a connection. Jonah's expressions, her visible concern, and her statement screamed that this was more than coincidence. I began to wonder if I should tell the agent about Jonah. *She did nothing wrong*, I thought. *Why involve her? She was innocent, and it wouldn't be right to put her in a suspicious light.*

The agent must have noticed that my mind had wandered, "Mr. McIntyre, you're thinking of something very important to this case. Tell me what it is."

How can he see through me in this way? Maybe I should tell him. Maybe, But not yet. I wanted to visit Jonah again. Maybe she would tell me something I could pass along without getting her involved.

"I'm sorry, there's nothing more I can say."

"Because you don't have the knowledge or because you won't say it?"

This man is very insightful.

"Honestly, Agent Thomas, I don't know what has happened. If I knew, I would tell you."

Neither one of us had moved a muscle, and the moment became a battle of wills. I fought to maintain a poker face, but I could feel myself slipping. If it went on much longer I feared I might lose control and blurt out Jonah's name, even though I was determined to keep her out of the investigation. As we both battled with our emotions and facial expressions, I admitted to myself that Jonah knew something pertinent to the case, and I had to find out what it was.

Agent Thomas finally relented and said, "I'm going to let you go, but don't leave town, Mr. McIntyre. I'm sure we'll talk again."

"No, sir. I won't leave town until you say I can."

Anne — The Discovery of Intelligence

I HAD FINALLY CHECKED my voice mail. I learned that Bob was being interrogated over the snake shirt incidents, but that he would be released soon.

I sat on the edge of my bed, thinking about the message. My mind went to what had become the central topic of the day—the shirts. The police had confiscated all the shirts at the Convention Center, but there was another one, and it was in my room, the one I had pulled from Jensen's box. *What is all the fuss about?* I wondered. *It is surely not the cause of so much pandemonium.* Even though I had promised not to, I worked up the determination to try on the shirt. I will prove, once and for all, to the entire world, that this shirt is not dangerous. And I'll do it in the bathroom, just to spite them! I picked up a shirt and marched into the bathroom.

I don't know which was most frightening, the attack or the subsequent realization. The attack was simply beyond any experience I could ever have imagined, let alone encountered. I slipped the shirt over my head and began straightening it. I looked down upon the shirt and myself pulling it here and there until it settled into place. Then I looked up to examine the view in the mirror. For a moment, all was normal, but normalcy didn't last.

First, my thought patterns began to change. It felt like my brain was slowing down. I wasn't losing consciousness but my thoughts were foggy and unclear. As I fought to understand the change, my vision changed. The edges became fuzzy. It was like looking through a sheer curtain with a hole cut in the middle.

Then I felt movement associated with my left breast. I looked down to see what was going on. It seemed that my shirt was in motion. I could feel something scraping across my skin. It felt cold, rough, and scaly. In my veiled-sight, I wasn't sure what I was seeing. I felt it more than saw it, but I began to believe that the head of a snake was detaching from the shirt. As the head detached it became three-dimensional. The body remained connected, but I could feel the transforming image writhing over my skin. The great head was now in front of me, looking at me, supported by the muscles of its massive body. It began swaying in the air, focusing on me, exuding a look of malice; it's tongue flick out and in. As though casting a spell, it bobbed and weaved its gigantic form before my failing sight. Occasionally the head would fall outside the clearer center of my tunnel vision. Outside that tunnel, the colors were muted and the form was obscure, but within the scope of that tunnel, it became a spotlighted specimen of a vicious reptile. Every few moments the massive mouth would open, revealing the fangs of lethality.

As horrible as the fangs appeared, it was the eyes that were the most terrifying. It felt like all the malevolence in the world was concentrated in those two piercing orange orbs. The lids never closed. *Never a blink.* It was a piercing, penetrating, invasive stare that chilled me to the core of my soul. As the motion continued, the tunnel of my vision continued to shrink until it was little more than a pencil's width. Small bits of the monster were clearly in view, but outside that, the cloudy image became increasingly horrifying. In slow motion, the mouth began to open far wider than I supposed it capable. Another set of fangs erupted from the bottom jaw. Both upper and lower fangs began to ooze blood-red venom.

In a lightning strike, the serpent took my entire head in its grip. Both pairs of fangs grasped me in its deathly clutch. It refused to let go, holding me for a horrifically, interminable expanse of time. I was aware, not of fang punctures and venom, but of a new danger; something was erupting from the throat of the snake. It was dark and wispy, like smoke from a coal chimney. It penetrated my eyes, my nose, and my mouth. It was suffocating, and as my lungs filled with the black, weightless fog, my mind darkened. In some span of time, I could not tell, I felt my mind begin to break and shatter into a million pieces. *Oblivion.* I lost all sense of existence.

When I regained a level of consciousness, I sensed a feeling of space around me, but space without form or sound; just space. I felt no tactile input, no extra-sensory *sensation* of any kind. I simply became *aware*, but there was nothing to be *aware of.* I could not detect my body, but I felt I was still alive. It was as if my essence was aware of my existence, but could not connect with my corporeal form, much less any other form, or thing, or life around me. It was as though my mind existed in a pure void. *I had no perception of anything.* Nothingness—complete and empty nothingness surrounded me.

My search was interminable. My only discovery—the feeling of despair. As I languished in that emotion, I began to comprehend a change. Vaguely, and changing ever so slowly, I became aware of something that I could not define. It was something I sensed, but could not see; could not feel.

One by one, I began to perceive them. Then, the rate of perception—at first quite slow—began to accelerate. As they appeared, their numbers ever growing, I saw them only as things. Suddenly, in an avalanche of recognition, I realized that they completely filled the infinity of space, or at least the space that was known to me. They existed by the billions, trillions, I thought. Then I knew that their numbers were beyond counting and impossible for me to comprehend.

There were too many to look upon, but with great surprise I discerned they were sentient; and they were, in turn, conscious of me. I grasped the idea that I was in the midst of billions of almost infinitesimally small intellects. My best description would call them tiny points of light, or energy, but each had the property of intelligence. No words or thoughts were exchanged, just the comprehension of awareness and mutual existence.

At length, I recognized that I was in a great sea of intelligence, from the simplest of intelligences, to complex and sophisticated intelligences that were beyond my comprehension; and all the members of this amazing sea of intelligence were perceptive, communicative, and responsive to all the intelligences around them, but in a realm and using methods that humans could not detect.

As my perception increased, I realized that many of these intelligences were solitary, while others were organized into collections, both simple and complex. The variety of formations and their complexities were innumerable. The countless intellects stretched into the vastness around me, their order beginning with the simplest of intellects—the lowest order—and rising to higher, more complex orders that were unfathomable. I understood that each intellect was not simply perceptive of their environment, but also communicative. The variety was astounding. Some seemed adept at comprehending the complex intellects around them; while others seemed limited in their comprehension. I saw millions of types of complexities, each with its own capacity based upon the level of its intelligence. It was mind-numbing to consider that such a realm existed. It was a realm I'd never thought of before, never read about, and I wondered if it had ever been detected.

Bob's Horror

THE QUESTIONS SEEMED TO go on forever, but during the long ordeal, I had forced them to stop twice so I could call Anne. The agent assured me that his office had called her cell phone, but that she didn't pick up, so they'd left a message. I finally convinced him to let me try.

Her cell phone rang but went to right to voice mail.

"That's odd," I said to the agent. "She always answers when I call."

The agent seemed unworried and assured me that she was fine, but something in the back of my mind wouldn't accept his words. I knew she had gone shopping, and I worried that something might have happened to her. After all, the city and its people were unpredictable.

I tried to keep my mind on the agent's questions, but it was no use. All I could think about was Anne, and the agent finally figured out that I was more worried about her than I was about myself. After more questions than I could count, he finally said, "Okay, Mr. Preston, I have no reason to hold you for now, but don't leave town."

"I won't," was all I said.

It took a few minutes, but I was finally released and on my way back to the hotel. As I hustled out of the Convention Center, I noted that there were still a few people waiting to be examined or questioned. I didn't know which. The whole mess had dramatically affected the convention. I walked out of the hall and into the heat and humidity of the city. There was a line of taxis available, so it was easy to hire one. It was a short ride, and I was there in minutes.

I jumped out of the taxi almost before it had stopped. I had already tossed some cash into the front seat, tip included. I hustled past the doorman who barely had time to open the door. I paid no attention to the hotel, guests, décor, or anything else as I rushed to our room. My only thought was of the shirt that Anne had promised not to wear and my hope that she had kept her promise.

I had the keys out before I got to the door. I fumbled a bit but had it open fairly quickly. As I entered the room, I called out her name. There was no answer. I immediately headed for the bedroom. She wasn't there, so I passed through the small entry hallway to the bathroom. The door was open, and as I rounded the door frame, I saw her. There she was, the love of my life, on the floor, her skin slightly gray-toned.

I slumped to the floor and took her arm, holding her wrist, searching for a pulse, but there was none. I checked her carotid. Again, no pulse. I jumped up and ran to the phone. Gratefully, the front desk quickly answered. I told them my wife was unconscious and to call 911. They assured me they would.

I ran back into the bathroom and began CPR. I rhythmically kneaded her chest, stopping occasionally to blow air into her lungs. She was cold and the air that escaped her lungs was cold. I continued the CPR in between my own gasps for air, my tears, and the cries that I uttered. Nothing appeared to be working. She didn't respond in any way. Her skin was cold and gray. In every way, she looked like the New Jersey woman who had died in Jensen's bathroom.

No, this cannot be!

I continued the CPR. *Where is the ambulance?* I wondered.

Within minutes, I heard the siren. It wailed a mournful warning to all in its presence that something was wrong. Someone needed help. When it stopped its piercing dirge, within moments, I heard voices and running.

"Mr. Preston!" a shout came from the doorway.

"In here—in the bathroom!" I screamed. "Hurry!"

A big man entered the bathroom and pushed me aside. I didn't resist. He quickly checked her pupils, her pulse, and her breathing. I knew that he'd found no sign of life. Another man entered, and their eyes met. The first one shook his head, and a "no" escaped his lips.

Slumping against the bathroom wall, tears flowed freely down my checks accompanied by a heaving chest, and deep sobs of despair and hopelessness.

"It can't be," I cried out loud and repeated it like a mantra three more times. My eyes focused on the snake shirt, and my heart began to fill with hatred. I'd never liked snakes, but this one received the focus of all my hate and frustration. Had it been alive, it wouldn't have been for long. I wanted to lash out. I wanted to pummel the head and fangs with my fists. I wanted to stand and stomp on the head until it's blood and brains spilled onto the ground. But I could do none of these things. Anne was within the shirt and a pummeling of the snake would only be a pummeling of some cotton and my now dead wife.

One of the EMTs bent over and said, "Come on, Mr. Preston, let's go into the other room."

I complied and soon found myself seated in the overstuffed chair, still weeping and feeling more dejected than I had ever been in my life. I started thinking through all the *if onlys*. *If only* I hadn't come to the convention. *If only* Jensen hadn't bought those shirts. *If only* I had taken this one away from her. I heaped the fault, the blame, and the pain upon my guilty soul. I felt accountable because I had let it happen. I should have known better. I should have done something to stop it.

While deep in my morass, I heard muted sounds from the bathroom. Within minutes, a wheeled-stretcher appeared in the door. My heart was so broken I couldn't watch as they wheeled her covered body out of the room. I was torn. Should I follow her dead body or stay here in the chair, deep in my personal pain? I was too heartbroken to move.

I don't know how long I sat there. It could have been minutes, or it could have been hours. I heard a commotion in the hallway and the sound of running feet. Although I heard the sounds, no hope filled me. It could not be anyone or anything that could appease my pain. But then an EMT pounded on the door.

"Mr. Preston, open up! I have news!"

I grumbled under my breath, "News? What good news could he have? They had pronounced her dead at the scene."

He pounded again and shouted, "It's about your wife! She may not be dead!"

Confusion filled my mind. I felt a glimmer of hope, but also a fear that I had misunderstood him.

There was an even louder pounding of the door, "Mr. Preston, open up!"

I struggled to get my feet under me. I tottered to the door, unsteady like a drunken man, my senses still mired in despair. As the door opened, an excited EMT stood there with a smile.

"Mr. Preston, come with us. Your wife may still be alive. We don't know for sure, but information about these deaths has begun to circulate. It appears that these people may not be dead. Come with us."

Still in a measure of shock, I let the EMT lead me down the hallway, onto the elevator and, finally, out to the ambulance. He opened the rear doors and motioned me in. My wife was still on the gurney, strapped in, but her head was uncovered. She had an oxygen mask over her nose. I felt a cautious hope.

The siren screamed once more as the vehicle surged away from the curb. I was grateful that people would respect our emergency and clear the way to the hospital. The ambulance jolted, twisted and turned, slowed, and hastened again. The horn blared occasionally to clear the unaware from our path. There were no delays, just a quick ride to the hospital, which was ten minutes away.

The ambulance came to an abrupt stop. The EMT in the passenger seat jumped out of the cab and ran to the back, quickly opening the doors. The driver moved to the head of the gurney. Anne was efficiently removed out of the ambulance. At first, I paid little attention to the facility, but eventually I realized it wasn't the emergency room. Instead they took her through a nondescript door into another area of the hospital. I followed behind the paramedics as they walked down the hallway to a suite of outpatient rooms. They pushed the buzzer. Almost instantly, the automatic doors opened, and they were on their way once more, traveling down another hallway, and through a very wide door. A medical assistant was waiting for them.

I stopped dead in my tracks upon entering the room. It was a good-sized room and it was filled with gurneys on which lay partially covered bodies. The paramedics gave Anne's gurney to some medical staff members who transferred her to a table. Within a few seconds a man in a white lab coat walked up to me.

He had been looking at a chart, but he soon lifted his head, "Hello, Mr. Preston. I'm Dr. Whitely."

I mumbled a "hello" in response.

The doctor looked neither happy nor stressed. After staring for a moment, I asked an obvious question. "Who are all these people, and why is everyone in this single room?"

Dr. Whitely set the clipboard down, which held a copious amount of paperwork, on a nearby table and said, "These are all victims of the same malady. We still don't know what it is, and I'm sorry to see that your wife is among them. The CDC has put their full resources behind the question, and everyone is working overtime to find a cure."

"They aren't dead?" I tentatively asked. "My wife isn't dead?"

"That is what we believe," replied the doctor, "even though they all appear to be."

Jensen's Dream

IT FELT GOOD TO be walking toward the Convention Hall exits. The interrogation room had become hot and stuffy. The cooler air of the hall refreshed me. I had, at last, been released from my ordeal of non-stop questioning, but before being released, I had been told that Bob had left an hour earlier. That was the good news. The horrifying news was that Anne had been found dead, in her bathroom, wearing a snake shirt. After sharing that news with me, I was asked again to explain the basis for this unnerving twist of events. There was nothing more that I could tell them, and I think they finally believed I truly didn't know and, therefore, couldn't say any more than I had already said. We were all at a loss. I was told that I could leave.

Outside the convention hall in the warm and humid air, I flagged down a taxi, which took me to the hotel. After paying the fare, I walked slowly and despondently to my room. I unlocked the door, ambled through the entry, and into my bathroom. The beautiful countertop and elegant facilities beckoned me to wash. The cold water felt good on my sweaty, reddened face. I dried my hands and went back out into the suite, sought the most comfortable chair and slumped into it. After sitting a few minutes, still miserable and unhappy, I got up and paced the floor, finally ending up in my bedroom. I flopped onto the bed and immediately curled into the fetal position. In that position, my tired body and exhausted mind gave up. Soon I was in another world—the world of dreams.

My dream world was not pleasant. It was a nightmarish world filled with creaky boards laid over hissing snakes. This delusional landscape became walled up, the barriers covered by the hairy and loathsome bodies of tarantulas. Each spider tapped its eight legs on the rough, wooden partition in a chorus that became a staccato background to the even more menacing buzz of a myriad of rattler tails, tuned to the rhythm of a chair that rocked back and forth over the creaking boards, driven by the sun-damaged and tawny legs of Mothe' Moses. The formerly gray hair of Mothe' Moses took on the terrifying appearance of Medusa, the gray strands the epitome of a writhing, but caressing tangle of serpents that fell from under the baseball cap, itself in commotion from the endless ebb and flow of the wiry Medusa curls. Looking up from her wittlin', her old gray eyes and yellowed and broken teeth, proclaimed the message, over, and over, and over again, "M' li'l babies ah vey p'otective. You be shua, check be goo tamora, too."

The horror of the old woman on the porch lined with spiders and snakes was wretched enough, but into my mind came the visage of the check, the check for two thousand dollars. There it was, my savior, the redemptive payment that could end the torment. *Yes, it will be good! It will be good!* I cried out in my sleep.

My hope for relief was short-lived as a score of paper-eating insects lit upon the edges of the fraudulent note. They at once began biting and chewing; chewing and biting; tearing the edges to pieces. Bit by precious bit, the insects chewed into the check, its existence and value plummeting into the void of my unraveling mind.

Already morbidly distraught by the gradual death of my salvation, I sensed a new terror. Countless fingers pointed at me, while their invisible masters, in cadence with the rocking, and the buzzing, and the biting, and the crunching, cried out, "You be shua! You be shua! You be shua!"

The shrieking was more than I could bear. It stole the beat of my heart, staunched the breath in my lungs, and pierced the drums of my ears. It wouldn't stop! It went on, and on, and on, until finally in my own scream, I jumped to a sitting position in my bed. With eyes wide open, and my consciousness fully returned, the rocking, and creaking, and buzzing, and tapping, and biting—fell silent. Everything stopped but the shriek, which continued its assault. It kept ringing incessantly in my ears like a telephone that wakes one from a deep sleep in the middle of the night.

That's it! It's the phone.

I don't know how many times the phone had rung; I just knew I had to answer it.

"Jensen, are you all right? I've been calling and calling your room."

I thought back to the incessant ringing before I answered, "I'm sorry Bob, I just couldn't get to the telephone."

I noted a mix of anxiety and something else in his voice, but I couldn't be sure what it was.

What I could assuredly hear was Bob's voice saying, "I was worried. I was about to call the hotel to have them check on you. I was afraid you'd put on one of those shirts."

I let Bob prattle on for a while. He had a lot to say about life, and death, and the hospital, but to be honest, I didn't care what he said, or even how he said it. Though he spoke the words, they made no connection to any sentient thought of my own. Whatever he was saying, I was sure I deserved it. After finishing his rant, Bob finally went quiet.

"Are you finished?" I asked.

"Yeah, I'm done."

"Good. I'm beat, and I've got to get some sleep. Good night, Bob. We'll talk tomorrow."

With that, I hung up without saying or waiting for a goodbye.

I lay back down on the bed and closed my eyes. Sleep didn't come, but something else did. I couldn't shake it. I couldn't turn it off. My mind was filled with thought after thought, and I couldn't make them stop.

Put on the shirt. That's all my mind would say to me. *Put on the shirt.* It repeated the phrase over and over. I thought of all the dead people who had put on one of those shirts. In my mind, in my heart, and in the pit of my gut, I began to feel the guilt, the unrelenting self-destructive pain, and the horror of self-blame. The guilt was alive, it reproduced, and it spawned an apocalypse that was impossible to shake. It was like acid-laced flames in my gut that could not be quenched or put out.

I have to do it.

Almost robot-like, I got off the bed and walked to a drawer where the last snake shirt lay neatly folded. Like the carrion of the undead to live brains, I picked up the shirt, turned, and walked into the bathroom.

I stood in front of the vanity. I looked into my own blood-red eyes. They lay dull and listless inside puffy and bloated sockets. My cheeks were aflame, and my hair was tousled. The reflection was not the man I knew as Jensen. I picked up the shirt, holding it with both hands. I slipped my hands and arms into the bottom and with a move practiced one thousand times ten thousand times, I slipped the shirt over my head.

My eyes immediately focused on the head of the snake. The mesmerizing eyes and the venomous malice were instantly an assault on my senses. I felt it in my soul and watched with my eyes as the viper came alive, weaving its head, watching my every move, and sensing my every thought. It held me transfixed and pulled me into another world where the only sound was, "You be shua. You be shua," repeated over and over, again and again.

I lost all sense of place, time, and balance. As the great, open-jawed, fang-laced head struck, my knees buckled, and I fell to the tile floor. Under the weight of the monstrous reptile, its cold, scaly skin pressing me into the relative warmth of the marble floor, my sight was buried in the mouth of the beast, a black smoke filling my lungs. The loss of consciousness could not have arrived too soon. It was a relief. My pain was consumed.

There are those who say that time is a human construct, that it doesn't exist; and that it can't exist unless someone marks its passing. I don't know if time passed in minutes or in eternities, but after some period I started to become aware. At first there was nothing of which to be aware. I was simply aware, if only of my awareness. There was no light; there was no darkness; only nothingness, a state I had never thought possible.

In the nothingness surrounding me there was no way to mark time. It might have been a mere second or a hundred eons, but none of that mattered because in that nothingness, I felt nothingness, and that was the horror of it. Then guilt began to push its way into my mind. It was the guilt of a thousand murderers as they were beaten with the stripes of their punishment. It was guilt in its most exquisite nature, beyond anything I could have imagined. It permeated my essence. It attacked me in a way that was impossible to defend. There was no defense, no falling asleep, no pill to take, and there was no ball to curl into that could relieve my suffering. I simply knew that I was born of guilt, and it would be endless torment. The unabashed pall of hopelessness was so extreme that, had I been alive, I would have certainly chosen an immediate death. I was at the bottom of a bottomless pit, and there was simply no reference point from which to look for hope.

Jensen: A Vision from the Void

IT WAS AS THOUGH I was dreaming it, but I became aware of an event that was going on around me. I heard the phone ring. I saw the hotel operator pick it up. A harried voice on the other end spoke of the man who was a guest in one of the Bourbon Balcony Entertainment Suites. The man said their guest might be ill and may not be able to reach the phone or the door.

"I'll send someone up immediately," the operator said, just as clear as the sun shines in daylight.

Within minutes an employee was knocking on the door. The knocking became pounding, and very quickly a key had opened the door. The lights were on in the bedroom so the employee looked there first. The bed had been disturbed but no one was there. He knocked on the bathroom door. Once more there was no answer. After a louder pounding, with no response, he opened the door. The guest was on the floor. The guest was *me,* and I was seeing myself from the void.

I saw the hotel employee run back to the telephone and heard him tell the operator, "Call 911, and get them here quickly. We have another guest who looks mortally ill."

The employee went back to the guest bathroom. I heard him mumble something about snake shirts as he carefully rolled me onto my back. The look on his face screamed surprise. He seemed to be jolted into a state of fear as the form of the venomous viper appeared before him. I heard the employee exclaim a guttural grunt as he swiped instinctively at the snake, trying to scare it away. But the snake held its ground, staring back with its hateful eyes. He squirmed back toward the wall. The snake held its place on the shirt, which was on my body. In this most bizarre of dreams, I suspected his thoughts. I had entertained similar thoughts. The snake looked too real to be bound by the material of a flimsy shirt. His audible gasps finally resolved to heavy breathing; the employee gathered his senses. The snake was only an image, a terrifying image, but only an image after all.

I could see the man's personal battle, seemingly able to read his mind. He wanted to help me, but the employee's mind flashed to his father's farm, the one he had been glad to leave when he came of age. He remembered the rattlesnakes, cottonmouths, and other venomous vipers. Each of his encounters had been terrifying, but none of those living snakes bore the evil intensity of the very large image on my shirt. While still shrinking from his duties, the employee heard the EMTs knocking at the door. He rose quickly to let them in.

When the door opened, the EMTs rushed past.

"He's already dead," said the timid employee as he fled into the hallway.

The EMTs went to work as though they knew I was still alive. In moments, my body on a gurney, partially covered, an IV solution flowing. They had worked quickly and wordlessly, and in less than ten minutes, they were pushing the gurney down the hallway to the waiting ambulance.

Caught up in my dream, I again saw the employee who had gone back into my room with his supervisor. I heard him ask, "What is going on?"

Fidgeting with his keys the supervisor replied, "I'm not sure. All I know is that this is the fourth hotel guest who has been removed while wearing one of those shirts, and each of them looked dead. The city wants this kept quiet. The hotel owners want this kept quiet. I've been told that all first response teams have been given instructions with regard to the people who are found unconscious in the snake shirts. They were told to treat them like they are in shock, and to transport them immediately, and with as little fuss as possible."

The two hotel employees stood looking at each other in silence, neither venturing to speak. It was finally the man who found me who spoke up first, "In all my years I've never seen a snake like the one on that man's shirt. I hope to live the rest of my life without ever seeing it, or anything like it, again."

The supervisor motioned toward the door. "Let's get out of here. I understand the police will be here shortly to search the rooms for more shirts."

"Will we have to help them?" the employee asked.

The supervisor, who had already started to walk out of the room looked back over his shoulder and said, "I pray to God that we don't have to help them. I've seen enough, and I don't want to know anything more."

The supervisor pulled the guest room door shut, made sure it was locked, and put a "Do Not Disturb" sign on the handle.

The dream was as real to me as any experience of my life. But it was a strange reality because it was the only reality I was aware of. It was like watching a holographic movie in a theater auditorium that had no form or substance. It was like watching from a state of nothingness and, as soon as the dream ended, once more nothingness was all I felt. I only knew that my name was Jensen, at least that's what my friends called me.

Anne Becomes Aware

As I struggled to understand the vast number of intellects around me with their varied complexities, I made a great discovery. Some of the intellects were of my same order. Some of them were like me. *No, they aren't **just** like me; they are also in my same circumstances.* It was an incredible revelation and seemed to spawn another reality, my physical reality.

As I began to comprehend my physical being, I felt a great relief. It was comforting to feel my body, but that comfort was soon replaced by a horrible craving. I felt cold, almost lifeless, verging on death. I shouted out in my mind that I missed the *warmth* of my body, its substance, its spectrum of senses. I felt like an addict craving a fix. I yearned for it, demanded it, and would have done anything to secure that comforting warmth of my beloved body.

The concept of surroundings and my physical discomfort triggered a stunning new awareness. We—me and the other intellects—were in some kind of physical assembly or room. Since my awakening, it was the first time I'd felt the physical world. Then I became aware the other intellects were clothed in bodies like mine and suffering the same experience. The other bodies were gray and cold just like mine.

Revelation upon revelation came to my mind, and then the most amazing comprehension enlightened my being. I understood I was actually made up of innumerable billions of those tiny intellects, like those I had seen earlier. Their simplicity had joined together to make up my complexity. It was the same for the bodies around me, and we had all come to the same conclusion. As the intellectual factions of our bodies began to comprehend one another, we all understood, together, that our corporeal partners—our bodies—lay nearly lifeless, and we had no power to influence them. They would lay there, inanimate—and this became my greatest shock—until something happened that would save us. We understood that the process of being saved was something we could not do for ourselves and could not control. We only knew that without that saving influence, death would overcome us forever. *That ultimate death was a horror beyond consideration.*

— CHAPTER ELEVEN —
SATURDAY EVENING: AT THE HOSPITAL

Bob's Memory

I WAS SITTING IN a small waiting room in my hospital prison, watching over Anne, when banging doors announced another ambulance arrival. There had been no siren; all the responders were to work quickly, quietly, and with tight lips. The local government wanted to keep the incident quiet. I'd now seen six people come into the treatment center in the same way. Each had been wearing a snake shirt. By my own count, the number had reached twenty-four.

I was in a small room hardly large enough to be called a waiting room. An eclectic collection of chairs filled the small space, but I was the only prisoner. The CDC had declared that the victims, or patients, had to be quarantined. Their families were not allowed to be in close proximity. I was the only family member in the facility, and I was here only because of my involvement. I was told that family members of the other victims were being notified. They would not, however, be allowed to enter the facility.

Victims, I thought. *It seems an apt term*. I couldn't think of a better description. As far as I was concerned, I was a victim, too. Well, maybe not. I did have culpability, at least in some way. I participated with full knowledge that there was something different about these shirts, so how could I claim to be a victim? But then again, almost everyone who saw them felt the thrill of danger. It had been something similar to an endorphin rush—terrifying, but life-enlarging. I felt like I was hunched down, out of sight, driving the Jensen again. Except this time, the consequences were much more serious.

It was more than curiosity that forced me to watch as each new emergency vehicle arrived. I wanted to know who the people were. Somehow, my life was wrapped up in their lives, and I wanted to learn all I could about each person. In the end, I might need to, in some way that I had yet to discover, assist in their rehabilitation. In addition, I hadn't heard back from Jensen. It was unusual for him to just hang up the phone, and the hotel hadn't called back. In the back of my mind, I half feared that Jensen might be on the gurney.

I left the room and went to the doorway where I knew the next victim would be brought in. A security guard watched me to make sure I complied with my order of self-willed containment. I watched the gurney as it was pushed down the hall toward me. Even with half a thought in the back of my mind, I wasn't prepared for what I saw as the gurney passed by me. It wasn't simply that it was Jensen; it was the *look* on his face. By the time I saw the other victims, their faces had taken on the look of repose. That all changed with Jensen. His face was not an expression of peace, but rather the exact opposite. So intense was his look of pain that I could almost feel it. His face was a twisted, contorted picture of exquisite agony.

Jensen had always been, of the two of us, the one who was most in trouble. He was, too often, willing to take one more step beyond the limits. He hadn't been a dangerous man or a man who would go much outside the envelope of propriety, but he had often taken enough steps beyond the boundaries to be in frequent trouble. He'd told me his business was doing well, but I wondered how much truth there was in his statement. Knowing now that he was guilty of fraud, I began to wonder what else might be wrong in his life. I felt sorrow for Jensen, knowing that he'd brought this curse, if that's what it was to be called, into his own life.

I watched in my own distress as Jensen was wheeled past me. I absentmindedly followed after him, my thoughts focused on Anne and her condition. At a fork in the hallway, I decided to go to her bed once more. I'd been given considerable latitude in the facility, because I was somehow involved in what insiders were calling "zombie snakebites." I didn't like the term, but I was in no position to change it. I was simply glad they let me stay by Anne.

I walked through a door and nodded to a nearby nurse. She nodded back, knowing my identity. The security guard at her side gave me a wave, and I was allowed to pass. It helped that the CDC considered me to be a valuable consultant. I'd answered any and all questions they had for me, at least as well as I was able. The CDC had not been as forceful as the police, but they were determined to gather every bit of useful information. I'd told them everything—*everything but one thing.* I hadn't told them about the tiny flower that was back in my room, nor had I told them about Jonah, the mysterious owner of the Voodoo Shop. Well, I hadn't told them about the frequent buzzing that both Jensen and I heard, either. I guess I actually held back a lot of information, but it would simply have to be that way.

The staff had kindly provided a stool for me to sit on when next to Anne's bed. Her face was ashen gray. Her skin was cold. As I held her hand, I searched for a pulse. I could feel none. She looked dead. I was amazed the doctors had detected life in her. I figuratively wrung my hands and pulled at my hair. *How can I help her? What can I do? I felt completely helpless and dependent; but dependent on what?* The doctors had no experience with this medical issue. The CDC had no record or data on such a malady. Everyone was at a loss. As I looked into the faces of the staff, I felt their helplessness. The status of my dear, nearly dead wife and friend cast me into a state of hopelessness. I was discouraged and wished that Mothe' Moses' shirs' had never crossed our paths.

Mothe' Moses was and is still an enigma. And what did all that travel through the swamp accomplish? It had taken all day and for what? A flower? What could a flower do? I thought about our trip through the swamp. I thought about the pungent lotion she had rubbed on me and the relief I experienced from the mosquitoes. I thought about my fear of the swamp. I remembered that, while under the influence of the lotion, I could understand her speech. She was a strange woman in a world of strange doings.

The police told me they'd asked her local jurisdiction to pick her up for questioning, but she was nowhere to be found. In an effort to locate her, they'd talked to neighbors and people in the community. Reports indicated that the community was generally tight-lipped about the old woman. No one seemed to want to cross her. I wished that the kind personage of Mother Moses was with me. I wished that I could introduce her to Anne. I was sure that if she would just look upon my dear Anne, that she could, and would, help her.

I brought our conversations back into my mind.

"This be for you," she'd said when she handed me the flower.

I remembered asking her what it was.

"I have no shirs' for you, but this be better. Better for you and better for everyone. We go now."

How can the tiny, frail bit of a flower be better for me and, even more strangely, better for everyone?

I tried to remember all the words she spoke to my best recollection. I tried to reconstruct them exactly as she had spoken them. She'd looked deeply into my eyes and told me, "Yuh be walking back to a hornet's nest. Yuh don't know yet, but Jensen set bad things in motion. His dishonesty do it. He may be friend to you, but not always good friend to all people. It be your job to control the events that are coming; that's why I take you to swamp."

After rehashing that statement, I wondered where I had gone wrong. What could I have done to control the events of the last few days? I don't understand now, and I remembered telling her I didn't understand when we were back at the swamp.

Her reply was as curious now as it was back then. "No, an you won't until more days pass. Then you understand."

I remembered asking her what I should do and when. She then

took the bottle out of her bag and held it up to the sun. Her words were strange, "This be life," she'd said. "It be life to maybe a hundred 'n twenty people."

Once again my mind latched onto the number. *One hundred and twenty people.* More forcefully it came to my mind that one hundred and twenty was the exact number of shirts that Jensen had bought. I remembered mentioning it to her, and her reply that I was a smart man. I still felt dumb but remembered, with even greater clarity, her kind response to my lack of understanding. I closed my eyes and brought the recollection as clearly as I could. She'd said, "Because you be humble."

Humble. How am I humble, and what does that mean?

I looked around the room. It had eight beds crammed into it, and one of those beds belonged to Anne. I could see the faces of the other people in the room. I knew many of them, but not all. In another room, our common customer, Marshal, lay upon a bed. I longed to hear his big Texas laugh. In another room was the woman who had been in our suite. Her beauty was gone, and her vivacious character had been reduced to lifeless clay. I looked at Anne and thought of the excitement she had shown at the idea of shopping in New Orleans.

"Oh, if only you had stayed home, my dear Anne."

I thought back once more to Mothe' Moses and her words about my character.

"Yes, I say humble. You willing to go with me, take da herb, and settle in a rickety boat. You willing to walk through sucking mud and lay in da grass while we talk. You not high and mighty, you de right man, you set things right."

How can I set things right?

I pressed my memory again and heard, once more, the parting non-verbal communication, "You good man."

Am I?

In a heartbeat, I realized that I had vastly under-rated the woman, and from that moment on I started thinking of her as Mother Moses. I felt like she deserved the distinction of a proper title.

Jensen Discovers a New World

I HAD NO HANDS with which to feel and no legs with which to kick, but I began to sense the floor and the sides of the bottomless pit into which I had sunk; for how long, I could not tell. Over some period, the walls began to disappear, and I found myself as though floating in a void.

I had no sense of the corporeal. I could detect neither my body, nor anything physical around me. I began to wonder if my inability to sense anything was due to the massive guilt that weighed on me. The guilt pressed upon me like a mountain with roots of fiery spikes. I could not tell which was more painful, the press of the mountain or the fire of the spikes. I began to suspect that the two pains obliterated all other senses.

As if the pain of the mass of the mountain and the fire of the spikes were not enough, I began to be aware of a tortured tumult of voices. They clamored loud and long. They wailed in pitches high, and they moaned in low groans. The uproar grew until even it became painful, matching both the mountain and the fiery spikes pressed into me. But then I nearly jumped for joy. I could feel my body! Despite the pain, it was a gift to feel, once again, something that I had once known and had lost in my experience. Now it was back, even if accompanied by pain. I also realized that I was actually *hearing* the tumult, not just sensing it.

My next recognition was that a physical world was developing around me, or at least my awareness of it. Into my mind came the shape of a large building. Within the building were many rooms. Each room was filled with a life seething with anger, and the anger was directed at me. In a horrid awareness I came to realize that all the lives in all the rooms were pointing at me and calling me their murderer. It was too much. I thought my mind would break, and I longed for the quiet press of the mountain and the burning of the spikes. I howled in my mind and cried for it to stop! *If there is a God in Heaven, make it stop!*

Suddenly it stopped. I could not tell what had happened, or why it had happened. The tumult was gone, the press was gone, the fire was gone. Something changed the world of my existence, but I was pitifully unable to explain the change. I cast my senses around, losing awareness of the building and feeling desolation of the void. My isolation was once more confined in nothingness. I began to wonder if I had ceased to exist, but, no, that cannot be true. I remembered Plato's great posit, "I think, therefore I am."

I began to feel some consolation. The pain was gone, my existence was ensured, but I still could not identify my status, other than my ability to feel awareness.

Bob's Escape

I HAD BEEN MUSING over the idea that I was a good man, at least as defined by Mother Moses. If that is true, there must be some way to break the conundrum of the dead and yet living people around me. *Surely, there is something in Mother Moses' words that I might take hold of.* Then I remembered more of what she'd said. It seemed to have been hidden from my memory. I hadn't thought of it before, nor had I mentioned it to the police. The words of the conversation began to fill my mind. I had been perplexed by her strange talk of humility. At last, I remembered my words, "You keep talking like I understand, but I have no idea what you are talking about."

She had responded in words that made no sense at that time.

"I make it simple. When people start to die, you take this plant to Voodoo Shop in French Quarter and ask for Jonah, but not before people die. You tell her it from me. She know me, and she understand. You do as she say. She save you and other people. She may save Jensen. We see."

I remembered the feeling of butterflies in my gut, after she spoke the words. It was like those I felt before my high school football games. I remembered that a quiet moment developed and remained for many minutes, neither of us saying a word. At the time, I was trying to figure it all out, but I could find no point of reference from which to analyze it. It was Mother Moses who broke the silence. "Yuh bes' get clothes, de dry now."

That had been her signal to be on my way. For some reason, the suggestion now filled me with resolve, and I knew what I had to do. But I had a problem. I was, virtually, in jail. The flower in the glass bottle was in my hotel, and Jonah was in the French Quarter. *Does she live at her shop or elsewhere?* I did not know.

Jonah's place of residence was unimportant at the moment. My immediate problem was that I had to get out of the hospital, but how? After thinking a few minutes, I realized there just might be a way. Security was supposed to keep people from entering the treatment area, if it could be called that. Everyone knew the victims of the zombie snakebite couldn't get up and leave, though jokes circulated about them rising up and eating the staff's brains. As for me, I'd become a willing fixture. I now hoped that I could use that to my advantage to effect an escape from my prison, and I knew just the place to make my escape.

As more and more bodies had arrived at the hospital, it became apparent there was not enough space to hold all of them. Along with my Anne, they had all been placed in the School of Medicine building on the ground floor. The great thing about the facility was that some of the restrooms were on the perimeter walls of the building, and there were windows to the outside.

I needed to know how closely I was being watched. I left Anne's side and went back to the waiting room. I'd been on the premises for several hours, and people were familiar with my identity. I had walked back and forth from the waiting room, to the treatment rooms, and the restroom a number of times. The security guard looked like he barely noticed as I made my way around the facility. The nurses and doctors moved around with little real work to do, and they paid me little attention. I left the waiting room and walked toward the restroom, the one where I'd noticed a window. I felt I needed to make my escape on the first attempt. Too much movement might alert them to my scheme. Near the door I bent down to retie a shoelace. It gave me an opportunity to survey the room, looking for eyes that might be watching me. I didn't see any.

I pushed on the door, hoping it was still unlocked. It yielded to my touch and opened. I passed through the door and locked it. I was alone in a locked room with a window. The window was closed and latched. Gratefully, the School of Medicine still utilized part of an older building where windows could be opened when necessary. I had no idea what might be outside the window. I didn't know what street it was on nor how far away from the hotel I might be. I decided I needed to postpone my escape until I learned more about where I was located.

I flushed the toilet, washed my hands, and left the restroom. I walked back to Anne's bed. I had to pick someone who would talk to me, someone who would volunteer information about the city, and where we were. I picked the most talkative person in the area. Her tag said her name was Jana. "Hello, Jana, how are you today?" I asked.

Jana looked up and responded pleasantly, "Why, I'm fine. How are you?"

"I could be better. It's so hard to wait and wonder what is wrong, and I'm getting a little queasy. Can you tell me if there are some sandwich machines close by?"

She gave me directions to the machines but, of course, I needed more information than that.

We chatted about our homes—mine far away and hers in New Orleans. We got to talking about the Garden District, the pre-Katrina and post-Katrina Ninth Ward, and all the changes. I already knew what their geographical relationship was, but I asked about it anyway. Knowing where the hospital was in relationship to these two well-known areas would be helpful. After a few minutes, I learned that the Medical Center was on Tulane Avenue. We chatted about the French Quarter and Bourbon Street. Before long I figured out that I was less than ten blocks from my hotel. The route was a little fuzzy, but I could always ask a stranger along the way. Better yet, I learned that Tulane Avenue was a busy street, and I was likely to find a cab, even though it was late at night.

I excused myself to return to the restroom, still talking about my queasiness. She offered to look for some antacids, but I declined. Once in the restroom with the door locked, I reached up for the window. The latch was out of reach. *A garbage can might be enough*, I thought. Soon I was standing on a not-so-sturdy-might-break-at-any-moment metal garbage can. The added height was still not enough. I removed my shoe, balanced on the can and reached for the latch. I realized that with just enough stretch I could move the latch handle with the toe of my shoe. I stretched once and took a swipe. I missed. I stretched a second time, missed again, and nearly threw myself off the can. I teetered on the brink of a fall, barely maintaining control. I took a big breath, and held it for a moment. I eyed the latch to make sure I knew how it worked. *Yes*, I thought, *I'm sure it will open.*

I steeled myself to stretch with all my might, but resolved that I might have to jump an inch or so. I pushed off with the foot that was still shod, thinking the extra height of the sole might make a difference, and it did. But it was not the difference I'd hoped for. The shoe added some clumsiness to the jump, and the steel can slid on the tile floor. Suddenly, I was falling to the floor and there was nothing I could do. I came down hard on my left side. I tried to stretch out my arm to cushion my fall but a nearby cabinet got in the way. I fell flat on my side in a clumsy, inelegant manner. Fire shot through my ribs, shoulder, and elbow. As bad as the fall and the resulting pain was, it was even more frustrating that the garbage can rattled across the floor, banging up against the wall. The hollow can made a racket that should have awakened the dead. I was afraid that in minutes someone would be at the door to see what had happened.

I was not wrong. It was Jana. "Bob, are you okay?"

Thinking quickly and disguising my pain driven voice, I tried to simply say, "Yes, I'm okay. I was tying my shoe, and I knocked the garbage can over. I'll be out in a moment."

Jana was a kind person, I could tell, and she offered once more, "Are you sure I can't get you something?"

"No," I tried to say calmly, "I'm feeling better already. The cold water on my face has made a difference."

"Okay. Let me know," she said.

I listened for the sound of her soft-soled shoes walking away, but could not be sure about her departure.

I wondered if I had broken a rib, the pain was so intense. I had certainly bruised my elbow and wrenched my shoulder. *Shake it off. Play with the pain.* I tried to use old tools learned in football to fight the pain. I moved the garbage can back to its place and focused on the latch. "One more time," I said under my breath.

I stepped up onto the can once more. This time, I took off both shoes and both socks. *Maybe I'll be nimbler in bare feet.*

With the shoe in my right hand I went through a couple of deep knee bends. I forced the pain out of my mind and pictured a quarterback that I needed to sack in the end zone for a safety. With all the strength I could muster, I coiled my body into a tight spring. I released the tension quickly and shot into the air. With the infallible application of hand-eye coordination the shoe neatly hit the handle of the latch, and it opened.

I was however, once more in midair with no place to go. It flashed through my mind that I simply could not afford to knock over the garbage can. A second ruckus would be too much to ignore. In a flash I saw a quarterback who had already thrown the ball and I had to avoid him. In a very athletic move, I pulled my knees up and rolled to my left. The good part is that I would miss the can. The bad part was that I'd be coming down on my already injured side.

I hit hard, trying to roll onto my back to diffuse the contact. It worked to a degree, but a flash of pain nearly took my breath away. I lay there for just a moment. If I didn't get up quickly, the ref would make me leave the game. I continued the game in my mind. I saw the pass was incomplete, and I had another opportunity. It was third and ten on their one-yard line. If I tackled the quarterback in their end zone, I could still get that safety. With those two points, the tie would be broken, and we would win the game. I painfully scrambled to my feet. The garbage can was still in position. I stepped up once more. The lower frame of the window was within reach. I hoped it wasn't stuck shut. I stopped to put my shoes and socks back on and prepared for another jump.

Using my right hand, I reached up and grasped the window. My rib cage cried out as bruised and broken bones screamed that I should stop, but I pushed through the pain, and the window pulled open. I had no idea what was outside, but had to take the chance. Once again, depending mostly on my right hand, arm, and shoulder, I boosted myself up to poke my head out the window. I felt like I might have just one chance, and that chance depended on the strength in my left side. Behind the goal line, the quarterback was trying to sneak through. If I stopped him before he got to the line, that elusive safety would be mine.

Thankfully, there was no sidewalk traffic. What I didn't see was a homeless man nursing his bottle in a doorway, just a few feet down the street. I scrambled through the window, buried my pads into the quarterback, and found myself on the ground once more, nearly stricken with shooting pain, but with the freedom gained by accomplishing the safety and the addition of two new points.

I could not lie there for more than a second. I rose to my feet and looked down the street for a yellow taxicab. I could see none. I started to walk toward the Mississippi River, which would take me in the direction of Bourbon Street. I whispered a quick "Thank you, Jana." As I walked, my left side was on fire, but I pushed on trying not to limp. A teetering man in New Orleans was a dead giveaway for a drunk who might need to spend a night in jail, while sobering up. A vision of my near-dead wife replaced the football metaphor.

I kept looking for a taxi. After a block I saw one coming my way, and it was available. I moved off the curb and raised my right hand to hail the cab. It stopped. I slid into the seat and told the cabbie to take me to a jazz bar on Bienville Street, around the corner from the lobby doors of the Royal Sonesta.

The cab ride was short; I paid my fare, stepped out of the car, and into the jazz club. I watched the cab pull away and returned to the sidewalk. I knew that Jana was a conscientious woman. She would watch for me and check back at the restroom when I didn't re-appear. Then she would call security when I didn't answer, thinking I was in some sort of medical trouble. Very soon, the police would be looking for me. I had to get into the hotel without drawing attention, grab the little glass bottle, and be on my way, all before the police arrived.

I found an alternate entry through a connected restaurant. I went straight to my room. Time was fleeting, so I took the stairs, despite the nearly debilitating pain on my left side. Each step was a lightning bolt of pain in my left rib cage. At the door, I fumbled with my keys. It was all I could do to get the key into the lock. The hotel used electronic keys rather than the key cards. At last, the door opened, and I was inside. I really needed to use the bathroom. For real, this time, but I felt like I could not afford the time. *Where is that bottle?* I wondered. I had thought little of it since leaving the swamp.

I went to my dresser where I thought I had left it. It wasn't there. I rifled through all the drawers; it remained elusive. I was becoming panicked. There was a drawer in the nightstand. I went to it and pulled it open. I closed my eyes before reaching into the drawer and said the smallest of prayers. I rifled through the drawer. It wasn't there, either. My panic had reached a crescendo. I would have to look through each drawer once more, this time more carefully and far more deliberately. I started on the top drawer of the dresser, and then I remembered. I had stuffed it inside an old pair of lounging socks that I kept for cold hotel floors. Those socks were in that very drawer. I reached for them, hoping to find them filled with a bottle. It was inside! I shoved the bottle into my pocket and started for the door. Suddenly I stopped. I went back to the shaving kit and grabbed a handful of anti-inflammatories and acetaminophen that I hoped would curb my pain, but that would have to be later. I turned, and in seconds, I was out the door. I made for the stairs again, hoping against hope that I would not meet the police on the way down.

I was fortunate. At the bottom of the stairs, I made my way to the inner courtyard. I walked casually around the pool, through a passageway that led down a hallway, and to a door that opened onto Conti Street. I moved out the door, turned right and walked to Royal Street where I made a left turn. Out of sight of the Royal Sonesta, I began to feel I might have made it. But time was passing quickly, and I knew I couldn't remain on the streets as a fugitive. I made my way down Royal Street, looking for a bar to get some water with which to take my painkillers. Sadly, it was a street filled with jewelry and clothing stores, with no bar to be found.

I finally reached St. Peter Street where I looked both left and right. On the right I saw a coffee shop. *Great!* I thought, *some coffee and a beignet.* I needed a new source of energy, and I was close to Jonah's Voodoo Shop. Whether or not she would be there was another matter, but I felt I needed a breather from my run as a fugitive.

The door swung open, and there was a vacant table with a view of the street. A server with a friendly smile greeted me and happily took my order for black coffee and a beignet. My nerves began to settle as I watched the street, looking for prowling police. None were in sight. I asked for a glass of water and downed the painkillers. I doubled the dose.

The coffee and pastry soon arrived. The hot liquid and sugary feast hit the spot. A refill was soon furnished and another beignet; both were delicious. I felt both time and need pressing me, so I left cash and hustled out the door. The Voodoo Shop was one block away, between Royal and Bourbon Streets. I was in a dangerous world again without any cover.

Searching for Jonah . . . and Hope

THERE WAS NO ONE on the street, so blending in was impossible. I was a lone man walking down a vacant street. If the police drove by, I would surely be questioned. Looking down the street, I saw the sign. The painkillers were beginning to have some effect. When I got to the door, it was just as I suspected—locked. The business was closed for the evening.

I didn't know what to do. I couldn't think of anywhere to go. It was clear that I had to make it to morning. *How? Where?* Using a credit card to rent a room would divulge my location. I was in too much pain to curl up like a homeless man on the streets, or in an alley. Besides, I could be rousted and identified; or mugged and killed. There was no good solution. I elected the most improbable of all choices; I started knocking on the door.

My knocks went unanswered, and soon my knocking became pounding. It was a delicate line. If Jonah's residence was at the shop, I had to knock loud enough to bring her to the door, a move that would be unusual. But I could not pound too loud, attracting unwanted attention. It was a long shot. I kept knocking.

There were dim lights in the shop that lit up the merchandise. As I peered through the door, they were as I had remembered them, a little mystical. I found it odd that the things I feared just two days ago now appeared as a coveted refuge. I pounded a few more times, showing persistence and hoping it would pay off. At last, a light flicked on in the back room. I watched intently, and there she was, at least there was her head. She looked carefully around the wall. She studied me for a moment. I have no idea what I must have looked like to her. My face would have been a shadow. I knocked again, not roughly, but pleading-ly. She moved around the wall with caution. She flipped a switch that lit up the shop and my face. Would she remember me? Then in a way that duplicated our previous encounter, she seemingly floated across the floor.

At the door, she stayed back and peered out at me. She motioned to the sign that said, "Closed." I held up my hands in a praying gesture. She shook her head and said, "No."

I was nearly apoplectic but fought to control my anxiety and my pain.

"Please!" I called out.

Once more, she shook her head, "No."

But then I had an idea. I pulled the bottle from the pocket. She flinched. Maybe she thought it was a gun. I quickly held up the bottle to the glass of the door, hoping she would recognize the flower inside, rather than call the police. She looked at the bottle. Her face changed from a look of annoyance to one of recognition. There was still hesitance, but she reached for the lock. I slumped in gratitude and hope. I was nearly exhausted, despite the coffee and pastry.

Jonah slowly opened the door, just a crack, and a heavy chain jangling to its full length.

Trying not to look and sound crazy, I spoke out. "Mother Moses said to seek you out. She said for me to tell you that she knew me, and to show you this little glass bottle with this tiny bloom inside."

I turned my head, looking back and forth, up and down both sides of the street. It still looked clear.

I focused once more on Jonah. "Please. I am desperate for your help. People may be dying. Some may already be dead. Please help me. Mother Moses promised you would help."

The recognition in her face began to change. As she considered that I knew Mother Moses, the look on her face softened, but she remained hesitant. Finally, she asked, "Are you the man who came to my shop with the other who had bought the snake shirts?"

I gave her a positive nod. She still looked hesitant. I knew I was asking a lot. It was the middle of the night, and she had no idea who I really might be. It could all be a ruse for a robbery, or worse.

Once more I painfully raised my hands to the symbol of prayer, "Please."

She seemed to come to a conclusion. Her face took on an empathetic look. She closed the door, unhooked the heavy chain, the door opened again, and she said softly, "Come in."

I quickly entered the shop. She glided deeper into the interior where there was more privacy and turned out the shop lights. I followed her around a corner where a table and some chairs were revealed. I was glad to sit down once more. Despite losing the powerful edge of pain, I was miserable. I needed help in more ways than one. She pulled some curtains across the opening between the store and the back room.

"May I?" I asked, motioning to the chair.

She nodded her head in affirmation; then she also sat down at the table, across from where I was seated.

"Are you in trouble? Are you running from someone?" she asked.

I said, "Yes. Those snake shirts seem to have caused people who wore them to go into some kind of catatonic state. In fact, they appear dead, and at first they were taken to the morgue for an autopsy. I guess it was in the morgue that they discovered some muted signs of life. I'm not even sure how they found them. My wife, Anne, is one of the patients. All the patients have been taken to a hospital where they are under observation. No one knows what to do. The CDC is testing them to see if they have some kind of infection. They are in quarantine, and there is fear of some kind of epidemic, although authorities believe there is some tie to the shirts."

I stopped to catch my breath and to let my words sink in. She remained silent.

I began again. "Because the CDC fears some kind of infectious epidemic, I was also under quarantine. But I remembered what Mother Moses said about you and the flower. I broke out, grabbed the flower from my hotel room, and—well—here I am.

Jonah seemed to consider the circumstances as I had described them. She sat for many moments considering—something. I elected to stay silent. The moments passed. I watched her jet black eyes. They were eyes of intelligence, and I could see the intelligence was at work.

At last she said, "Is your friend one of the victims?"

She had used the "victim" term. That was not a good sign.

"Yes."

"How many are affected?"

"Twenty-five," I said.

Jonah rose; there was a small hot plate on the counter and a tea-kettle. She lit the burner and returned. "What did Mother Moses tell you?"

I told Jonah of our trip into the swamp, of the lotion she had me apply, and the retrieval of the tiny blossom. With a sheepish smile, I recounted her words, "She said I was humble, and that I should come to you if people died, and bring the blossom.

I set the bottle on the table. The tiny blossom floated in the water. It looked like it had just been picked. Up until that moment, she hadn't touched the bottle. Taking her eyes away from mine, at last, she looked down at the fragile little flower. She picked up the bottle and began studying the blossom. While she studied the flower, I began to feel foolish.

What on Earth am I doing? My wife is dead or dying in a hospital, and I am with a strange woman in a Voodoo Store who is looking at the most fragile-looking blossom I have ever seen. How on Earth is any of this going to help?

Jonah looked up at me, almost as though she could hear my thoughts. Her mouth opened as though she might speak, but then she stopped. I was feeling desperately drained, full of emotion, fear, dread, and fatigue. All I could do was wait for her to speak again.

"You said your wife was named Anne. Is that correct?"

"Yes, and she is one of the victims."

"A woman named Anne came to my shop today."

That revelation surprised me. Anne was not into voodoo.

"Did she say where she was from? We live in New York."

Jonah's expression visibly changed. "You are married to a very nice woman. She and I talked for an hour. When she left I felt as if a friend had left my store."

I thought about it, not for long, and remarked, "Yes, she is a good woman. I love her very much, and if you have the power to help me save her, I'm pleading for you to help us."

Jonah was clearly in her own state of turmoil, but I didn't understand why that was so.

"Mother Moses and you are asking me to do something that is rarely done. You are asking me to call on the elements that surround us. You are asking me to me to coax them into serving your needs. Only a humble man could make such a request. A proud and vain man may ask for such help, but it will not come. Nature will not help a proud man in this way. Are you truly a humble man?"

My thoughts were racing. I've never given my humility any consideration; it simply hadn't ever occurred to me to wonder whether I was proud or humble. At last I said, "When Mother Moses said I was humble, I was both surprised and a bit confused."

She did not respond to my words, but once more studied me. It was as though she was seeking counsel. After a very long period of what I considered to be intense scrutiny, she apparently made a decision.

"Very well," said Jonah. "I will do as you have asked, but only because Mother Moses has requested it, and because I met your Anne, and she is an innocent party. If you are truthful, we may be able to save your wife, your friend, and those who have been poisoned. But the poison is strong. It attacks in a way that is not understood. Left alone, it will eventually bring death, normally within just a few days."

"But, how can this be," I gasped. "How can a shirt cause this poisoning?"

"There are many elements of the universe that are not understood. I do not understand it all, except to know that the elements seem to make their own decisions. Sometimes they help us; sometimes they punish us; sometimes they can be called upon to give assistance to those who are worthy, or to punish the proud and arrogant.

"And Mother Moses believes I am worthy?" It truly was a question.

"Apparently so," she responded. "And as I listen to you and sense your character, I believe she is right. Remember I said there might be a lesson in this for your friend?"

I simply nodded my head in affirmation, not knowing what else to do.

"There will be a lesson, and I hope he learns from it. I hope you learn from it, as well. It is a priceless lesson, and in that lesson some of the secrets of our existence are revealed. Whether you ever understand in fullness remains to be seen, but your understanding is not required. It is your humility that is required, your kindness, and willingness to believe in something that's true, but unseen. Do you possess those traits?"

Suddenly the teakettle began to whistle. It seemed like the sound of mourning. Jonah rose from her chair and reached for the small pot. She poured hot water in to a dingy, gray-white mug. It reminded me of the one that Mother Moses had used. She sat the mug in front of me and turned to a cupboard. A number of opaque glass containers were lined up on the shelves. Each was secured with a metal band that pulled over the top. She opened one and spooned out some of the powder, and poured it into a small piece of cloth that looked like cheesecloth. She opened two more jars and added some of their contents to the mixture. Then she quickly tied it up with a string and dropped the blend into the mug. She swooshed it all around in the mug and said in a matter-of-fact tone, "In a few moments this will be ready. It will calm you. It will relieve you of most of your pain. Later, I will also rub your side with a lotion that will help you heal. For now, drink and rest. You may lie down on the cot on the other side of the room. You will fall asleep. I will wake you when the time is right."

I was so grateful for her help that I drank the entire contents of the mug, as quickly as I could. It was neither bitter nor sweet. It felt nourishing. Very swiftly, I began to feel its affect.

"Go lie down. You are in great need of healing."

I struggled to get up, made my way to the cot, and nearly collapsed into it. My senses told me the cot was uncomfortable, but my body sunk restfully into its care. As I lay in comfortable repose, Jonah turned and reached into her cupboard. At the end of the line of herbs, or whatever they were, sat a container unlike the others. I was becoming sluggish, losing my understanding, but I knew this container was somehow different from all the rest. I saw her turn and look at me; then she looked at that particular container. As my vision faded, she turned and walked up a stairway I had not noticed before. In seconds, I was asleep. I didn't even know for sure that she was gone. There was no thought of "where" and no consideration of "what."

— CHAPTER TWELVE —
SATURDAY: MIDNIGHT AND DESPAIR

Jensen Battles the Monster of Quiet

THE VOID, THE QUIET, the nothingness was relentless. Nothing permeated the emptiness of my existence, except for my feeling of guilt. At first, the quiet was a relief from the pointing fingers, and the raucous, accusing voices from a former time, but then it lost its comforting qualities. It had become, in and of itself, a raging voice in the vacuum of an empty hole.

If I had ears I would have closed them, but I had no sensation of ears. And if I had them, what would I hear? I would hear the great roar of nothingness.

Such was my misery. I am Jensen, locked in a misery that seems to be never ending. I have no reference of space or time. I have no reference of the physical or the ethereal world. I only have a mild awareness, and it is startlingly unbearable. I cried out, seeking relief, but there was no sound, and no one to hear me. I was isolated and lost in depressive wretchedness.

Anne's Intellect

I SENSED THE PHYSICALITY of my body and felt hope that it still existed; so did the other intellects. We all sensed it. We could not communicate in words, but we mutually felt a simple awareness of the existence of each other, our bodies, and of our proximate gathering. I became even more convinced that some of the intellects belonged to beings like me. These other intellects had been familiar with the same life, motion, and thought, as I had known. My conclusion was that they were humans.

But, just as curiously, we all became aware of other intellects—living intellects, human intellects. And we began to suspect they were trying to help us. There was comfort in that thought, although no real relief; our state was still too unsettled.

At one point I wondered if one of the intellects, the living intellects, might be Bob. Then I was surprised I had actually thought about Bob. It was the first time I had thought about him. There was something familiar about a particular presence that had been near me, spending more time with me that the others. But he (if it was *Bob)* had suddenly vanished, and I no longer felt that particular presence. I wondered where he had gone and wished for his return.

My existence was so confusing. All my musings were unreal. Their progress was slow, and it seemed hours before one thought could be fully developed. There was initial progress from feeling like I was in a complete void, to a point where I had sensed other intellects, and then the progress stopped. For what seemed to be a long period my awareness continued as though on a plateau. Then, with great alarm, I began to realize that my awareness, which had been at best cloudy, was deteriorating. There had never been any light in my awareness, but there was no dark either. It was very weird. How could my existence be without either light or dark, formless, indefinable? But those questions seemed to be unimportant because the sensitivity of my senses was fading. I was less aware, less sure of what I had earlier discerned. It was as though a much larger void was taking me, and I was helpless to stop it. What I began to conceive was the terror of a failed existence. *Could this be death?* I wondered.

The Frustration of Dr. Whitely

THE RESULTS CONTINUED TO be reported, each one landing on my desk, and none were enlightening. In between patient visits I would sit and study the results of testing, of questioning, and the coordination of information. No matter how hard I searched, I could find no valid, scientific, or realistic rationale for the malady and, therefore, I could find no hint of a cure. There was no toxin in the blood or tissues of the patients. There were no puncture marks from needles or fangs. No abnormal bacteria had been cultured from the patients. We found no viral infections. The catatonic state of my patients had no apparent cause. The only thing I was able to determine was that they were all gradually sinking into a continually deeper state of limbo, and in the end, they would all likely die if we found no cure.

EKG recorders were almost worthless. The normally recorded sine waves indicated no normal heart function. There were no distinct sinus rhythms, just long lines with minute fluctuations. Rather than being pumped, it was like the blood was seeping around their bodies. We found that our best indicators were the real time EEG monitors. However, we did not have enough EEG monitors to record the brain waves of every patient. More had been requested, but they were arriving slowly. We had attached the EEG monitors to the first patient and to subsequent patients. We began to see troubling results. The EEG activity of our first patient, the man most simply called Marshal, had at first alternated between bursts of activity and long periods of very little activity. The problem was that the numbers of bursts were diminishing and the periods of near-inactivity were getting longer. If the current trend continued, it appeared that he might soon be brain dead.

We had gathered all kinds of metrics for each patient. Hospital and doctor's records had been provided, as well as geographic, social, and work records. Marshal, and in fact, all the patients, had been healthy people. As I read Marshal's reports, I pictured a robust, confident, possibly loud character with nearly infinite energy and activity. That image was a far cry from the gray, cold body that lay nearly lifeless on the bed.

I had instructed the nurses to start an IV solution for each patient, but it soon became apparent that the IVs were of little use. There was so little blood pressure and actual movement of the patient's blood that the IV solutions were not being absorbed by the bodies in a normal way. We concluded, however, that even the low rate of saline intake was better than nothing. The treatment that appeared most efficacious was the oxygen we were giving them. The lungs were barely functioning, but the pure oxygen that we added did improve their 0_2 saturation levels.

The CDC had been running tests around the clock. Their tests had gone far beyond bacterial and viral cultures. They had tested muscle tissue, organ tissue, bone fragments, and even bone marrow. In every case, the results were normal. We'd found no cause, so we could affect no cure. It became the most little understood malady the world had ever known, and we were but a few hours into the mysterious event.

There was only one vein of investigation that resulted in some potential parallels. We learned of rumors from people of the bayou, of men and women who had become sick and lay in their beds for days without putrefying. Most of the stories were rumors, old wives' tales as some described them, or concoctions in people's minds, as others put it. The only substantive information came from ME records that indicated the time of death was usually five to seven days from the earliest documented doctor's visits. In the backwater swamps of the southern states, records were often incomplete, or non-existent. What we did begin to understand was that this current epidemic was not the first indication of the malady we were attempting to treat.

Of course, there were rumors of voodoo, of witch doctors, and old women who would cast spells on people, usually people who had done some great wrong; and those spells had forced the victims to their beds and to their eventual deaths. Wagging tongues among the current staff were prevalent. The terms "zombie" and "snake bite" were added. Most amid joking and laughter, but I noted that a few people seemed to actually believe in the possibility. I chatted with the seeming believers. In each case, they were children of the people of the swamp who had broken out of the old ways and become educated. Still, it seemed that old superstitions lingered in their minds. Though unwilling to say too much, the unexplained experiences of their early lives were so indelibly written in their minds that they could not be completely cast out.

Suddenly, a nurse burst through the door of my temporary, make-shift office. "Dr. Whitely, we think Marshal may be dying."

Oddly, as I jumped to my feet I thought, *Why do we call the man Marshal? He has a full name!* In the moment, however, I could not think of it. He had simply become Marshal. All who had ever known him, including the current nursing staff, just called him Marshal. Somehow, it was right. In just a few moments, I was at his bedside. "Okay, Marshal, what's up?"

Of course he gave no response, only the continuously diminishing results of his EEG. His heart rate showed not even the smallest fluctuation. He had essentially flat-lined. I wondered how there could be any real brain activity. My mind shifted back to the swamp stories. I looked at Marshal and wondered what he could have done that might have brought about the onset of— whatever the hell this is.

I was still thinking of Marshal and the other patients when the security officer came up to me. "We have a problem," he said. "The husband of the patient named Anne broke out of the facility. He managed to get out through a window."

I shook my head back and forth, wondering if it really meant anything. He'd seemed unaffected by the malady, and I didn't believe he could be carrying any dangerous bug or virus. I didn't think there was danger in his leaving but thought it would be nice to have him back, if only as a control subject.

"I guess you'd better call the police and put out an APB on him."

The security officer nodded and left to make contact with the police department.

I stood there silently and shook my head once more. I was stumped in a way that I had never been before. *Why would the man leave when his wife is here being treated?* I wondered. *He must have some good reason.*

I began to have some kind of hope that the man would return with an answer to our dilemma. It was a thought, a thought that seemed improbable.

Bob's Enlightenment

I SLEPT THROUGH THE night, but just as the sun was rising I began to stir. My head was clear and the pain from last night's escape had diminished, but not gone. Jonah was filling her teapot with water. She turned to me when she saw me stir.

"Good morning, Bob."

Scratching my head and stretching, I uttered my own, "Morning." I wasn't sure if it was a good one or not. The events of the last few days, the escape, and the run through the night were on my mind. And there was Anne. She was back at the hospital, in an unknown condition.

"Did you sleep well?" she asked as she held her hand near the burner to feel its heat.

"Yes, and other than a little pain, I feel good. What did you give me?"

She wagged her head back and forth and said, "It's complicated, but suffice it to say that it's a concoction of herbs that I felt would help calm your mind and strengthen your body. It looks like it worked. You were quite hysterical."

In daylight, and with proper lighting, Jonah took on the look of a more human form. It was the first time I'd seen her in real daylight. Gone was her demeanor of floating. She appeared and talked like every other human being I had ever known, not the ethereal and mysterious host of a voodoo shop. I had a million questions but forced myself to stick with my most urgent needs. "So what's the deal with all this— death?" I shrugged my shoulders not knowing how to describe it.

"And then there's the snake shirts, and the flower, and Mother Moses—and—well, you?"

A smile spread across Jonah's face. The smile contained kindness and warmth. Somehow it became reassuring. She walked to a chair near the table and sat down.

"What I'm going to tell you is fantastic, and you may not believe me, but you've asked. You're embroiled in an event that you have no control over, and Mother Moses apparently felt like you would be receptive."

I had no idea how to take her statement. Like everything else in this crazy experience, it made no sense. I raised my eyebrows, pursed my lips, and told her, "Go ahead."

She hesitated for a long moment, as though searching for a place to begin.

"Are you ready to believe in something that is true but unseen?"

I warily nodded my head, "Yes."

The one thing that hadn't changed was the tone of her voice. It was beautiful and it carried authority. I decided I was ready to believe.

"The world around us contains an unseen and undetected mystery. It is made of principles that are unknown to most, undetected by science, and controlled by but just a few. The only thing that might give you a way to grasp what I'm about to tell you is the idea of Karma. Others call it the Law of Restoration. You see, to each of our choices, there is a consequence. It may be large or it may be small. The consequence may be pleasant or horrifying. Your friend, Jensen, made a decision and acted upon it. That decision and action set off a series of very negative consequences. I don't know why Mother Moses sold him those shirts. She is almost as strange to me as she is to you, but I know she had a purpose. When the two of you first came into my store, I began to believe the purpose was for both of you, not just him. Now, I am not so sure who will gain the most. Only time can tell that tale."

"I don't understand; you are talking in mysteries."

"Yes I am, because it is a mystery. I don't know how it works, but I am familiar with the consequences."

"Enlighten me," I begged.

"As humans, we talk about Mother Nature, and we often label her with traits that suggest life and intelligence. All I can say is there appears to be more truth to that than we suspect. I've learned from Mother Moses that nearly everything around us, perhaps *all* things, has some kind of life force, some kind of ability to perceive and act. Going back to Karma, it appears that nature around us truly responds to us in hidden ways, in ways we don't understand or even suspect. There are a few who do understand and who live in that world of understanding. Mother Moses is one of them.

"Mother Moses is a being who comes and goes. Occasionally she'll come to me. It's as though she is checking up on me. The last time she was here, she brought that shirt, the one with the snake on it. She told me not to sell it, merely to keep it, that at some point it might become useful. I think that point may be upon us."

My head had begun to swim. The clarity I had felt moments before was becoming misty. "I just want to know how to save my wife."

"Is that really all you want?" she asked.

I had considered that and gave her a thoughtful answer. "No, there's more. I want my friend to be healed, and I want all those people who are sick to be healed. I want things to be right again. I wish Jensen had never gone to the swamp. It has become the ruin of us all."

The room became silent after I spoke the words. Jonah looked as though she was still surveying me, sizing me up, and evaluating me. At last she spoke, "I think Mother Moses was right. I think you are the man who will make things right. You will need my help and the help of the goodness around us, just as I have described. You won't understand it, but you will be given a gift, a gift only you can use— for the benefit of others. In that benefit to others, you will find your own healing."

Now, it was my turn to evaluate Jonah. She was beautiful, almost beyond description. She was smart, and she had an air of confidence about her. In my short evaluation, I felt a great welling of trust in her words and in her message. "Okay," I said, "I'm willing to give it a shot. What do I do?"

It wasn't a smile that she gave me, it was more the look of satisfaction, possibly of fulfillment, I don't know for sure. All I know is that we now had a bond of trust, and I was grateful that she had become my ally and benefactor.

"First, you'll drink some more tea."

Jonah rose and, once again, poured hot water into the aged mug I had been using. She went to the same container as before and spooned a small amount of powder into the mug, plus a little more from this or that jar, put it in the cheesecloth, which she put into my mug. She swirled it around for a few minutes, handed it to me, and said, "Another dose will continue to calm your mind and open your heart."

I did as I was told.

"I'll be right back," she said as she turned, and in seconds she had slipped up the staircase and out of sight, just as she had last night.

Bob's Peace

I sipped the tea from the mug. The dark, hot liquid felt peaceful as it passed my palate, warming me from head to toe. I remembered the sensation I had when Mother Moses rubbed the lotion on me. My fear abated, and my hope increased. I still didn't understand what Jonah had told me, but it felt right. For the first time I looked around the small back room. It was not a stockroom per se. It felt more like a personal space, a place one might enter to relax, to feel peace. I turned to look behind me, when a jolt of pain reminded me of my possibly broken ribs. I peered through a doorway into another room. That room appeared to be her stockroom. It was filled with boxes on shelves and boxes on the floor. It was neat, orderly, but full of an amazing variety of goods that she sold in the storefront.

My sight and mind came back to what I had now labeled "the room of peace." One small window was before me, built into the wall at the bottom of the staircase. The glass was frosted, and the light was diffused. I would have to describe the quality of the room as being brighter than half light, but not full light. There was a lamp on the table and a light fixture hanging from the ceiling, but they were both off. The short counter was void of everything but the burner with the teapot. The doors were closed to the cupboard above, but I could see in my mind's eye the line of jars with metal loops that held the glass lids tightly to the jars. I imagined a sealing ring or better yet a fit that was so precise as to completely, and perfectly seal the contents inside. Below the cupboard a half-dozen hooks had been attached to the wall. Five mugs hung from five of the hooks, my mug had likely been taken from the number six hook. The walls of the room were covered in a variety of materials. They were painted a peaceful tan, and trimmed in a somber brown. It made me think of burnt umber, an oil paint color that my mother loved to use in her paintings. Over the paint hung a variety of woven rugs, paintings, and photos of the bayou. There were knick-knacks and bric-a-brac. Some hung on the walls and some sat on shelves. All in all, the room was the epitome of organized clutter, but it was a homey room, and I felt that if even one piece was moved, or removed, the ambiance would have been ruined. I felt at home.

I was brought out of my thoughts by Jonah's appearance at the foot of the staircase. I was surprised that I heard no creaking as she glided down the steps. She held two containers. One was small, the other large, and seemed to slosh as if it were filled with liquid. She juggled the two containers, setting the larger one on the counter, next to the hotplate. She stepped toward me with the small container.

"Please move to the cot," she said. "I want to put this salve on your ribs."

So great was my trust, I did as she asked, without question. In a moment I was lying on the cot with my shirt off. She dipped her fingers into the small container. They came out coated with aromatic salve. The concoction of smells made up a blend that I cannot describe, although I did pick out the smell of eucalyptus. As she applied aromatic ointment to my skin, it felt warm and healing. Not only did it warm my skin, the eucalyptus opened my sinuses and refreshed my senses. Her touch was sure and pleasant, like the hands of a well-trained masseuse. All too soon, she was finished, but, even though the soothing touch was gone, the ointment gave me the impression of deep healing.

She interrupted the calm of my healing. "Now sit up and put your shirt back on. We have work to do, and I'll need your help."

Once more I complied without question.

She pointed to the counter and said, "Underneath is a larger hotplate. Please get it out, set it on the counter, and plug it in. Set the large pot on the large hotplate. While you are doing that, I have some things to gather," and she walked into her supply room.

I reached down and opened the doors under the cupboard. One of them squeaked as the hinges opened. The hot plate was under some smaller pots. I pulled it out of the lower cupboard, surprised that it was not dusty. Sitting it on the counter, I plugged it in, and picked up the big pot. There was about an inch of clear liquid in it. The pot was heavy. I turned on the hot plate, and within seconds, I could smell the heat from the coils. The liquid in the pan was clear, and it had no odor.

Jonah stepped out of the supply room. She had two bottles of liquid in her hands, and of all things, the snake shirt she had once shown us. I watched as she sat them all on the counter. I was very leery of the snake shirt, but she handled it without the anxiety that I was experiencing. She left once more and returned with a very large pot, almost two feet tall and more than a foot in diameter. She sat this largest pot on the table. She went back into the room and returned with a blanket. It went onto the table.

Jonah then opened the two bottles and poured them both into the pot that was on the stove. The liquid in that pot had begun to gently boil. She turned down the burner, then opened the cupboard, securing both leaves and powders from several glass decanters, and added them to the lightly boiling solution on the big burner. She then turned to me.

"I must now take the bottle and the blossom that Mother Moses gave you."

I had almost forgotten about it. It was in my pocket. I quickly pulled it out and handed it to her without saying a word.

She took the bottle, held it up to the light, examining it. She studied it with both reverence and analytics, as if to assess its potential efficacy. She rotated the bottle, looking at the frail blossom from every angle. Apparently satisfied, she finally said, "Good, the blossom is still fresh and undamaged." Then, in an instant, she opened the small bottle, unceremoniously dumping the blossom, water, dirt, and all into the big pot. I thought it odd that she dutifully studied the tiny blossom but was cavalier in dumping it into the pot. Mother Moses considered to be of such great value. Jonah's attitude toward the flower seemed mixed.

Giving the solution a stir, she turned to me and said with a pointed air of authority, "You will need to stay here and watch the pot. I don't want it to boil too hard. Keep it on a low boil, and it simply cannot be allowed to burn. The burner is not on high so it shouldn't scorch the contents, but you are to watch it carefully to make sure it doesn't burn. Stir it frequently." Turning away she reached for her purse and added, "We need some blankets. Since the police are likely searching for you, I'll go buy them. I'm sure you'll be safe here. It's almost opening time, but I'll keep the closed sign on the window. Hopefully, no one with your persistence will come to the store."

She gave me a slight smile. I responded with, "Or my problems." Her smile grew broader but continued to be kind and not mocking. I chuckled to relieve my own tensions.

In a flash, Jonah was out the door. She didn't even say goodbye. She just hurried out. I gave the solution a good stir and set the timer on my watch for five minutes.

I thought about Jonah and her actions. The tiny blossom seemed to be the most important part of her plan, Mother Moses certainly believed it to be important. What is it about this tiny flower that can change the solution into some kind of healing agent? It seemed an unsolvable mystery.

Waiting for time to pass, and after giving the mixture another stir, the storefront became my personal adventure land. It was quite a different experience from the day when I stood in the doorway nagging Jensen to leave. The awesome lights weren't on, but the goods were still amazing. Remembering how ill at ease I was at our first visit, it was surprising that I perused the shop in calmness. If the attraction didn't appear to be fragile, I would pick it up and carefully examine it. Interestingly enough, there were no voodoo dolls. That was puzzling—*a voodoo shop without voodoo dolls?* That would be a subject to pursue when Jonah returned. For the next forty minutes, the mixture was stirred every five. The task at hand was important; there could be no failure, or so Jonah had made me believe.

While I was giving the mixture a stir, Jonah unlocked the door and entered the shop. She left the "Closed" sign on the door and locked it again. "How is the soup doing?" she asked with a smile. *Was she serious? Was this really soup? No, it can't be.* She looked into the pot, dipped her finger into it cautiously and tasted the mixture. "It tastes just right and is nearly ready," she said.

Maybe it is soup, I thought.

We sat for another hour. Jonah rose and stirred the mixture occasionally. Each time she dipped her finger in it and gave it a taste.

"Why do you do that?" I asked.

Jonah looked at me without speaking at first, as though she was trying to decide what to tell me. At last she simply said, "It has to be at just the right temperature and with the correct flavor. Anything more or less, and it won't work."

I was overcome with curiosity. "What is it supposed to do?"

"No, no, no," she said. "It isn't yet time for you to know. You shall know, in fact you'll become intimately acquainted with your task, but for now just wait patiently."

— CHAPTER THIRTEEN —
SUNDAY: HOPE

The Blankets

THE MIXTURE HAD BEEN gently boiling for two hours. I had tried on several occasions to get her to tell me more about the flower. She simply wouldn't share her knowledge and kept our conversation general in nature, but at the two-hour mark, Jonah rose from her chair and tasted the solution once more. "It is almost done," she announced. "Now, I want you to pick up the snake shirt and put it into the boiling mixture."

Once more I did as I was told.

"It must boil for another five minutes, then you'll remove the shirt," she instructed.

We waited the five minutes, and I used some tongs to grasp the shirt, lifting it out of the pot. She picked up another pot and said, "Put the shirt in here."

I complied.

"Now it is finished. Here, help me lift the big pot. We'll move it to the table and pour it into the larger pot."

It wasn't terribly heavy, but it was awkward. Using hot pads, we picked up the pot, pouring its contents into the second, and much larger pot to a quarter of its capacity, my ribs gently complaining. Jonah turned to the counter and the sink. She turned on the hot spigot, filled another empty pot with hot tap water, and said, "Now, help me pour this water into the pot on the table."

Once again, it was an awkward process, but we did it, and I survived the jolt of minor pain.

"Perfect," she said. The pot on the table was now about half full.

She turned to me. "You must do this next step alone. I cannot help you. The act has to be selfless and honest. I didn't tell you this earlier because I didn't want you to think too much about it. Clear your mind of fear, doubt and especially anger or hatred. Think only of the good you will do for your—friends. She hesitated for moment as if undecided about something, and then continued.

"You asked about the flower. The truth is I cannot tell you much, except to say that it is a very special flower, and its qualities are known to very few. What I have learned is that it is the essence of purity, and that purity, in some way that I do not know, combines with the malice in the image of the snake to create a solution that concentrates the good in the world around us."

The idea of a pure flower, the malice of a snake painting, and concentrating good seemed impossible to fold into something of which I could make sense. However, her words carried authority. I tried to believe her. I carefully considered them and wondered if I could shed all doubt.

"If you at first doubt, simply fill your mind with a desire to believe," she encouraged me. "The rest will be taken care of if you fill your heart with desire."

After making that statement, she looked at me again, as though continuing to analyze me and said, "You are now going to make a covering for your friends using these blankets. They will be saturated with the purity of the blossom and the concentrated goodness that is in the solution. Take the first blanket and put it into the pot. The water is hot, but will not burn you. Make sure the blanket is completely saturated with the mixture."

The blankets that Jonah had purchased were sized for a single bed. They were light and thin. Doing as instructed, I placed the blanket in the water. I swished it, swirled it, making sure it was saturated, and then looked up at her. My shoulders shrugged and my head tipped.

"Yes, that is enough," she said. "Now you must wring it out. The mixture is precious. Please keep the spills to a minimum.

That process was not easy. I twisted and squeezed and twisted and squeezed some more. The water stayed mostly in the pan. Jonah didn't correct me, but watched me do the work. At length, I felt like I had completed the task. Jonah reached under the counter and pulled out a long and low plastic container. "Put the blanket in this container and follow me." She headed to the stairs, and like a servant, I dutifully followed.

Drying Time

As we climbed the stair the décor changed. The rustic and dim appearance of the ground floor transitioned into a room with brightly painted walls. The carpet was a remarkable white and the furniture was light-colored. I followed her to the bathroom where modern conveniences contrasted the old facilities downstairs. She pointed to a curtain rod. "Unscrew this end and move the curtain rod so it is centered over the tub," she instructed. It was an easy task and soon completed.

Jonah added, "Make sure the rod is securely pressed between the walls."

I checked it once more and believed it was secure.

She gave me more instructions, "Now, place the plastic tub in the bathtub, fold the blanket unevenly over the rod so one corner hangs low."

When all was done, I looked at her and asked, "Now what?"

"Go back and do it again. I have eight blankets. Hopefully there is enough mixture to saturate all eight blankets."

The process was completed eight times. The fluid that dripped from the blankets was carefully placed in another small pan and poured back into the biggest pot downstairs. I was afraid the weight of the saturated blankets would make the rod fall down, but it held. And we didn't waste a drop. In fact, she treated the liquid like it was gold.

At one point she stopped, looked at me seriously and said, as though knowing my thoughts, "This is more precious than gold. It brings life, rather than corruption."

I considered her words over and over again as I worked, suspecting that the blanket would be laid over the victims. Once more I wondered, are they victims or patients? I decided it didn't matter.

After the eight blankets were hanging and a row of tubs and pans were collecting the drippings, she said, "Now we wait. They must dry."

I considered our location: New Orleans. The air was warm and that would help, but it was humid. *That's a problem*, I thought.

Then Jonah brought in two fans and turned them on. "This will help," she said.

We went back downstairs and waited. Our talk became simple chitchat. Where did I live, and what were my days like? She wanted to know about Anne. I spoke freely. We discussed the hurricane, Katrina. She told me of her experiences riding out the storm. She hadn't left her shop but stayed upstairs. "I was protected," she said. I thought of Mother Moses when she said that.

We chatted over a simple lunch of crackers and cheese. In the evening she fixed a delightful dinner. It was simple—boiled crawdads in some kind of seasoning, rice, and steamed broccoli. I liked it all but the broccoli, but I ate it without complaining. I suspected that she knew, but nothing was said. She seemed to know much about me, almost as though she read my thoughts, or sensed various aspects of my life. The effects of her tea potions were clearly present, so I didn't feel invaded.

After dinner, she put on some music. Of course it was New Orleans styled jazz. Jonah checked the blankets occasionally. By 10:00 p.m., they were nearly dry. She prepared a late night snack. It was a spread that we ate with crackers. It tasted different from what I'd received earlier. It had a sweet flavor to it, but she hadn't put any sugar in it. After we finished she said, "It's time for bed." She pointed to the cot and added, "Have a nice rest."

Jonah at once climbed the stairs and was gone. I was left alone to think and ponder, but in just a few moments, I was fast asleep.

After what felt like a second, I was jostled from my wonderful sleep. It was Jonah. She was all business.

"We have two hours before the sky lightens. I have a car. I will drive you to the hospital. You must come with me now and put the dried blankets into this box."

A cardboard box rested on the wooden floor on top of a throw rug.

I looked at her nervously, "How will I get back into the hospital, and what do I do?"

"I have a friend. She will get you into the hospital. Her name is Jana. She is my cousin."

I smiled, "Yes, I met Jana. She is a very kind and caring woman."

"She'll help you get into the hospital. Despite our relationship, it was difficult to get her to agree."

"I'm still not sure what I'll be doing there. Will she understand it?"

"She believes that you missed your wife so much that you returned out of love. That much is true. She also believes that you simply have some blankets to put over her patients. She will accept your magnanimous offer."

"But I only have eight blankets. How do I explain who I've chosen to cover with blankets?"

Jonah thought on that question for a few minutes and finally said, "Tell her you're covering the ones who have been sick the longest since they seem to be in the greatest danger."

I thought about that for a moment. *If I were merely covering people with blankets, wouldn't I cover Anne first?* Could I possibly be that unselfish? In a way, I guess I was being unselfish but I had justification for it. I didn't have a better answer so I concluded to take that course.

Within minutes, I had neatly folded the slightly damp blankets, placed them in the box, and loaded them into the car. She wouldn't touch them and said they were for me only. In fact, before starting the engine, she gave me strict instructions, "Do not let anyone else touch these blankets. They will be effective only if handled by you. You were the one who received the blossom, a blossom of purity. It bonded with you and you alone. Its efficacy is tied to you and no one else and is now a part of these blankets. And remember, I spoke of concentrated goodness. We don't want the goodness spoiled by the touch of an evil person."

I gave her a dumbfounded look. In less than ten minutes, we were at the hospital.

Fear, Hope, and Despair

"I HAD TO CALL Jana and have her come into the hospital," Jonah explained. "This is not the time of her shift. Her excuse is that she had forgotten something very important. She doesn't know it, but it's true. That important thing is you and the blankets."

After pulling up to a nondescript door, she reached out, putting her hand on my shoulder. "You are a good man, just as Mother Moses said. And you are humble. Remember to maintain the desire to believe. That's all it takes. As the blankets do their job, you will understand."

"But what do I do?"

"Have Jana show you the patient who came in first. I think it is the man you call Marshal. Put a blanket on each of the first eight patients. You will leave the blankets on until each patient opens their eyes. You must stay nearby and watch. It is very important that you remove the blanket at that time and take it to the next patient. Each person will be different. One may take an hour, another more, still another less. You will have to watch, and react quickly and do so before the staff removes the blanket."

"What if the staff touches the blanket?" I asked.

"If they touch it during their service, it will not matter, but do not let them remove the blanket once the patients open their eyes."

She stopped talking and looked steadfastly into my eyes. "Your service is very important. The lives of these people are dependent on you. Be courageous, do not be deterred, and believe."

Her eyes remained locked onto my eyes, but she said kindly, "Go now. Jana is at the door."

I stepped out of the car, crossed the curb, and went to the door. Just as I arrived it opened a crack. An eye peered through the slit. It gave a look of recognition and then opened enough to let me in.

"Hurry," she said.

I moved through the door and looked down a long hall.

"Come quickly and follow me."

Jana had made a nice gesture, but I already knew how the patients were arranged. I moved quickly and placed the first blanket on Marshal. He was the number one victim. Jana offered to help. I said, "No, many of these people are my friends. Please let me do this."

Jana nodded her head and simply said, "Okay."

I was grateful that she had given in, even though she intently watched me as I placed the eight blankets on the first eight people who were brought into the treatment center. It pained me to know that my wife, Anne, lay uncovered, but I was determined to follow Jonah's instructions.

There were chairs in another room. I asked Jana if I could get one to sit on. She agreed. I brought the chair into the room and waited. My thoughts swirled about the events of that last few days. The convention and my experiences were the stuff of fairy tales. It was beyond anything I might have imagined, all a blur, and yet, now very convincing.

I pulled up a chair and sat at Marshal's bedside. I already knew the schedule. Each patient was checked every thirty minutes to see if there were changes in their vital signs. A nurse checked him for the second time in the last hour, and I noticed a change in her expression. It was subtle, but the change was there. She didn't look at me, but turned and walked away quickly. I watched her, wondering what was wrong. She left the room, turned, and walked down the hallway. Within moments I heard the mumbling of voices. I couldn't tell what they were saying but I sensed concern.

The hushed voices began moving closer, then the nurse and a doctor appeared in the doorway. They went quickly to Marshal's side. The doctor gave me a sidelong look, and the nurse suggested that I move back to give them a little room. Their focus on Marshal was intense. Something was definitely wrong.

I began to watch the monitor with more interest. It was hard for me to tell, since I'm not experienced in such things, but it appeared that the heartbeat was even less frequent and less powerful. The EEG waves looked considerably weaker. I didn't know what it meant, wanted to ask, but asked no questions. I didn't want to lose my privileges. I simply watched and listened, suffering through each agonizing moment.

After a few minutes, I heard voices in the hallway, and Dr. Whitely hurriedly entered the room.

"What's going on?" he demanded.

The other doctor kept looking at the monitors and simply said, "I think we're losing him."

Dr. Whitely didn't say word, at first, then simply uttered, "Damn."

The two doctors and a nurse stood there as if in a trance, each held by circumstances that were unfathomable and in a situation where they felt hopeless. Dr. Whitely finally broke the silence and asked a simple question, "Do either of you have any ideas?"

Neither the nurse nor the other doctor responded.

My heart sank, my head dropped to my hands, and I felt the burn of bitter bile rising in my stomach. I'd been nursing the good feelings that Jonah spoke of, but with the doctor's last question, the good feelings vanished. My mind became a blur of the disheartening events of the last few days. I was tired, and it felt like Jonah's potions were not working. I began to feel pain and felt a need to let my tears flow.

Now it was my turn to hurriedly leave the room. I simply could not control the torrent of emotions that convulsed in my heaving chest. I half stumbled, half ran to the bathroom from which I had made my earlier escape. I turned on the cold water letting it run over my hands. I splashed it on my face, poured it over my head, and rubbed it on my neck. I stopped cold, looked deeply into my own eyes and wondered where the goodness had gone. I felt forsaken. I felt like my only companion was fear and loathing. My world was dark. If Marshal was not improving, if he was not getting better, but was, in fact, slipping further into the abyss of death, then what hope did I have that Anne would live? What hope did I have that my life would ever be the same? I had viewed the trip to New Orleans as a fresh start for Anne and me. Instead, I feared that it had become a bitter ending.

Leaving the restroom and walking back into the hallway, I found it silent—deathly silent. I don't know how long I had been gone, but when I went back to the room where Marshal lay, the doctors were gone and the nurse was checking other patients. She looked up when I entered the room. Our eyes met, and she read the question in mine. Her answer was simple, just a slight back and forth shake of her head. At that moment, all hope fled.

I pushed the chair back up to Marshal's bedside. *Why am I here*, I thought?

I sat with my head down, slumped nearly to my chest. With great effort, I thought back on the time I had spent with Jonah. I remembered that she hadn't made me any promises, but she had offered hope. Definitions of hope flashed through my mind, and I concluded that *hope* came from some kind of substance or evidence, at least, that *hope itself* was justified. I thought about Jonah's first instruction, simply to have a desire. I reached deep into my soul, trying to plant a new seed of desire. It was not easy.

Planting the Seeds

"I SAT UNMOVING UNTIL I began to feel numb, all the while wrestling with the concept of goodness. I stretched my mind, trying to bring belief into my thought process. I thought again and again about Jonah and the counsel she had given. Before I lost all the feeling in my legs and feet, I stood. I looked at Marshal's blank, pasty face. I looked at the blanket that covered him and thought of the goodness that it was supposed to contain.

I wondered in the depths of my soul. *What is this goodness?* I wondered once more how a simple blanket, saturated with herbs and the essence of a white flower could have the power to raise the dead? *How can it be?*

I lifted my hands cautiously and laid them on the blanket that covered Marshal's body. I expected it to be cold, but it was not. It wasn't warm either, but whether it was my imagination or reality, I thought I detected something that I could not describe. The best I can say is that it felt like there was life in something that was supposed to be lifeless—a blanket.

Standing for too long, I realized that my lower legs and feet were nearly asleep. It snapped me out of my mental machinations. I reached down and rubbed my legs, raised them, and bent my knees. I stamped my feet, and worked my joints, trying to revive the circulation. At length, I began to feel again, not just in my legs but also in my heart.

I sat back down on the chair and began to nurse the sprouting green bud of new hope. I must have sat there for an hour or more, I'm not sure, and then it happened. I saw Marshal's eyelids flicker. It was like the shiver of first movements of a butterfly wing, impulsive and unmanaged. I stood up to get a better look, a feeling of joy erupting in my heart. Marshal's eyelids began to do more than flicker; they began to blink. And then his eyes came fully open.

I grabbed the blanket and quickly folded it, remembering that the staff could not touch it. Even though Marshal's eyes were open, he appeared to be in a fog, like someone awaking after being anesthetized. I called excitedly for the attending nurse. She came rushing in. She raised her hands to her face and covered her mouth in amazement. She pressed a button on her communication device and nearly shouted out the news.

"Marshal has opened his eyes!"

Within moments, the room had four people in it, including

a doctor. Marshal's eyes were indeed open, but they were fixed and dilated, at least that's what medical personnel said. I noticed the EKG machine began to show a slightly stronger heartbeat. The staff virtually cheered as they examined Marshal. It was clear that he was not completely conscious, but he seemed to have turned a corner.

I carefully watched the other patients. The next to respond was the client who left our suite and went into the bar across from the hotel. I gathered up his blanket, too, before the staff noticed. The man made a gurgling noise, and a nurse rushed over. After checking him, she shouted out, "This man has a heartbeat, too!"

An excited commotion had now filled the room. Yesterday, it was full of gloom and discouragement. Now the ambiance of the room had changed, almost as though it had begun to feel happy. The feeling of jubilation was catching; each staff member was experiencing it, as well. Medical technicians from the CDC were also present and just as excited.

Three people had opened their eyes, then a fourth one. I scrambled to grab the blankets before the medical personnel could touch them. Then to my dismay, the fifth and sixth patients opened their eyes at the same time. I was standing by the sixth one and froze with indecision. To make matters worse, a nurse was standing next to the number five patient. Excitedly, she put her left hand on the blanket, pulling it down a little, exposing more of the patient's body. I broke from my frozen spot and ran to number five before the nurse could do more. I grabbed the blanket and ran back to six, wanting to remove the blankets in order, just as Jonah had instructed and without that blanket being touched by someone other than me.

Now I was in a real dilemma. Two people had awakened at the same time. I was afraid to leave the room. I didn't want to take the blankets into the other room, fearing another patient would awake in my absence. I couldn't take the chance that the nurses would touch *another* blanket. I grabbed the box and began putting the blankets in it as neatly as I could, keeping them in perfect order, while at the same time watching the last two patients. Gratefully, their awakening was not concurrent, so as they awoke, I was able to scoop up the blankets before they were touched by anyone else.

One by one, the eight people in the first room revived to one degree or another. Their EKGs varied in strength, but none showed signs of consciousness. It was as though they were in a coma, which was a significant improvement from being "undead," but still not in optimal condition.

I took the box of blankets into the next room and laid them over the next eight patients. I had kept track of the blanket that the nurse touched, keeping it in the same order, as it was to cover the fifth person in the second room. I knew the patients were to be covered in a specific order, but I wasn't sure if the blankets had to be kept in order, too. I decided to cover the patients not only in order of their admission, but also using the blankets in the same order. I noted that the fifth blanket covered the fifth person in room two.

Again, I sat and waited. As I pondered the recent events, I wondered if the staff would become suspicious of the blankets and their effect on the patients. I began to see a general pattern that varied slightly from one person to another. The patients seemed to awake after 60 to 90 minutes. Over the next hour and a half, all of them passed from the realm of death, near-death, or whatever it might have actually been, to a coma-like state, except for one. That patient was the fifth patient who had been covered by the fifth blanket, the one that had been touched by the nurse. I remembered Jonah's instructions, and I became panicked. I didn't know what to do. *How should I use this fifth blanket, or should I use it all?*

I had been able to manage the next set of blankets without another touching incident. Seven of them were in the box, but I was waiting for the person who was covered by the fifth blanket to respond. I decided to take the seven blankets into the next room and gamble that the woman wouldn't revive while I was covering the next seven people.

My thoughts turned to Anne as I began to cover the people in the third room, the room where she lay. Then my blood ran cold!

Anne was the fifth patient.

I didn't know what to do. The fifth patient in the second room was still "undead." *What was I supposed to do?* Jonah hadn't prepared me for this possibility. I wanted to put the sixth blanket on Anne, for selfish reasons. But then I realized I didn't know the consequences of covering her with the sixth blanket. The words of Jonah echoed through my mind. "*You are an honest man.*"

Am I? What would an honest man do? I thought once more.

I had to make a decision. I didn't know the current status of the fifth patient in the second room. I knew what Jonah had told me, but I didn't know what had truly happened. If I placed the sixth blanket on Anne, would I be doing it for selfish, personal—*actually dishonest*—reasons? Would my personal interests overshadow the proper course?

I thought of the many movies where people were willing to sacrifice nations to protect their loved ones. I had always wondered what I would do in such a case. *Would I bow to my selfishness, or would I do what was seemingly right?*

The problem was that I didn't know what was right. *What would happen if I put the sixth blanket on the fifth patient? Would that affect the healing process? Would it dilute the virtue of the flower that saturated the blankets?*

I could not put off the decision. I bowed to the idea that things had to happen exactly as Jonah had prescribed. It was the hardest thing I had ever done in my life.

As I covered the sixth patient with the sixth blanket, my heart bled with the horrific idea that I may have just sealed Anne's fate. Leaving my wife uncovered, I may have consigned her to the death of a living hell. If that was a possibility, I decided it was better that she passed into a more peaceful, but literal death. But now my forgiving and loving heart was filled with undiluted, wretched anguish.

The Terror of a Choice

AFTER COVERING THE seven patients in the third room, I went back into the second room. The fifth patient was not responding in the way that the others had. After a few minutes, I supposed that I knew all I needed to know. The touch of the blanket had negatively affected her awakening.

I decided to go back to the first room to see what had happened to the fifth patient. I couldn't raise attention to the purpose of the blankets, so I had to ask general questions. At length I learned that all eight patients seemed to be in the same condition. That meant that patient five was doing as well as any of them.

On the way back to Anne's room, I stopped again in room two. The woman under the fifth blanket was in the same condition: catatonic. The other seven patients continued to show signs of revival, but not number five. It was then that I realized she had been the one who had succumbed to the snake shirt in our hotel suite. My guilt became overwhelming when I thought of what was happening.

I left the catatonic woman and went to Anne's room. She lay there, uncovered, and in the same catatonic state. I sat by her side on the now familiar stool. I grasped her hand, which was without warmth, feeling lifeless. I watched her face, stone cold and gray. Looking past the visage of death, I saw the contour of her cheeks, the perfect shape of her nose, and the fullness of her lips. She had been a beautiful woman—and still was.

I lay my forehead on hers as tears began to flow. I was barely able to hold back the sobs that welled in my chest and beyond caring if the staff saw my distress. I just needed the relief of letting go. My emotions poured out like water from a pitcher. The range of terror, fear, happiness, joy, hope and desolation poured into the mix of teardrops, wetting her cold body.

I sat unmoving for the longest time until all of the ache in my heart had been let go. With the pain expelled, there was nothing left. I felt no hope, no faith, and no belief. I could muster no emotion. My psyche had flat-lined.

Despite my neutral mood, I had kept track of time. I don't know why, but something inside forced me to watch my smart phone. At the sixty-minute mark, I began to look about the room. It was then that I decided to take a gamble. I got up and ran back in to room two. I wanted to see how the woman was doing. It took but a moment to see that nothing had changed. I turned and went back to Anne.

I stood in the center of the room where I could see all the patients. My experience told me that they didn't awake by their order. As I watched them, I continued to watch Anne. Feeling a need to put some life back into my body, I began to pace. I walked from one bed to the next, anxiously looking for changes. It was nearly at the ninety-minute mark, when I finally saw the eyelids of another woman blink. I removed the blanket and called for a nurse. They came running, ecstatic that these patients were also responding.

In a pattern similar to the first sixteen people, those in the third room began to awake.

Once more they each had heartbeats, but I did learn from the staff that their brain function had only slightly improved. I wondered what that meant and so did the staff. It was at this point that I became included in the conversation. At first ignored, I now became a focus of their attention. They began discussing the fact that the patients had changed after I had covered them with the blankets. Questions were asked, but I knew I could not tell them the truth. They wouldn't have believed it. I tried my best to joke about the blankets, their design, and label, etc. Some had wanted to touch them, but I wouldn't let them, exclaiming that if they touched them, the magic would be taken. The levity of the idea seemed to quell their need to touch and feel, but I knew it wouldn't hold them off forever.

The third room was a little more crowded; there were actually *nine* beds. *Jensen* was in the ninth bed.

Watching over Anne

I HAD TAKEN THE blanket off the first patient in the third room who had awakened. I placed it over Jensen. Again, I went through rough moments of wanting to cover Anne first, but Jonah's instructions ran through my mind, and I placed the blanket on Jensen. Anne remained unconscious on her bed, without the hope of a healing blanket. When the second person awoke, I quickly grabbed up the blanket and spread it over Anne.

In addition to Anne and Jensen, there were seven more people who needed to wake. I continued to survey the room, watching for the next sign of improvement. While waiting for these last seven patients to respond, I thought of the last two bodies, Anne and Jensen The scenario troubled me. Jonah had given me strict instructions. "He is the twenty-fifth man. He must be the last to be covered. Fail in the progression, and all will be lost."

I wondered if Jonah had known that the twenty-fifth body was Jensen. I suspected she did. Of course she couldn't have known that one of the blankets would be touched and damaged. She couldn't have known that I faced the choice of covering Jensen before Anne. *Or had she seen the future and understood?*

The staff, now watching me with purpose, quizzed me once more about the blankets. In an odd way I was glad for the distraction. I simply said, "This is my way of serving these people. Many of them are my friends, and I feel responsible." I pointed to Anne and said, "She is my wife, and he is a close friend."

Gratefully, they gave me the space I needed, and went about their own work, which they felt was still critical. I'd heard little news about the people in the first room. They hadn't regained consciousness, and the staff, though hopeful, was still clearly worried about them. In a way, I was pleased with that turn of events. It kept them focused on the patients and not on my blankets and me. As they continued to give me free reign, I accomplished my duty, which had truly become an act of love. After all, I knew most of them, and I cared for them.

To this point, most of the patients had been close friends, business acquaintances, with just a few strangers. None of them were as emotionally close to me as Anne. I had certainly felt a sense of relief as the others revived, but the fabric of my world was tied to Anne, and I desperately wanted to her to react and revive. I thought once more about the goodness in the blanket and tried again to imagine what that could be. *How can an inert object, soaked in a potion, have an effect on a dying woman?*

These thoughts were tempered by the idea that the blanket may not even be efficacious for Anne. I began to wonder if I might be sabotaging that goodness because my faltering belief was causing chinks in the virtue of my thoughts. The battle for Anne was so much more important to me, and that increased my anxiety. I wondered if I could maintain the apparent requirements of belief and goodness long enough for Anne to regain her life.

Anne's Nature

It was as if time did not exist. I didn't know if it had been hours, days, or years. It might have been an eternity. It had been sheer torture to live with only my mental awareness, an awareness that was without physical sensation. It was its own kind of literal hell. Then without any warning, I noticed a change. I decided that I had been in a slow state of deterioration, but it seemed to have stopped. My awareness of the intellects around me became more certain, just slightly, but it was an improvement. The change in my ordeal gave me a greater sense of hope. Just as I had been aware of the other intellects like me, I realized there were also even more intellects moving around us, interested in our state, in a seeming effort to help.

My mind shifted to a new realization; there was a host of simple intellects in numbers too large to comprehend or count. I could not communicate with them, but I sensed comradery as they gathered around me. They radiated a feeling of kindness, of mutual existence.

They came to me—covered me—began to warm me—then it *dawned* on me; I had actually felt the warmth. It was my first awareness of the return of my physical body. The warmth was barely detectable at first, but it increased. As I searched my surroundings, I started to believe it was coming from all those simple intellects that had so kindly gathered around me, covering and bathing me in their warmth. It was something I had not experienced before.

No. That is not true.

This experience was different from any previous one, but it caused me to reflect on small moments in my life when I had been guided to something important, when some kind of sixth sense whispered both what to do and what not to do. There was a similarity; I felt a warmth in my heart, in my chest, which encouraged me to have *hope*.

While un-marked time passed, I felt as though the intellects were gathering more closely around me. In some way that I couldn't conceive, they were healing me. As they did, the warmth increased—*and this was the precursor to a miracle*. I could feel my body again. I felt happiness beyond description, realizing the gaping hole of discontent and misery spawned by the absent sensations of my corporeal being, was being replaced with the physical. Simply put, I had missed my body in a way that surprised me. The reuniting of physical sensations with my intellect was almost more than I could bear in terms of happiness and joy. It felt as if tears were beginning to flow, and I could feel the pulse of blood throughout my body.

Jensen Gains Understanding

ALL I HAD KNOWN was the void that had persisted. It had seemed endless. *There was no hope. There was no future. There was no next minute.* All had been stripped from me. I didn't seem to be thinking real thoughts, only surmising the ghosts of awareness. It was a fate worse than death itself. In fact, the best I could do with the meager resources of mental sensation was to hope for death. I wished for a death that would take me away to a state of pure darkness where even thought and awareness were non-existent. I deemed such a state to be better than the current residence of my thoughts.

While enduring an endless void of eternal quiet, I began to sense something. It was far away. I could not tell what it was. There was no identity around it, but I could tell one thing; *it was not friendly.* I felt it was *angry* with me. It didn't seem malicious, but there was no doubt it *was* angry. The sensation began to surround me. In a strange way, this gathering anger was a relief, definitively better than the previous nothingness. I still had no sense of time or space, just this angry entity coalescing around me; but suddenly it fractured into a million pieces.

Then it began. I could see uncounted fingers pointing at me. At first, everything was bathed in quiet, except for the pointing fingers. Then I felt rumblings, deep rumblings, and vibrations that suggested the dawn of a physical reality. It was the tactile sensation of the *physical* world for which I had *longed*, for which I had *yearned.* But the pointing fingers muted my yearning.

As I labored under the weight of my misery, I had a new experience. It was thrilling, terrifying. My ears burst with the return of sound, almost more than I could stand. Just as suddenly, I felt the emotions of my heart. But the emotions were bitter, and I began to dismay. And now voices accompanied the host of fingers. They shouted, they roared, hissed, and snarled. "Murderer!" they bellowed. "Destroyer of life, harbinger of death!" With fingers pointing they cried, "Dishonest, liar, bearer of falsehoods!" I felt simultaneous waves of guilt and terror and hopelessness.

I didn't understand. I cast my mind about trying to comprehend, but all I knew was confusion, prompted by the return of physical awareness and the myriad fingers that continued pointing at me; even the shouting became more intense. All at once, events of the past days came flooding back. I remembered the o-wom'n, Mothe' Moses. I remembered her admonition, *"You be shua,"* and *"Check be good tamora, too?"* The feeling of greed, like a black and poisoning dart, pricked at my skin. I remembered the check, and how I had stopped it. The snake shirts came into my mind, and the venomous eyes bored once more into me, in a repeat of the moment when the gaping snake mouth swallowed me up in agony. The tongue licked my face and with every touch, it screamed, "Impostor, deceiver, swindler, cheat!"

In this unreal state, the great mouth opened once more. Venom dripped from the vicious fangs. From the lower jaw came a second set of fangs. The toxic ooze seeped from both the top and bottom fangs set in a hinged jaw, which *unhinged*, opening wide, then wider still. Once more it took me into its black gullet. The repugnance was revolting. Terror struck me to the quick. I was filled with fear and loathing, and I recanted my rejoicings regarding the physical world.

Then, in the flash of a moment, I was looking about with different eyes. The world in my new view was cast in blues, and oranges, and reds. I saw colors shifting before me. I hated them. I hated the smell that pierced the pits on my face. I flicked my tongue. I sampled the air. Something was there. It was too large for prey, but it had to be killed. It was in my domain. I was cornered. There was no way to escape but to fill the intruder with my poisons.

I struck and missed. I struck again and missed again. I struck, I struck, *and I struck*. With each lightning strike, my fangs found only thin and sickly air. Then I realized I had been tricked. Nothing was there but flashes of color. At once the colors began to sting my eyes. The pits above my mouth burned with smells so toxic that I recoiled. I rolled into a ball. I was completely defensive. I played dead.

I held my flicking tongue and tried to sense through my viperous pits alone. The smell was overpowering, and I passed once more into oblivion—an oblivion that satisfied my need to escape. It was done. I was beyond all understanding and all pain. All I knew was *nothing*.

Jensen's Heartbeat

I WAS STANDING BY THE TABLE where Anne lay, while watching Jensen from a distance. He was the last one to have been covered with one of the untouched blankets. But most of my attention was focused on Anne. In those moments all the marital annoyances, frustrations, and disappointments became as nothing. I reflected on the good, the kindness, and the happiness I had experienced with her. The sputtering spark of love, concealed deeply within my heart suddenly burst into full flame. I felt as I had in the first moments of our meeting. My mouth went dry, and I remembered the fear I felt in searching for just the right words. *What should I say? What should I do?* The common pickup lines seemed trite. And besides, she was someone I really wanted to know. So I simply said, "Hi, my name is Bob."

I remembered the look she gave me, as though sizing me up.

I remembered sweating.

In my memory she turned toward me, still silent.

I felt a gut-wrenching spasm so deep in my core that it nearly made me retch.

In that moment, I was terrified and yet filled with hope, futile hope perhaps, but hope.

At last she said, "My name is Anne."

That was the beginning and though stricken with a flash of anger at some of our later experiences, I was convinced once more that she was the one I loved. I could feel the fabric of our love. It was strong and beautiful, a tapestry of the finest material and weave; a tapestry that I wanted to preserve. Then the anger disappeared.

I was shocked from my reverie and impressed with my renewed commitment to Anne as I heard the beep of Jensen's EKG monitor. I turned toward him. His eyes were wide open. I jumped up and rushed to his bed. What I saw was a vapid stare that turned to terror before my gaze. I could see that he was in pain, and it was a pain greater than I could imagine. He began gasping, and his mouth opened. He hissed three guttural and barely distinguishable words. *"No. No. No."*

While removing his blanket, I wondered what had taken him. His reaction was unlike the other patients. I called for the doctor. A nurse rushed to his side. This was clearly a new reaction to her. She, too, called for help and a debate ensued. "What shall we do?"

They appeared in a quandary, standing transfixed, as if mesmerized by the man hissing, *"No!"*

It was the sound of the EKG that broke the seeming trance. In the quiet of the moment the beeps became a thunder. His EKG showed that his heart was racing. His EEG, which I had learned to interpret, showed impossibly active brainwaves.

"Should we give him a sedative?"

"No!" cried one doctor.

Another said, "He is seizing!"

"No! It doesn't fit!"

The staff was clearly frantic with confusion.

Jensen's Choice

I RETURNED FROM NOTHINGNESS. My great head, still in the form of a snake, was weaving back and forth. Playing dead had changed nothing, because I was alive once more with both pain and the threat of the intruder. Bluff and bluster became my tactic. I opened my mouth and hissed. I looked for the eyes of something or someone that I could mesmerize. There was nothing—nothing I could bite or intimidate. My frantic attempts were all failing. I twisted and curled, writhed and struck into the air. My eyes were burning with brilliant colors. My sensing pits were on fire, and my frantically flicking tongue tasted the bitter air of my environment, but I could find no enemy. Consumed by fatigue and fear, I gave up once more. I lay still, not faking death, but feeling death. "Fine. Let it be. Whatever it is, let it be. I surrender."

Snakes cannot hear, but we feel vibrations, and it was the vibrations I noticed. Typically, I would be searching for the vibrations of a mouse or a rat. That was not what I felt; these vibrations were different. They grew in intensity and, as they grew, I felt a change in my surroundings.

I began to feel as if thinking creatures surrounded me. Well, not creatures per se, but they existed and they had thoughts.

In one voice they asked, "Have you suffered enough?"

With all my heart, for I had no voice, I cried, "Yes! Yes, I have suffered—and suffered enough!"

"There is one who can save you and justify you—if you change."

"Yes! I will change! Please take me from this wretched existence!"

Then I saw something. It was an apparition of some kind. It had no body, but it had a form. I recognized the form but not the personage.

"Who are you?" I asked.

"I am one who can assist you. I will touch your heart when you need me, and show you the way when you falter. However, I will leave you if you purposely turn away from me."

"I will do as you say."

"You have wronged many. You will need to redress your wrongs."

"I will. I will!"

"You must travel a new path. The path will be difficult, and you will want to turn back, but remember your misery, let it guide you, and you'll find the strength to succeed."

As Though in Unison

I WAS WATCHING JENSEN'S face. It had been contorted like one being pricked by a thousand needles, but suddenly it changed. It changed to one of peace. His heart rate changed to a normal sinus rhythm on the EKG. His brainwaves also became normal. Then his eyes began to blink. With each blink, his pupils became more and more responsive until they appeared normal. The doctors and nurses looked at each other in astonishment.

Jensen took upon himself the look of recognition, and a smile spread across his face. "It is done," he said, and he sat up.

I looked at Jensen in amazement. He was awake. He looked healthy and happy. And then something very amazing happened. Almost as one, the other seven patients in that one room raised their heads. I heard a Texas holler that could only have come from Marshal. It was all very exciting. The medical staff wore great smiles. The fully awake patients were clearly relieved, but they seemed to be holding back as if they were unsure of their current status and completely puzzled by their experience.

Despite the jubilation, I went to Anne's bed and sat calmly by her side. She was the discord to the event. She was the one who had not raised her head from a place of near death. But then I remembered there might be another. Without saying a word, I slipped away to look at the fifth patient, the woman in the second room. It was an incredible contrast in emotions. Just as the staff and patients were celebrating the joy of the moment, one very emotional doctor was covering her with a blanket.

I walked up to the bed, and he turned to me. I couldn't speak, but didn't have to. He understood my question.

"I'm afraid we've lost this one. Her heart has ceased to function and her brainwaves are nonexistent."

He pulled the blanket back from one arm. I saw a deep surgical cut. There was no oozing blood and no inflammation around the cut.

The doctor volunteered an explanation. "We made an incision to see if she would bleed. She didn't. We don't know what was different, but for some reason, this woman didn't survive."

I looked at the woman. I remembered her loud northeastern attitude. She had not been one of my clients but I knew of her. I knew she had a family, and that she ran a successful retail clothing business. It was sad to think that something so seemingly inconsequential as the touching of her blanket could end in such bitter finality.

And then I thought of Anne. I ran back to the third room. I was terrified that in the few moments I had been gone, some medical technician would be making the determination of her life or death. I burst through the door frame, nearly hitting the far side of it. In an instant my mind found some level of relief. There were no white-coated doctors standing over Anne with scalpels in hand. But that was a small relief in pressure cooker of emotion.

Culmination

I watched Anne more closely than I had any of the other patients throughout the ordeal. My thoughts were swinging back and forth like a pendulum, from hope to despair. I tried to apply Jonah's instruction to believe. *I struggled to believe.* I struggled for *goodness,* not knowing from minute to minute the level of my success.

I continued to sit by her side. The moments turned into an hour. The room was busy with doctors and nurses giving the patients complete physicals right there in the room. The medical staff was consumed with the need to understand what had taken place. There were lots of questions, sprinkled with the joy of victory.

Occasionally, I could both see and sense that they were looking at me. Jensen was the most consumed with his interest in Anne and me. His bed was close, and I could easily hear him asking the medical team about Anne's condition. Sadly, there was nothing they could say. They still had no answers. There was one negative, of course, the woman in the second room had passed away.

In my agony, I clung to Anne's hand, hoping desperately to feel a change. Then almost imperceptibly, I noticed something. Slowly, very slowly, a bit of color returned to her face. I said nothing to the staff, although they were constantly looking my way, each with their own version of anticipation. I didn't want to break any kind of positive Karma that may have existed. I also realized that her cold hand seemed to be slightly warmer. The time was interminable; the progress slow. *But then it happened.*

I saw her eyelids flutter, ever so slightly. Then her heart monitor beeped, and there it was, the glorious sinus rhythm of her heart. I cannot express the feelings that filled me. I leaned over her. I kissed her on the forehead. Her eyes opened, but appeared vacant. And then I saw it. A tiny tear slowly formed in her eye and trailed onto her cheek. I began to believe the worst was past.

I grabbed the blanket and called to the staff, "Her heart is beating, too!"

All at once, the medical personnel rushed to the last patient who seemed to have turned a corner. They rushed to *see*, but there was little they could *do*. In fact, all they could do was monitor her vital signs. It had been the same for every patient. They knew that this patient, Anne, was my wife, and they also knew that there was nothing anyone could do but wait. If the patients were to improve, each would have to revive from their coma. They cautioned me and told me they didn't understand what was taking place. I didn't understand either, but I still had my desire to believe that Anne would be completely healed.

Some might say I had developed faith and, after giving it some thought, I think that may be accurate. I considered that my desire to believe had pushed me into this state of faith. I knew that for hours I had been walking the path *toward* faith, but I also felt something else. *That walk of faith had been the precursor to hope.* I had seen evidence of improvement, and I believed it would continue. The staff seemed to note my demeanor, and I knew I'd been the subject of whispered discussions. I'm sure they would like to have asked me about it, but circumstances didn't allow for such Q&A. I noticed the look of respect as they watched me, my beloved Anne, and the connection that existed between us.

Wrapping Up

THE DOCTORS BEGAN ASKING QUESTIONS. There was a different answer for every patient in the three rooms. Not one agreed with another. Later, under more controlled circumstances, each patient was interviewed, but there was still no agreement. What I learned, later still, was that the patients were afraid to speak of what had really happened, so they all spun stories that hid the real truth.

Since no civil laws had been broken, the police backed off. The CDC identified no bacteria or virus, so they all went home. The doctors could establish no medical cause. It was left to the psychiatrists and psychologists. Initially, authorities believed the patients would all need counseling. That turned out to be untrue. One thing became clear in their psychological evaluation. None were telling the truth about their experience.

After a day of endless discussions, the city and the medical establishment decided to make a statement. News of the odd illness had spread, despite their best efforts to control it. People wanted to know if they were in danger. Before things got out of control, the police located all 120 shirts. Just to be safe, and with Jensen's agreement, they were incinerated at a biohazard facility. The official line was that the ink that had been used in the shirts was tainted and had made some people sick. They went on to say that after the shirts had been removed from the patients, their bodies had fought the contaminants, and their immune systems overcame the ink poisoning. Eventually every patient, except the woman from the northeast, returned to good health.

In the few days of convalescence, while they were still together, the patients quietly and surreptitiously discussed the reality of their experience with each other. They concluded that the authorities and the public would never understand what had really happened. The decision was unanimous and a private pact was established. They would never reveal the truth of the details of their experience to the authorities.

I tried to stand on the sidelines of the discussion but was helplessly drawn into it. A very stark reality existed. Everyone knew the patients had recovered after I placed the blankets on them. That's why I had returned them to Jonah. I simply told the authorities and the patients that I had disposed of them. I convinced them that I was sure the blankets were only a coincidental element of the story.

It became apparent to me that two of the patients had slightly different experiences, and as such, they had a different understanding of what had taken place. Jensen and Anne had held back their complete experience from the other patients, including me. Of course none of the patients were aware of the details being withheld by my wife and friend, but I knew there was something more. First of all, I knew the entire story. Secondly, I saw the whispering between Jensen and Anne and the knowing looks they shared. Not wanting to be left out, I pressed Anne. After serious consideration, she told me the complete story.

Jensen said I was his best friend, and he had to come clean with me with all the details, even those he did not share with the group. After considerable discussion, they both agreed to include me in their circle.

One night, Jensen and I sat up late, alone, just the two of us. He began to tell me his story from the beginning, which had actually started long before the convention. He told me of his misdeeds, right up to the point when he had put the stop payment on Mother Moses's check. He told me about a very large debt that was hanging over his head and about other people he had cheated in hope of retiring the debt. He told me of his dream in the hotel. Most importantly, he told me of his experiences while under the spell of the snake. My skin truly crawled as he explained the void, the pointing fingers, and the voices. My heart nearly froze when he told me of the snake and how, in the end, he had *become* the snake.

It was at this point that Jensen told me his secret—a secret that he and Anne shared. He told me about the appearance of a *figure*.

"Who was it," I asked.

"I don't know," was his response.

Facing him, I asked, "Was it God?"

Shaking his head, he said, "No, I don't think so."

"Was it Jesus?"

Still shaking his head, he replied, "No. I don't think it was Jesus either."

After his last response, we sat quietly for a rather long period. At last he spoke, "I don't know, but since that time, I've felt it with me. I think it's some kind of spirit. It touches me inside in a way that is quiet and still. The voice was not a voice at all, but more an impression. All I know is that it brought, and *still* brings, me comfort."

I sat quietly after his last revelation. I believed Jensen's story and appreciated his candor.

"Did Anne have the same experience?" I asked.

He was hesitant but finally said, "It was similar."

He was quiet for a few minutes, and then he said, "Though there were similarities, there were just as many differences."

In that moment, I was the only other person who knew the true and complete story of the two accounts, and it made a difference to me. Our lives were changed in ways we never expected.

Extra Time

ANNE AND I DECIDED to spend some extra time in New Orleans, extending our stay at the Royal Sonesta. We felt it was important to face the events in every way we could. The staff could not have been kinder and more courteous. They treated us like royalty.

On our last day, we walked to Jackson Square. I told her I wanted to walk the same route I ran in the middle of the night. We went to the same coffee shop and, at last, we went to the Voodoo Shop. To my surprise the door was locked and a sign had been placed in the window that said, "Permanently Closed." I peered through the windows into the store. The room was dark and there were no goods to be seen. I expressed disappointment to Anne. I had disclosed my feelings about Jonah to Anne, and I wanted one more visit with Jonah that could have been a shared experience. My time with Jonah became a treasured memory. Not only had she calmed my nerves, her potion had healed my broken ribs. More importantly, she had helped to heal twenty-four patients. And as I looked at Anne, I knew Jonah had helped heal our marriage.

Perhaps the biggest miracle for me was the lesson of what it means to be a good man, a humble man. I would carry that lesson, mingled with thoughts of Mother Moses, with me for the rest of my life and knew my life would be different because of it.

I held Anne's hand as we walked past where the old pastry shop once was. We understood it had opened elsewhere, but we knew it wouldn't be the same, and we didn't want to change the memory. We walked hand in hand to the Café du Monde. The beignets were still as they had been, delicious to the last bite.

After leaving the beignet shop, we walked along Decatur Street. As we continued on I noticed a horse-drawn carriage for hire. I suggested that we take a ride. Anne agreed.

The driver, a woman, took us through the French Quarter. She said she had a treat for us. Taking back roads that avoided busy streets, we ended up in the Garden District. We rode under the dappled shade of old, sturdy, and often sweetly scented trees. The feeling was pastoral. It was free and easy, and we were filled with romance.

Finally, we arrived back at Jackson Square. We had been gone more than two hours, and I wondered if there would be an added cost. I asked the driver if we owed more than the original fare. "No," she said. "The extra time is my gift to you."

I dipped my head and said, "Thank you, but please let me give you a larger tip."

I opened my wallet and pulled out a $50 bill. When I held out the bill, a very small and wrinkled hand reached for it. The hand surprised me. I had never looked directly at the female driver. I thought about asking her how she maneuvered us to the Garden District without crossing the busy streets of New Orleans. I didn't think such a route existed. I decided to leave things as they were. They were just too perfect to disturb.

We turned to walk away, but I heard a strong voice, in broken English say, *"You be a good man, a humble man."*

I stopped in my tracks and turned, but the driver slapped the reins on the horse's back. At once the carriage was on its way. I watched as they clip-clopped into the distance. The driver had a familiar form. *How could I have missed that?* She was hunched over and wearing an old faded baseball cap from which hung her gray and wiry hair. I watched for a while and then turned toward Anne. She had walked a few steps ahead. But suddenly an odd feeling came over me, and I could swear that I heard the sound of rattlers, and an echo of the words, "Ma babies respec' yuh." I turned around to look once more, but there was no carriage and no old woman.

POSTSCRIPT

It had been six months since I'd seen Bob, but I wanted to talk to him. I called and arranged a lunch appointment on my next trip to New York. We chatted light-mindedly about this and that and had a good meal. I wasn't particularly surprised when he asked me a serious question.

"How are you, really, and how is business?"

I was only too happy to answer, and, in fact, it was why I had called him.

"You know, I've changed. I've changed as a person, and I've changed the way I do business. I used to think I had to cheat people to make a buck. After our experience, I made a commitment to be honest with people. And, you know, I've actually made more money being honest. I guess I've been trying to live up to the counsel that Mother Moses gave to you, to be an honest man. And speaking of Mother Moses, I drove back out into the bayou to pay her cash for the shirts. She wasn't there. The old store and the gas station were still there, but they were boarded up. I knocked on the door of the trailer and at the house on stilts. No one answered. I asked around and was told that she had suddenly left, and no one knew where she was. Her reputation remains, but she has disappeared. It was as though they were protecting her disappearance. She's an enigma, Bob, a pure enigma."

I watched Bob's face as he mulled over what I had said. He finally responded, "Yes, she is an enigma."

We sat in the quiet restaurant, uncommon in New York, and for a period of time said nothing. I had something to say but felt guilty and embarrassed, therefore I was hesitant. At last I spoke up.

"I've got something I need to tell you."

Bob sat his cup down on the table. He looked at me seriously and nodded his head. "Go ahead."

"I had an odd experience. One day, while having lunch alone, a man approached me. He introduced himself as a researcher at a university and was studying the culture of the swamps. He told me he had heard about the incident in New Orleans. He wanted to interview me, and he offered me a very large sum of money for the interview. He told me the purpose was not to publish the story, but to research the information in the story. I told him I'd have to think about it.

"I contacted Marshal and some of my friends and clients who were patients and asked them if they would approve of my sharing the story with the researcher. Since we had made our agreement of secrecy as a group, we decided to get together as a group. I called Anne, too. I'm assuming she said nothing to you?"

A look of surprise spread across Bob's face. "You all discussed this without me?"

I dropped my eyes, "Yes, without you."

Bob gave me a look that doubled my feelings of guilt and asked, "Why didn't you include me?"

Still staring at the table, I answered the question. "I'm sorry. It was a group decision, and although you were critical to our return to health, we were the ones who felt the intellects around us. The man was specifically asking about the intellects. He is studying similar stories and wants to learn if they are real or a figment of people's dreams. He was also tying bits and pieces of stories together that came from other people who seem to have had, or still have a relationship with—things. Not with people, but with things."

Bob just sat there looking stricken. After a long moment, he spoke up. "Anne told me about the intellects in her experience. In fact, we have discussed them at length. Certain ideas have grown out of our discussion. Many people believe that Mother Nature is more than fairy tale. Anne's story painted a picture of a world that is alive, not inanimate, as we so often consider it to be. Anne has developed a feeling that life exists on a level and state that we cannot see or detect. In fact, she had been reading a theory by a physicist who talks about truth and intelligence and relates it all to matter. I think she has developed a personal conclusion that the physicist's theory might be true."

Now it was my turn to process Bob's words and the reason I had called him to meet me. I continued with my purpose and explained, "Knowing that you didn't know, has bothered me. And I couldn't be sure that Anne would keep our secret. I want to be an honest man, in all respects. I wanted to come clean with you. I contacted the group and gained permission to discuss the matter with you. I didn't just call you out of the blue, I wanted to tell you about the researcher."

Bob picked up his fork and clinked it against the plate a few times, and then he sat up straight in his chair. His look was kind and he said, "I can see that you are an honest man."

A smile began to spread over his face, and I broke into a smile of relief. Inside I felt a wave of liberation. I felt like my penance was complete.

We sat for another moment, this time in comfortable silence. Finally, Bob spoke up and said, "Have you had any more contact with the researcher?"

"No," he said, "not a word."

Bob moved in his chair, as though trying to become more comfortable and said,""I'm going to mail you a copy of the scientific papers that Anne has been reading. They are entitled "The Theoretical Operation of Truth and Intelligence." It is an amazing read, and the thing is, the subject sounds just like the subject your researcher is questioning." Bob hesitated, but I knew he had more to say. I waited for his next line.

"Jensen, you have changed, and I think you'll find the theory to be an enlightening one, especially the theorist's concept of truth and intelligence. And you'll have fun reflecting on the changes in your life. There is still so much that I don't understand. I don't understand how a flower, some herbs could be combined to create a solution that seemed to focus the goodness of the world upon each of you, healing you. I don't understand it, but it happened, and it also made me a better man."

I focused on Bob's eyes. I could tell that he meant what he had just said. I felt the satisfaction of peace in the kind words of my best friend—and the echo of the words, *"You be shua."*

I LOVE MY SAN FRANCISCO CONDOMINIUM on Russian Hill. From its vantage point, I can look over the San Francisco Marina, the crest of Lombard Street, the island of Alcatraz, and the distant city of Sausalito. To the right is the grand landmark of Coit Tower. Behind it is the critical transportation artery of the Oakland Bay Bridge. Off to the left is the ever present, and universally loved, Golden Gate Bridge.

It was early, and I had stepped out onto my balcony with a steaming cup in my hand. The sun was just beginning to peak over the mountains to the East that look down upon Oakland and Berkeley. It was the golden hour of dawn. The Oakland hills were still dressed in shadow. Alcatraz Island was just beginning to brighten in the rays of the morning sun. The orange paint of San Francisco's most treasured landmark gleamed gold.

I stood in awe of the beauty of the Golden Gate Bridge glowing in the morning light. The scene seemed to testify to the idea of constancy. I took in a big breath of fresh ocean air, filled my lungs, and stretched my arms. With great vigor, I exhaled, expecting to see the white condensation of my breath in the chill of the morning. To my shock, the vapor was wispy black, and my mind instantly and revoltingly shrank from the image of the dark throat of the viper and the release of its evil black smoke. All at once, constancy, and the satisfaction of my new lifestyle seemed in peril . . .

ACKNOWLEDGMENTS

Designing a cover for *Cajun Justice* was more difficult than normal. This book had to have a snake on the cover, but that idea was unsettling. Nevertheless, I searched the Internet for images of snakes with their fangs extended.

Serendipity is a wonderful principle and in full effect when I found a most unusual serpent image. I had never seen anything like it before, either in person, in the media, and certainly not like any snakes on our farm or at our current property. And it was nothing like the rattlesnakes I found in some of the fields I worked as a young man. The image also had no label, and no photographer's name was attached.

It took several months to find the original photo on Flickr where the photographer had uploaded it. His original photograph had a caption that partially explained the condition of the snake. It read: "The festering evil carcass of a juvenile Bamboo Viper (Trimeresurusalbo labris). Lantau Island, Hong Kong." (https://www.flickr.com/photos/cowyeow/6099623176/in/photolist-ai1asq-ahxmkr-ai1aqq)

At last, I found the photographer's name, Daniel Rosenberg, was able to contact him, and received permission to use his photograph. Brian C. Hailes is the artist who created the cover painting using Daniel's photo image as the model.

With gratitude, I acknowledge Daniel Rosenberg, who captured the image of the carcass of the Bamboo Viper. Mr. Rosenberg is a world traveler and many of his photos can be viewed on his Flickr account: https://www.flickr.com/photoscowyeow. The dead snake was found in a water conduit (cement canal) on Lantau Island, Hong Kong.

The amazing story about this serpent was that it seemingly froze in death in the act of striking, with fangs extended. Kevin Messenger, who accompanied Mr. Rosenberg on their "herping" (searching for reptiles) expedition in Hong Kong, made this comment. "It was a dead juvenile Bamboo Viper that seemingly died in mid-strike . . . it was really weird.

The snake obviously baked in the sun, but the striking 'motion' seems like an odd way for an animal to die." I will add that it had either drowned, starved, or became dehydrated in the empty water conduit in which it was found in it's still angry striking pose.

Kevin Messenger, from Huntsville, Alabama, was visiting Daniel Rosenberg to go "herping." Mr. Messenger is a dual PhD candidate. If you are interested in his four-day field report, check out this link: http://www.Fieldherpforum.com/forum/viewtopic.php?f=2&t=9668. You can read about their experiences with cobras, kraits, and more.

Both Daniel Rosenberg and Kevin Messenger are excellent photographers and have posted wonderful photographs of their many journeys. If you are a herpetologist, you'll enjoy looking through their work.

— Lee R. Hadley

ABOUT THE AUTHOR

Lee R. Hadley is a leader in thought and action, and no blind follower, who draws from his diversity in mixing truth, fiction, and genre types into unusually fascinating tales.

He describes growing up on his father's Idaho farms as an animating paradise. Exploring the endless banks of the Payette River, riding horses along the Snake River, and driving fast cars over open roads were some of the formative backdrops for his young imagination. In his youthful wonderment, he never imagined the wide range of his future interests and delights.

Creativity is Lee's natural instinct, yet he was drawn into a career of sales and marketing. Outside of work, Lee relishes DIY projects. He redesigned and built his home, and rebuilt car engines for both driving and racing. Along with landscaping and gardening at his home, Lee processed film and printed photographs in his personal darkroom. He became a videographer, creating superb amateur videos. Lee is a modern Renaissance man winning awards in Retold Story, music composition, engineering, and music video production. Traveling to forty-six states, China, Europe, and the countries of North America, he has seen much of the world. His diverse interests often caused him to joke about what he might do when he finally grows up.

At the center of Lee's happiness is his marriage of forty-three years. He and his loving wife, Sandra, have five upstanding children and seven delightful grandchildren. His life is filled with the joy of family, teaching religion classes on Sundays, the roar of Hemi engines, and the interplay of light, matter, music, and emotion in photography and videography. Lee is known for his heart, compassion, and in seeing the good in others.

Nearly fifty years after leaving the family farm, Lee began writing a novel. Today, it is a trilogy known as *The Towers Series. Book One, Origins,* imagines an apocalyptic scenario, all too timely for our day.

Book Two, Morning of Despair, and *Book Three, Providence*, carry the story forward in this geopolitical thriller with a supernatural conclusion. *Despair* and *Providence* are in final edit. *Towers of Peace*, the trilogy that follows, is in composition. Lee attacks his writing with vision and passion, and has clearly answered the questions of his vocation.

Please enjoy the Prologue
to my first book
in my trilogy, *The Tower Series, Origins.*
If you like it, please send me a message on my Facebook page
at https://www.facebook.com/leerhadleybooks/.

—Lee R. Hadley

ORIGINS

Prologue

"Will there be monsters? A smile spread across Haleema's face as the game began. FarZan, her seven-year-old son, feared monsters but loved to be scared by bedtime monster stories.

Tucking the bedding around him, she answered, "That depends. What is a monster?"

"Monsters are big and strong, stronger than men, and they have sharp teeth and eyes that are red as coals—and they roar at you, rrrraaahh."

FarZan's hands sprang into the air, fingers curled like the claws of an Iranian cheetah. She saw look in his eyes—they projected courage, which Haleema knew would slink away after the lights went out. Haleema noticed at the same time, FarZan nervously watching the shifting projections of shadow and light on the plain wall behind her, which were cast and transfigured by the blowing and billowing window curtains. A playful growl escaped Haleema's throat, and her eyes opened widely to express the potential incarnation of bedroom monsters. She envisioned the workings of FarZan's mind, thinking he might conjure evil shades of gray and black pierced by shards of occasional light; the combination translating into both his thrill and fear—monsters.

Haleema was born in 1985, six years after the Islamic Revolution of Iran. She was sixteen years old and married with three children. Satisfied with the comfort and repose of her daughters she continued to lavish her attention on her only son, FarZan.

It was just after sunset and the family had completed the evening Salaat, known in Islam as Maghrib, the final prayer of the day for Shia Muslims. Merchants in the Grand Bazaar were closing their shops and securing their outdoor displays, the activity sourcing the erratic light displays.

"No my son, the story has no scary red-eyed monsters, but there are monsters of another sort."

"Another sort, what does that mean?"

It means that they are monstrous in what they do but they don't have sharp teeth and scary red eyes."

"What do they look like?"

"They aren't animals like Cheetahs or lions. They don't walk on four legs."

With large feigning eyes he asked, "Are they snakes?"

"Oh no, not snakes my dear, our monsters don't slither across the ground, but they are cunning and devious."

The monster game had become a nightly ritual which Haleema often used to teach new principles to FarZan.

"How will I know if I see one?"

Haleema added a new facet, "You can't always tell them at first. Some monsters look scary. Other monsters may look beautiful or handsome, but if you could see inside, they would be scary."

"You mean their tummies are scary?"

Chuckling she responded, "No, that's not what I mean by inside."

"I don't understand," FarZan said in a more serious tone.

Haleema moved closer to FarZan, and in a quiet voice continued, "We don't have real monsters in our world, but there are those who act like monsters. Some people call the monsters man, but I don't like to use the word man because I think mankind, as a whole, is good. I believe that the worst monsters are simply inside some men."

Not quite catching the change from childhood games to real life, FarZan playfully asked, "Men, you say the monsters are men?"

"Some men are monstrous, but not all. Most men are good. Women can also be monstrous, but that is more unusual."

FarZan finally caught the shift from fantasy to reality, and more thoughtfully asked, "How can I tell if a man is a monster?"

FarZan was very intuitive and Haleema confidently believed, that over time, he would understand.

"You have to watch very carefully. We all have monsters inside of us. Most of the time, our monsters are controlled and hidden away. Sometimes the monsters in men act like monsters in caves. They come out in their fierceness to attack their prey then slink back into their cave for its protection. A man's monstrous nature may show in his face then slink back into the shadows of pretense. We see the evidence of a man's monster in his actions."

As Haleema spoke, her mind flicked to an image of her husband, and her self-applied label of "monster". She wanted FarZan to grow into something more benevolent than her husband.

"Some men purposely let their monsters out to feed them, making them more powerful. To know which men have fed their internal monsters you must observe them, watching carefully, examining their actions. If they do many bad things, their monster has become strong and powerful, and that man may have grown into a monster. If they do good things, they have likely learned to control their monsters. The great majority of mankind has monsters that they have learned to control."

Lovingly brushing a wisp of hair from FarZan's eyes, she uttered her inner prayer, that he would become a man who controls his monsters.

"If there are monstrous men around, will you protect me from them until I can tell who they are?"

"I will as long as I am with you. But if I should ever leave, Allah will help you recognize the monsters and keep you safe."

"I hope you are always with me, Mother."

"So do I, my dearest son."

"Since there are no real monsters, will this be a true story?"

"It is a story with both fiction and truth. It is for you to recognize the truths in the story. Just remember that most of the story is fiction but you may gather truths and use them for your good."

"How did you learn the story?"

"I learned it through life."

Haleema watched FarZan as he turned to look at the window with skittering light along the edges. She saw him look back across his small bedroom to the phantoms playing on a wall void of everything but a poster of the Persian Tree of Life. She loved the evening moments when she told FarZan her invented stories. Haleema leaned over and kissed FarZan on the forehead, at the same time anticipating his quiet tip toe over the wooden floor of their urban apartment seeking her reassurance that there were in fact no monsters. That solace was often brief or unattained, his father's stern and scolding voice too often sending him hurt, and scurrying back to bed. Even worse was his monstrous unwillingness to let her go to FarZan's bed to comfort him.

"Okay Mother, you can start now." FarZan looked at her seriously, revealing both his fears, and a growing understanding. He added, "But help me know who the monsters are."

"I will, my son, I will. As long as I have breath, I will."

As FarZan nestled close to his mother, she told him a story that included far too much reality. It came from her heart, experiences, hopes, and from deeply held fears. But most notably it came from her dreams; dreams that tormented her troubled mind over and over in the dark hours of the night. The substance of her dreams was unfathomable. It ebbed and flowed, in and out of her midnight sleep like the unrelenting waves along a shoreline; and they made no sense. From her point of view, everything should make sense.

The focus of her dreams was an ethereal view of her world hurtling through the cosmos. She saw the planet coursing through the silence of space, and began to understand that the ever-present activity of mother Earth is rarely sensed by human intellect. Plunged into daytime thought by her unrelenting dreams, Haleema became fixated on the planet where darkness reigns through half of every rotation, while the other half enjoys the light. Clearly, the light that crept around the Earth, driving the darkness before it, was life evoking, animating and illuminating. She wished that her dreams could be illuminated like objects in the light of day.

Haleema was not a believer in the chance or "somehow" of life. Only an Alpha/Omega planning session by the great Allah could have created the annual orbit as a life-giving cycle for the teeming, living inhabits. To her it was impossible that a hyper-lucky throw of the dice, trimmed in coincidence, could locate life in such a system, in a perfect orbit where life was conceived, and progression continually striving to better itself. How could it be a matter of chance?

Haleema believed that life on Earth was glorious. It was a superb realm for the living. However, along with the celebrated moments of life, she was all too aware that beauty was required to coexist with the ghastly; both states simultaneously existing within the Earth's perfectly established orbital trek.

Looking toward the Earth from the vantage of her dream-point, she saw the ferocity of the Earth's core. It was heart stopping. Constantly in motion, she saw that the Earth is not the semi-tranquil home that surface life enjoys. From her cosmic, x-ray view, she knew more assuredly that the roiling center of molten iron and an ever shifting rocky crust belies the seeming passivity of the planet. Many and notable have been the geological events of time, but her dreams suggested the beginning of something beyond the most those episodes.

Inside Haleema's dream-scape, in the earthen depths of her spinning globe, an unimaginable event was unfolding. Molten magma was forcing itself to the surface in plying fingers of diverse liquid elements. Each thrust and reach was tendril-like—a probing and exploratory penetration of suitable cracks and fissures. It seemed a purposeful search for the most direct paths of outward travel, coupled with an unwillingness to follow previous volcanic channels through the Earth's mantle. She began to understand that the sentient surface dwellers, in her midnight visions, were oblivious to the rising calamity. Then, all at once, in a lucid moment, Haleema realized that each molten shoot had a specific terminus on the Earth's surface. It was as though they had chosen their individual destinations, and she feared that her beloved city was a targeted objective, providing the dreams were a true portent of the future.

Pushing through the mantle and into the crust, she saw fiery molten shoots which took on a form previously unknown, and undefined by men. None could have hypothesized the phenomenon. Almost as swirling tornadoes, elements within the fiery tendrils mixed and cooked under great pressure. A concoction beyond human imagination was forming in the deeply hidden cauldrons of the Earth. The blend became a fabrication that Haleema, in her dream-state, watched again and again as it breached the surface of the Earth in multiple worldwide locations, shooting up like great pinnacles of rock, including her beloved city of Tehran.

The thrusting pinnacles of peculiar rock were not the only amazing elements in Haleema's world of dreams. She also saw great traces of light, lifting from the ground, and arcing through the sky. Blinding energy exploded from the pinnacles of stone colliding with the arcing lights in brilliant bursts that seared her mind and ended the moment of the dream; but not the return of the dream. It came to her, again and again, all too often and with too much anxiety.

Haleema could not have known the myriad forces of thought and action; the precursors to the dream. After all, they had started at the beginning, at a time and moment that may be unseeable and unknowable when looking back. Unaware of the beginnings, all she could do was wonder at the meaning. Are my dreams a portent? Are they a warning? Or are they just dreams?

As Haleema walked the course of her life, she would, in the end, gain an understanding. Its message is one that she could not have guessed. In the suddenness of a moment she would learn the meaning of the arcs and the nature of what would become known as the Towers: both as destroyers and saviors. She would come to know her place in the dream and in the ongoing story. The retelling of that story is a step by step discovery of the clashing forces. One must always go back to the beginning to understand the end, if for nothing less than the assurance that monsters do not fill the Earth.

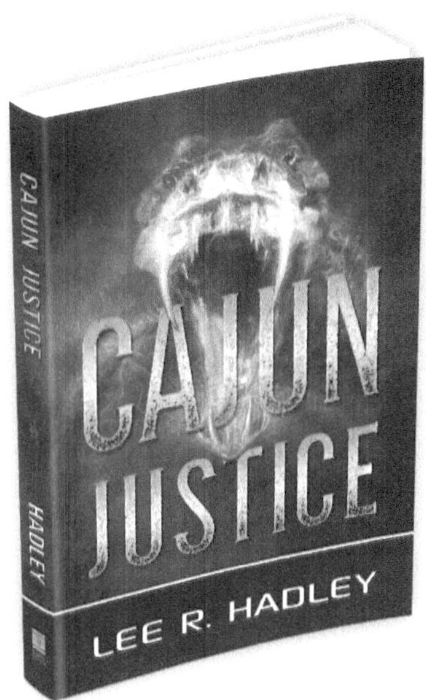

AVAILABLE NOW!

at Amazon.com or www.LeeRHadleyBooks.com